Embracing Eternity

A thin line

By

Hedir Al-chalabi

Dedication

To my cherished life partner - the unwavering anchor of my journey, whose love and support have been the guiding stars during every twist and turn.

To the architects of my being, my dear parents, who have tirelessly poured into me encouragement that not only shaped my character but carved my path as a writer.

To my cherished sister, whose friendship, steadfastness, and shared stories have filled the pages of my existence with warmth.

And to the unsung heroes, those who have touched my life, steering its course and enriching my narrative - your influence is forever engraved upon my heart.

This book stands as a testament to all of you, the bedrock upon which my world is built. Your unwavering faith and love have transformed dreams into reality. This is for you.

Table of Contents

Chapter 1

The Psychiatrist Ward Experience

As a seeker of truth through words, refrain from judgement, and embrace empathy's depths. – Hedir

I have read many books in my lifetime. Despite this, experiencing the vivid emotions articulated in numerous biographies felt remote and unattainable. I remained a spectator to the myriad emotions—joy, sorrow, hope, pain, defeat, and victory—that sculpted the histories of others. Yet, here I am, attempting to transcribe my narrative. This isn't a typical paparazzi tale filled with frivolous anecdotes or childish rhymes; it's a chronicle of solitary battles fought against the currents of prevailing thoughts.

On a particular Monday morning, the sun, in all its glory, had claimed the sky. I found myself speechless, standing before a building I had never envisioned visiting. The possibility of my presence there was limited to perhaps visiting an admitted acquaintance. A nurse and a security guard escorted me towards the entrance. The nurse, a towering woman around forty-five, with strands of grey marking her existence beneath the nurse's cap, led the way. Her floor-length uniform swished against her black, flat soles as she moved.

The guard, donned in purple and sporting a barely readable badge, followed suit. Our destination was a two-story building bathed in muted orange, nestled in a serene locale, away from busy urban centres where you can hear your inner thoughts and nature.

While I love hearing the chirping birds and murmuring streams, being engaged with individuals experiencing severe psychiatric conditions, such as depression, bipolar disorder, schizophrenia, or even worse accentuates my isolation. This entrapment heightens my despair, and I find myself grappling with questions of my presence amongst those genuinely struggling with mental health conditions. "What were they thinking when they decided to put me in such a place for patients with severe mental health conditions?" I could not just gather the dots. The decision to entwine my fate with those with severe mental afflictions baffled me. Whatever it was, I knew it would be sorted out in the end. Nothing was wrong with me, but they would continue arguing, especially as I was a new patient. Before they would prove me to be mentally fit, they must do their work and ensure that I was OK, but within me, I knew that they would only waste their time trying to run evaluations and diagnoses. However, I maintained my determination, trusting that my sanity would remain intact despite the upcoming evaluations and diagnoses.

Ufff, expressing my perspective to the world has proven to be quite a formidable task. That is one of the challenges I have come to encounter in life. I have always come across people who, most times, think that I am weird; they often misconstrue my uniqueness as eccentricity or madness. However, it is not so. This misunderstanding stems not from a place of malice but from my vehement pursuit of independent thinking—something society often strives to cage and mould according to its conformities. My quest for freedom and individuality results in inevitable friction with societal norms, a circumstance I've learned to embrace.

As I stood before the building looking around, I could see many passersby walking in and out, and I sometimes thought, how does the society in which they live treat them and pattern their thoughts? I was not truly concerned about those individuals- but those I am directly concerned with. These people around me who seemed not to mind what was going on in my mind could represent those who tried to bend my mind and scatter my rules, but it has always been a tough war. Yes, a very tough war between my society and me, but I was not ready to give up.

Standing in front of the structure, I scanned the diverse array of faces passing by, each one a reflection of their societal mould. I wondered how society had sculpted their thoughts and shaped their beliefs. It wasn't about them, though, but about those whose lives intertwined with mine, those who were seemingly indifferent to my internal turmoil. They might be symbolic of those who sought to twist my mind and shatter my principles. It had always been a relentless battle, a fierce war between societal norms and my convictions, and giving up wasn't an option.

I started walking towards the entrance, my eyes catching the sight of fences, towering walls, and ubiquitous cameras surveying the surroundings. The metal doors emanated a sense of disquiet, their austerity amplified by the unadorned, pallid walls. White coats floated around—doctors and nurses—interspersed with guards in blue uniforms. The patients donned identical home pyjama clothing, some looked hopeless, and I kept wondering how long they had been there and how much discomfort they had been through. The air was dense with untold stories of endurance and struggles.

My heart froze, and I mumbled, "Soon, that will be my outfit." The thought struck at my sense of security, but self-pity was a luxury I couldn't afford. I moved forward, encountering faces marked by sorrow and some by fleeting joy. Life, with its capricious currents, could turn the most joyous into the forlorn the very next moment. The people who wore bright looks might become the saddest ones the next minute. I clung to the memories of a carefree childhood, a time synonymous with joy and devoid of troubles, a stark contrast to the labyrinth of adulthood, where challenges were relentless companions. Adulthood comes with many difficulties, and sometimes those obstacles are overwhelming! However, resilience and perseverance were the essence of the human spirit; navigating through opposition was our inherent trait.

Hospital protocols, with their rigid adherence, were a source of discontent for me. Plus, there are strict rules and regulations regarding patient visitation. I dreaded the idea of being submerged in medication, compromising my clarity and ability to argue rationally. I need to be sane and have the lucidity to talk and give arguments when needed.

As I got to the ward, I meandered my way through a painted white corridor; two people were walking behind me, a nurse and a guard. The corridor has many rooms with many inscriptions, like "Consultation Room, Dressing Room". I did not pay much attention to that.

"Turn to your right", the nurse ordered me. I obeyed and turned to my right, which led me to another corridor teeming with many occupants. Some sat on the chair while some stood. Some were pacing up and down. We continued walking down the hallway until we got to the entrance of a room, where I was ordered to stop. They searched me before I got to my room.

Upon my arrival at the chamber, confusion danced in my thoughts, the reason for my presence there remained a puzzle. "I am fine! Every fibre of my being is fine!" I wanted to scream.

I became more confused. The reason was that I did not know why I was brought there "I am OK, everything in me is OK". I almost shouted.

That experience was not only depriving me of my freedom but stigmatizing me. To the doctors and nurses, I was not OK, I was a subject who needed immediate intervention! How could these people's perceptions be so divergent? Regardless of their professional assessments, my determination was to stand my ground, assert my mental well-being, and fight against the unseen chains seeking to imprison my spirit. The journey was not just a physical traverse through hospital corridors; it was a metaphorical battle for self-validation in a world quick to brand and isolate.

How distressing can it be when you are being observed through lenses tainted with doubt? Everything you say is a question mark for them. The atmosphere I found myself in did little to inspire my confidence. The entertainment room, cluttered with chairs, sofas, and tables, felt oddly sterile, with a large TV adorning the wall, standing out starkly in this devoid space. Strange look that I would prefer to avoid. Some curtains give a little contrast to the white walls and ceilings. I opened the curtain to reveal what was behind, it revealed an uninspiring view of shrubs and flowers. I saw some cars parked in orderly rows and quickly pulled the curtain back.

"Nothing intriguing," I muttered to the silence.

A middle-aged nurse approached; her demeanour was quite friendly as she outlined the rules. "Today exploration is permissible within the confines of the building; three meals would be given, and 9 pm is the designated bedtime. Besides that, you would have the possibility to have one-hour walks daily with supervision which is conditional on good behavior. We expect our patients to behave themselves. That is the internal law here."

"She's talking about law. This is it! Law this, law that. Can't these people be flexible?" I wondered silently.

She continued, "If you do not listen to the doctor's orders, you will not have the freedom to leave your room. That means you must help yourself so that everything will be easy for you as long as you are here. Everything depends on you. Tomorrow, you'll meet Doctor James. He's going to evaluate your situation".

"Which condition is he going to evaluate?" I thought about it without speaking.

Her persistent emphasis on the 'law' here grated on me. "Can't there be a semblance of flexibility?" I wondered quietly. My response was merely a nod, my mind silently protesting my placement here. The prospect of meeting Doctor James for an evaluation further fueled my subdued contemplation.

The nurse put on the air-condition and smiled at me as she walked out, closing the door behind her.

I stood for some minutes, lost in my thoughts. The room felt like a prison, echoing the lost freedom I yearned for. There is an inherent desire in everyone for the unbridled expression of thoughts, a luxury, I found, often limited to the realm of the mind.

Shortly, the door reopened, revealing a concerned pair, a woman and a nurse checking in on my well-being. My affirmation of my condition was met with further probing, to which my response remained firm.

"Ma'am, we are sorry, we just want to check on you and to know if you are okay."

"Of course, I am okay", I replied.

The aged woman, dressed in a green overall with glasses on, asked me again. "Are you sure?"

I was confused about what she was trying to say. "I am fine", repeated that time in a different tone.

"If you have any questions, let us know please.", the nurse continued. "I do not have any questions", I responded.

"Okay, if that is the case, we would have to leave you here for now. Your meal would soon be brought in."

Assuring them I was well, I stayed silent to their further remarks. Once they departed, I reclined on a crisp white-sheeted bed, inhaling the unmistakably sterile scent of the hospital that permeated the sheets, but I did not mind.

I mused to myself, "I wonder if they even have rules against napping in the afternoon here because they are always about rules. They want to control the way people think if possible", I grumbled.

I dozed off briefly, but my nap was interrupted when the door opened to reveal a strikingly beautiful nurse. Her beauty wasn't just conventional but deeply reminiscent of my daughter's features.

"Good afternoon," she greeted warmly. I replied with genuine enthusiasm, instantly drawn to her presence. Another staffer informed me they'd brought my lunch.

A fleeting thought crossed my mind about querying the food's specifics. But recalling my surroundings, I remembered my limited autonomy here. "Hospitals have their regulations," I thought.

She mentioned, "We won't be administering any medications until the doctor evaluates you tomorrow." "That's alright," I replied.

Internally, my anger flared because they insinuated that I required medication.

"We'll leave you now and will return to check on you later."

After they exited, I eagerly approached the food tray. Its inviting aroma was too tempting to resist. Yet, my rapid indulgence wasn't solely due to hunger. There was an underlying frustration. Bound by the institution's protocols, I felt a loss of the simple freedom to eat when and how I desired.

After my meal, I reclined and let my gaze wander to the ceiling, contemplating the true essence of freedom. True freedom meant autonomy over one's life and decisions. I always took pride in my sense of self-worth and independence, but here, those feelings had been replaced with a stifling sense of confinement and powerlessness. How can I share my unique perspectives when I'm labelled as 'unstable'? The weight of these thoughts lulled me into a deep sleep, which surprisingly, lasted for a couple of hours. "They must have checked in while I was asleep," I mused, swinging my legs off the bed. With my phone out of reach, my usual diversion, I felt a void. I longed for a good science fiction book to immerse myself in and temporarily escape this reality. I sat on the chair and looked around through the window. That felt monotonous and I lost interest.

"Perhaps a stroll outside might help?" I thought. But a nurse's words echoed back, "If you won't follow the doctor's orders, you'll be confined to your room." It struck me then, the depth of my isolation. That means I must listen to orders to leave my room. At that moment, I felt intense loneliness and started thinking about my family members. Did they truly believe I needed this evaluation? To them, their perspective was irrefutable, while my attempts to showcase a parallel truth were futile. "One day, they'll understand," I hoped without uttering a word.

The door opened, revealing the nurse who had charmed me earlier. My spirits lifted instantly, her presence offering a brief. I smiled sheepishly.

"We are on the evening ward round. I want to make sure that you are okay. My shift will end soon".

"Okay, are you on afternoon duty?", I asked. She was a bit surprised by my question. "Yee...eess", she replied.

After some casual conversation about the hospital, she departed, and my dinner arrived. However, the realization that I'd be spending the night in this foreign environment robbed me of my appetite "away from my home?" I queried.

"Why can't they see I'm fine? But they're so set in their ways and 'rules'." I sighed, feeling trapped once again.

After a few bites, I left most of my meal untouched, setting the tray aside for someone to pack them up as they did in the afternoon.

Glancing at the clock, I realized it was almost 10 p.m. "Time to wind down," I thought.

Lost in contemplation about how to occupy my time, a staff member entered to clear the dishes. Seizing the opportunity for conversation, I inquired, "Can you tell me more about what goes on here?"

"Like what?" she probed.

"The leisure hour," I elaborated.

"It's a communal time, mainly in the afternoon. You're free to explore the premises, but venturing beyond the gates is off-limits. Those are the rules here," she explained.

"Rules?" I echoed, feigning ignorance.

"Yes, rules. I thought whoever admitted you would've briefed you on our procedures. But don't worry, once you receive the appropriate treatment, things will get better for you."

I bit back a reply. In my heart, I knew I was fine, contrary to her assumptions.

Sleep eluded me that night, perhaps a consequence of my earlier nap. The soft bustle of the hospital, with nurses and doctors making their rounds, was oddly comforting. On one of her visits, a nurse noticed my wakefulness.

"Do you need anything?" she asked, genuine concern in her eyes. "No, I'm alright," I assured her.

"Why are you still up?"

"I think my afternoon nap has thrown off my sleep," I admitted.

She nodded thoughtfully, "Just be aware, if Dr. James thinks you aren't getting adequate rest, he might recommend a sleep aid."

"I did get some sleep earlier," I reiterated.

She seemed satisfied with that response and left me in peace, her footsteps receding down the corridor.

The next morning, I was still in bed when the door opened to reveal a nurse accompanying a doctor into my room. The doctor, a middle-aged man of average build, was dressed in a green uniform and clutched a stethoscope in his hand.

"Good morning, madam," he greeted, offering a reserved smile. "Good morning," I replied.

"I'm Dr. James. I hope you had a pleasant night's rest." I nodded.

"Follow me please to my office", he continued.

Upon arriving at his workspace, he stepped closer to examine me. My attention was drawn to a large framed quote on the wall. It read: "...I will not give deadly medicine to anyone if asked, nor suggest any such counsel... Should I trespass this Oath, may the reverse be my lot!"

The words resonated deep within me, setting off a flurry of emotions.

"Does he know what I'm thinking? No, that's impossible, unless someone informed him," I pondered internally.

Curiosity getting the better of me, I asked, "What does that quote mean?"

Meeting my gaze, he explained, "That's the Hippocratic oath—a moral and ethical code doctors pledge to uphold. It's why we can't just resign ourselves to the inevitability of death. We'll fight for a patient's life until it's evident that nothing more can be done. Our conscience does not allow us to think differently. That's why it's preposterous for us to view death as an ordinary event. It's our duty to save lives. Do you think it's fair to place such a weighty request on us? Isn't it rather selfish?"

I paused, collecting my thoughts before replying, "Where is the flexibility in our culture? How can a culture be so rigid and inconsiderate? Every individual should have autonomy over their life, especially when it comes to living and dying. I can't comprehend when choosing one's fate became a crime. How do we advance? Are we still reasoning as in ancient times? Hippocrates believed in Gods- the thing that, after the standards of modern societies, is unthinkable. So yes, we should learn from our old teachers and use their knowledge, but we should still advance in science, knowledge, and wisdom. Our world has evolved—our mindsets, technologies, and information have expanded over the years. We have been building unthinkable things and still explore and discover new things daily. While many cling to life, believing in its worth, they have every right to. But why should anyone dictate my choices or force me into a life I never sought? I'm not making a frivolous demand. What I'm asking it's not a whim! It's a right that I should have! A right as a person, a right as an adult who knows the consequences of such thought. So, is it selfish to want that autonomy? I yearn to find someone who understands this perspective. It's not a complicated stance and it's not selfish."

The doctor gazed at me intently, then began, "I've gone through your file and noted the court's reasons for bringing you here. Initially, I'd like to conduct some standard tests—blood and urine samples. Alongside that, I have a few questions for you."

The weight of his words caused a throbbing in my temples. "How audacious of the court to dictate my fate. Why can't they comprehend that I'm fully aware of the implications of my request?"

He continued, "No matter how passionately you believe in your rights, our hands are tied. The laws in this country are stringent and, I believe, similar in most places globally. Regardless of technological advancements, the act of willingly ending one's life remains contentious. Science seeks to preserve and enhance life. The very notion of ending it is anathema to our societal norms. Understand this: every individual has the right to live. Death, when it comes, should be natural and inevitable. Thus, the court's intervention to send you here for a mental evaluation is entirely within its jurisdiction. And that is what I will start with you until we are sure that you are mentally fit to leave this place. However, we cannot determine the time frame, but we will ensure you get better soon."

I resisted the urge to shout back in frustration, realizing it might further validate their assumptions about my mental state.

"But I'm perfectly sane," I interjected.

His voice remained steady. "That's for us to determine. Our role is to assess your mental well-being and determine when you're fit to leave. The duration is uncertain, but we aim to ensure your well-being."

I decided against further protest, allowing him to proceed.

"Ready for the questions? Afterward, the nurse will escort you for the physical tests."

Determined to prove my sanity, I nodded in agreement. "Yes, go on."

His first question was direct. "Have you ever used drugs or alcohol, and if so, has it altered your behaviour?"

Taking a deep breath, I replied, "Drugs? No, I've never used. Although, I had one minor encounter with marijuana during my first year at university on a trip to Europe, in Spain. A friend mixed it with tobacco, but I took only a couple of puffs. I didn't enjoy the taste or smell. As for alcohol, I drink sparingly—only on special occasions like New Year's Eve. Just a glass of wine, martini, or beer, never to excess. Everyone reacts to substances in their own way, but in my case, I'm naturally outgoing and don't rely on alcohol to be lively. If anything, drinking makes me tired. So, my experiences with both alcohol and drugs have been minimal and well within the norm."

The doctor looked intently at me, searching for any signs of distress. "When you're about to drift off to sleep, do you ever notice unusual things on your ceiling or perhaps hear sounds no one else does? Do you ever experience vivid hallucinations or night terrors?"

I met his gaze steadily. "No, I've never experienced any of those, not even as a child. I've always felt grounded in reality."

He studied me for a moment, as if gauging my sincerity, then ventured further. "How do you perceive those who brought you here? Do you see it as some sort of conspiracy against you?"

I sighed. "Not a plot, per se, but I do sense they doubt my judgment, which I find absurd. I've always been a critical thinker since childhood. Many have told me my views on life are unique, even extreme. To me, things aren't always black and white. Perspectives can vary, and what's clear to one person might appear differently to another. Do you understand what I'm saying? Am I right?" I sought affirmation from the doctor.

He nodded slowly. "I get your point; you are right to some extent. Perspectives can indeed differ. White could be black, and six could be nine in another circumstance. However, when it comes to the sanctity of life, societal norms are stringent. The court's decision in your case stems from the belief that every life is invaluable. This belief is deeply ingrained in our constitution."

I remained silent, absorbing his words, and he proceeded with his line of inquiry.

"Given these unconventional beliefs that others find perplexing, do you feel they've caused a rift between you and reality?"

I answered earnestly, "I can differentiate between reality and fantasy just fine. My views aren't fleeting whims but grounded beliefs shaped by deep introspection."

He looked genuinely perplexed. "But there is nothing logical here. We are talking about life. Wanting to end one's life without any clear medical justification or history of trauma doesn't seem logical." He queried, "Has there been any instance in your past, perhaps in childhood, where you felt mistreated or harmed?"

A hint of amusement coloured my response as the doctor looked into my past. "Abused? Quite the opposite. I have never been mistreated. I was the apple of my family's eye. Everyone adored me."

Dr. James persisted, "What about more distant relatives? Any untoward incidents involving uncles, cousins, or anyone else?"

I shook my head, "Absolutely not."

"And your school years? Were you ever a target for bullies?"

I chuckled at the memory. "Hardly! I was surrounded mostly by loyal friends. Sure, there were disagreements and folks who challenged my viewpoints, but isn't that part of growing up? Learning to appreciate diverse perspectives?"

He asked me, "Are you making excuses for any specific events or do you think those challenges influenced your current mindset?"

"How could they?" I countered, looking directly into Dr. James' eyes. "I've always held my beliefs independently, particularly concerning this matter. Choosing life or its end doesn't need to be tied to trauma or pain. I've given this deep thought and it's my informed decision, not a fleeting whim. My childhood was better, but I am opting for this because I feel it is normal for people to choose life or death. I am not a kid, and I am fully aware of this. I have subjected it to critical thinking and have seen that it has no adverse side effects on me."

He sighed, making a note. "We'll conduct a few more tests and continue this discussion tomorrow. Rest up and have a nice day."

He exchanged a brief, unspoken communication with the attending nurse, she understood that the session was over and escorted me back to my room.

Finally, alone with my thoughts, I replayed our conversation, pondering the depth of each question.

Chapter 2

Childhood Flashbacks

The next morning, a gentle knock on the door roused me from sleep. Half-awake, I spotted a lab technician in the typical green uniform.

Choosing to ignore him, I drifted back to sleep, craving the solace of a few more minutes. I thought he stayed for a short time. I needed more sleep and did not want anyone to disturb me. Later, I was woken up by another nurse. By then, I had more strength to reply to their questioning because I had noticed one thing about hospitals.

Generally, they could question one until you lose your patience. The annoying thing about them is that as they keep coming, they ask you almost the same question as if you need clarification on the information you gave in the first instance.

This time, a nurse unfamiliar with the previous day's encounters. "Hi, I'm Susan," her voice had a raspy quality.

"Morning," I murmured, stretching. "Victoria."

Her eyes held a hint of pity, "You've been referred here for psychiatric evaluation..."

I interrupted, irritation flaring, "Is there anything in my behaviour that suggests I need a mental evaluation?"

She hesitated, searching for words. "Mrs. Victoria, are you saying that the court was wrong for calling for your treatment?"

"Definitely wrong. You can see that I talk sanely, and what other confirmations do you still need?"

"But we still have to do our job. You are not the one to tell us how you feel. We are the ones to give authentic results to the court of law. Our role is to observe and report. The court has its reasons. So, equip yourself with patience."

"Reasons that seem quite misguided, given our conversation," I countered, confidence returning.

She sighed. "Doctor James will be the one to decide. Has he seen you yet?"

"Just once. He promised to return for more questions and maybe some tests." I explained.

She nodded, "Until then, try to relax. We're here to help. The tests that will be carried out will certify you to be mentally fit." With that, Susan left, and I laid back, contemplating the uncertainty of my situation.

I sat up from the bed and on the chair, leaning against the wall. Immediately, I started thinking about my family members. "Why are they not here to check up on me? Have they been banned by the court not to come around to check up on me until I am certified, okay?

After all, there is nothing wrong with me in the first place, and I do not know why they are not here. I hope they come around to check on me before today ends."

As thoughts of an impending visit flitted through my mind, a flood of memories washed over me. I was transported to my idyllic childhood, where love and devotion from my father, David, were the constants.

We were his world; he always put us first. Born into a humble background, David was fortunate to receive a formal education, courtesy of his British parents. Both his mother and father worked, and despite their relative awareness, they were unaware of the implications of their shared AS genotype. This genetic mix resulted in David being diagnosed with Sickle Cell Disease (SCD) as a child.

Relentless symptoms plagued him: frequent colds, exhaustion, pounding headaches, and more, confining him to his home. His schoolmates, misunderstanding his condition, labelled him weak and often ostracized him. Despite the emotional scars, my father's intellect shone bright. Upon completing elementary school, he made a seemingly audacious declaration: he wanted to study physics. His parents, hoping to spare him any added stress, gently pushed him towards the Arts. But David's determination was unwavering. They stopped trying to persuade him to change his mind when they saw that he was determined to study physics.

He passed his examination into high school, and that phase came with another stigmatization from his peers. They often laughed at him, jeered, or ran away whenever they saw him coming. High school proved challenging. His peers' ridicule and avoidance weighed heavily on him. Recognizing his struggles, his parents considered relocating him to a more accommodating school. Even as his teachers, recognizing his academic prowess, especially in the sciences, tried to dissuade the move, David's well-being was paramount. The decision was made. Leaving the school was a form of relief for David and his family. He flourished under the protective watch of understanding teachers at his new school. His brilliance was undeniable, and slowly, respect and admiration from both peers and educators replaced the shadows of his past.

Despite his luminous intellect, David's health crises cast periodic shadows over his life. Hospital stays often pulled him out of school, but each time he returned, his academic prowess shone even brighter, much to the astonishment of his peers. They soon dubbed him the "book wizard," an affectionate nod to his unmatched brilliance. In the face of his frailty, his academic achievements made him stand tall, an inspiration to many who yearned to emulate his success.

One vivid episode, as my father recounted to us, took place unexpectedly in class. His sudden health scare left his classmates stunned and concerned as teachers swiftly ushered him into the school's ambulance, taking him to the sick bay for immediate care. The episode prompted a hasty summon of his parents, who rushed to the scene. His father spared no expense, procuring every necessary medication and remedy to stabilize his son's condition. Miraculously, of these intense episodes, though distressing, were fleeting. David's resilience, combined with timely medical intervention, saw him through, allowing him to complete high school and advance to higher education, where he passionately pursued a degree in Physics. His parents were pleased about the feat, and arrangements were quickly made for his comfort because of his health status.

University life wasn't devoid of health challenges, but his father had now become adept at managing his condition with medications and other treatments. His efforts bore fruit as he graduated at the top of his class. After university, fate introduced him to Diana, my mother. She was the soothing balm to David's battle-scarred heart. Past relationships had been tumultuous for him; he'd faced rejections from women who couldn't see beyond his condition, especially those who'd witnessed his health crises firsthand. These experiences deeply wounded his spirit.

Yet, during these university years, he found an unwavering pillar of support in George, a classmate and close friend. George, empathetic and understanding, often took the lead in getting my father medical help, sometimes reaching out to his family only after ensuring he was receiving appropriate care. Through the highs and lows, George stood steadfastly by David, embodying the essence of true friendship.

Growing up, we often mistook George for a blood relative, assuming he was our uncle because of his tight bond with my father. It wasn't until later we realized that their deep friendship had effectively made George an honorary member of our family. One of my father's challenges was finding a partner who would love him truly. Love was tough to find because of his situation. I remembered an incident my father told me one day while we were returning from school. The protagonist of this tale was Jody, a brilliant and stunning girl in his class. Although they began as friends, my father found himself irresistibly drawn to her. Her chats with other guys often left him simmering with a quiet jealousy. However, the trepidation of rejection, especially given his health condition, left him reticent. George, ever the motivator, urged him to confess his feelings.

In time, my father mustered the courage. One day, post-lecture, as they strolled towards the university gate, he struck up a conversation with Jody – the first outside the bounds of academics. On that day, her simple response made him feel on top of the world. It marked the first time they would have a conversation despite being in the same department. My dad was happy because he had overcome his first fear of getting Jody's attention. However, fears later crept in because of his health status. Their relationship blossomed, and as they grew closer, Jody too began harbouring feelings for him. My father, valuing honesty, decided it was time to share the truth about his health with her. He picked a serene evening after their summer exams for this heart-to-heart. My father said that he was afraid of her reaction, but he was determined to say it regardless of what happened after that. Recalling that night, my father described the tension after he broke the news. Jody sat frozen; her face devoid of expression. The unexpected revelation caused her to break into a nervous sweat. The clatter of her fork dropping startled nearby diners. My father, equally tense, could hear his own heart pounding and ragged breaths. He locked eyes with Jody, searching for a reaction. She seemed paralyzed, and unresponsive even after he called out to her multiple times. Worried, he moved closer, gently shaking her, hoping she was okay. He said that Jody almost fell from the chair because she was already lost in thought and just sat there looking like a mannequin. Pulled back to reality, tears filled her eyes, mirroring my father's. The ambience of their date was irreversibly altered, ending with both seeking solace in each other's company before exiting the restaurant.

In the aftermath, Dad started having mixed feelings since the incident. He confided in George about the night's events, revealing the whirlwind of emotions he felt. It soon became evident to my father that Jody's feelings had shifted. While she outwardly maintained their friendship, her emotional distance grew, becoming more pronounced with time. My father, ever hopeful, thought she might just need space to process the revelation.

The true extent of Jody's feelings became clear during a party they all attended. That night, Jody grew close to another attendee. Seeking guidance, my father turned to George, who advised him to discuss matters directly with Jody. When confronted, Jody's words cut deep.

Referring to my father as a "walking corpse," she coldly stated she could never envision a future with him. Her words pushed my father into a depressive abyss, further deepened when he learned of Jody's subsequent marriage to her new beau. He had no choice but to move on. However, life has a way of turning tides. Eventually, my father met Diana, my mother. In her, he found the unwavering love and understanding that he had yearned for, finally building the family of his dreams.

My mother always stood by my father through thick and thin. She knew his health status and was determined to love and support him that way. However, it was a tug of war initially because her family did not want to approve of the relationship. Nevertheless, they later accepted after seeing my mother's resilience and determination to stay with my father. My father had some crises in the marriage but never let it define him. Despite various hardships, Dad remained positive and determined to live fully, creating the best family for himself. We had a wonderful childhood experience. My mother had secured a job that required travelling. She was often not around, but she was always there for my father until we grew older and could care for him—at least for now. While his crises occurred less often than in the past, they were occasionally quite severe.

Growing up to see my father in unnecessary pain sometimes made me more critical about life because I was helpless whenever he was in distress. Many people even said he was luckier because children with SCD challenges hardly live long. Some even die in infancy. Who could be blamed in such situations? His parents? Fate? Or Science that has not gotten a permanent solution to such things as they have for other health-related problems? Whatever it was, my father was innocent of the challenges he passed through, and anything I saw him, I cried secretly.

One of the reasons I bonded with my father was because I was his favourite. I was loved, but my father loved me most. I thought that one of the reasons for his intense love was because I chose to study Science course as against my brother, who preferred Sports and Art related courses. Whenever my father was less busy, he would often teach me Mathematics, Biology, and other subjects. He made me see Physics and Chemistry as my best subjects, even when many complained about them as the most difficult ones. I usually excelled in those courses, which motivated me to pursue a career as an architect.

My father had a zest for life that was infectious. His love for adventure was unparalleled, a trait that my brother Adam and I inherited. While mom often travelled for work, Dad ensured our childhood was rich with experiences. Adam launched his own business at the young age of 23, and I was into university life, pursuing architecture. Dad's vivacity masked the challenges of his Sickle Cell Disease (SCD); it was only in our later years that we understood the gravity of his condition. He bore his difficulties with ease, showing us the value of strength and resilience. As kids, our focus was purely on joyous moments, and they were aplenty.

Among our cherished memories is a family vacation to Italy. The sun gleamed brilliantly on the day we set off from Italy to Moneglia in our rented SUV, a vehicle choice typical of my father's penchant for spaciousness, despite the narrow roads of Italy.

Navigating through the mountainous, one-way tunnel road of Italy was both a thrilling and slightly nerve-wracking experience. Just imagine… as you approach the entrance of the tunnel, the scenery around you fades away, and you find yourself in complete darkness. The only light comes from the headlights of your car, which are reflected off the wet walls of the tunnel, casting eerie shadows on the road ahead.

The road is narrow and winding, with hairpin turns and switchbacks that require careful attention and skilled driving. The sound of the engine seems to reverberate off the walls, amplifying the noise and making it seem louder than usual. The air inside the tunnel is cool and damp, with a faint smell of diesel from the other cars that have passed through before you.

As you set off from your starting point, the road begins to climb, and you can feel the gradient increasing as the scenery around you changes. The air becomes cooler and fresher, and the scent of pine trees and wildflowers fills your nostrils. As you drive deeper into the tunnel, the darkness seems to close in around you, and you can feel the weight of the mountain pressing down on you. The tunnel seems to stretch on forever, and you start to wonder if you'll ever see daylight again.

The journey from the dark tunnel into the embrace of the radiant sun was like bursting into a painting. Suddenly, the world around was alive with rugged mountains and the scent of the crisp mountain air. Every twist and turn of the road unveiled panoramic scenes of sea meeting mountains. Those sheer drops might have made one's heart race, but the rewards for those daring enough were views that left us breathless.

The character-filled mountain villages we passed were like snippets from a storybook. Stone houses, terraced vineyards, and locals deeply engrossed in their daily routines. And of course, there were the pit stops – a delicious bite of the region's cuisine or a refreshing sip of its wines.

However, as thrilling as the mountain passage was, there was a palpable shift in the landscape as we neared Moneglia. The towering mountains gave way to sweeping coastal vistas. The blue of the sea sparkled in competition with the colourful houses perched on the hills. The symphony of the ocean waves and the bustling town streets grew louder as we descended into Moneglia, a gem on the Ligurian coast.

Travelling through a one-way road tunnel in the mountains can be a thrilling and unforgettable experience. While it can be a bit scary at first, the payoff of emerging into the stunning mountain scenery is well worth the momentary discomfort. It's a journey that should be taken slowly and enjoyed thoroughly, with plenty of stops along the way to soak in the stunning scenery and experience the local flavours.

As we drove through the winding roads that led to Moneglia, I remember how amazed we were every time by the stunning views of the Mediterranean Sea and the colourful houses that dotted the hillsides. The scent of freshly baked focaccia and seafood filled the air, making our mouths water with anticipation. Our cosy vacation rental was tucked in the heart of the old town. The charming two-bedroom apartment had a balcony with a breathtaking view of the sea, the perfect retreat for my parents sipping their morning coffee or enjoying a glass of wine in the evening. For us was every second an adventure. Days were passing by like minutes. We never wanted to leave that place. For Adam and me, each moment was an exploration, each second a treasure.

Mornings were a ritual. A hearty breakfast followed by a beeline to the beckoning beach. The shimmering waters became our playground, as did the surrounding area. From building sandcastles and indulging in luscious gelatos to hiking the verdant trails of Portofino Natural Park, every day was a fresh canvas. Not to forget our escapades to the enchanting Cinque Terre villages, with their cliffside trails, vibrant houses, and verdant vineyards.

Evenings in Moneglia had their charm. Strolling through its winding cobblestone lanes, we stumbled upon hidden culinary delights.

Fresh seafood, mouth-watering Italian dishes, and the ever-inviting passeggiata, an evening stroll by the promenade, which framed the sun's majestic descent into the sea.

When we were older and wanted to try other things… we took a boat tour to see the coastline, where we got up close and personal with the towering cliffs and the hidden coves that could only be reached by boat. We swam in the pristine waters, snorkelling among vibrant fish, creating a tableau of memories with every stroke.

Ending each vacation felt like closing a cherished book. The sweeping landscapes, tantalizing cuisine, and the heartfelt warmth of the locals rendered each trip unforgettable. My parents would exchange vows of returning, echoing their commitment to each other, and these moments became the fabric of our family lore.

These memories often dance through my mind, especially those with my father, tightening the bond we share. While Dad was a true adventurer at heart, Mom was his serene counterpoint. Her frequent travels had instilled in her a yearning for the comforts of home. She cherished our short local escapades, be it a simple day trip in our neighbourhood or a calming walk on the beach. Mom's idea of fun was muted, and she held a strict compass to life, prioritizing different aspects over sheer adventure.

I recall one dinner after plates had been cleared, where I voiced my dream of becoming an architect. While Dad listened intently, Mom met my revelation with a barrage of questions. She wasn't one to readily embrace my architectural ambitions. Her scepticism was evident that evening, setting the stage for many heart-to-hearts about my chosen path.

"Why architecture, Vicky?" Mom asked, her eyes searching mine for clarity. "Out of all the available choices, why that?"

"It's what I'm passionate about, Mom," I replied with determination.

"But you know it's mostly a male-dominated field. Won't you feel out of place or struggle to make your mark?"

"That's not where my concern is, Mom. I'm focused on where my passion and interest lie."

"But sweetheart, why not consider becoming a doctor, dentist, or even a food scientist? Fields where you might find it more balanced and can easily develop without stress?"

"I've always wanted to stand out, to be different," I explained, a hint of exasperation in my voice. "Dad understands this, too."

Across the table, my father shot me an encouraging smile. We shared a bond that went beyond mere parenthood; he was my confidant, my guiding light. Not to diminish my relationship with Adam, my elder brother, but Dad had always been my go-to for advice.

"I had always known that you would hardly bend the moment you make your rules. I know that studying architecture is good and it is also a lucrative job, but I am just afraid because of..."

"Because of what?... Your daughter's always been strong-willed," Dad interjected, addressing Mom. "I believe in her choice. Architecture is not just rewarding but can be a platform for her to break norms. She's shown exceptional aptitude in her studies. We should stand by her."

Adam chimed in, "Vicky's always marched to the beat of her drum. It's hard to sway her once she sets her mind to something. We should support her, and I'm confident she'll rise to the top."

Mom sighed, her face softening, "Well, she's always been headstrong. Whatever field she chooses, I believe she'll shine."

"Anyway, let's see. She is the stubborn type and I am sure she will always succeed in any field she chooses". My mother concluded.

The air, thick with tension moments before, now held a promise of understanding and support.

I was happy because I had achieved the first feat by convincing everyone about what I wanted my future to look like career-wise. Had it been that my father did not support me, it might have been hard to convince them. I assured them that I would strive to establish myself as one of the most respected architects.

Another thing that fascinated me about my family background was our religious aspect. My family was one of those families where there was flexibility regarding traditions. We attended church from time to time without being pressed by it. The religious rules in my home were simple and flexible, not long hours of prayers, even during the holidays when we were not choked and defined by time factors. Like other people, we celebrated Christmas, Easter, and New Year's Eve.

We had many friends across all religious spheres, especially when we relocated. We had Muslims, Christians, Buddhists, and even Atheists. Yet, we practiced our religion away from our social lives.

The only aspects of religion that shaped or affected our lives were the codes of living like "thou shall not lie", "thou shall not bear false witnesses", and other aspects of "thou shall not". Our parents endured that we were brought up in strict morals. We had rules that included coming back home on time. My mother especially did not tolerate staying late outside, even during the day. She was the strict type and she mostly determined the rules of our childhood; maybe that was responsible for some of our little frictions. Father was flexible and would want to welcome other ideas even if he would later correct some aspects of them or would even discard them. However, my mother would hardly give room for that, and if she would later agree to your views, you would have to convince her ninety-nine times.

Meanwhile, I noticed something about my father and mother; they rarely argued with each other, unlike my mother's frequent disagreements with us on matters. Sometimes, we went for days trying to argue an issue before she would succumb. It was not that she did not always allow us to have freedom of conscience and speech, but she always wanted to guide us, sometimes, out of that motherly care, she went overboard, and as a strong-headed type like she is, we were sometimes at each other's throat. My brother, Adam, was the agreeable type like my father. He hardly raised his voice or questioned anything. He would obey without talking back. I was just the opposite, with a knack for looking at things from different angles, and I was always inquisitive.

My father had a unique bond with me, despite his naturally peaceful disposition. I believe my inclination towards science and his innate fondness for me strengthened this connection. Adam and Dad - their relationship was evident during their strolls, especially when I would be busy in the kitchen alongside Mom. As Adam matured, their discussions evolved, spanning topics from academia to football, wrestling, religion, and politics. During such heated debates, I often sided with Adam, particularly when the discussion veered toward modern times versus the past. Yet, in other matters, I staunchly backed Dad.

Amidst these familial debates, Mom usually remained neutral, preferring to avoid taking sides. However, when it came to board games like Ludo or Chess, she had no qualms about favouring a player, and we did the same when she was in the game. Such trivial disagreements, especially between Mom and me, were commonplace. We often had contrasting views on many matters, leading her to occasionally feel exasperated with my personality. I sometimes sensed she favoured Adam over me. His calm and unquestioning nature contrasted sharply with my inquisitive and sometimes challenging demeanour.

I wasn't only a puzzle for my family. Some friends often remarked on my analytical and questioning nature. "Why are you so critical, Vic?", was a refrain I heard often growing up. Some of my high school teachers also grappled with my personality. I wasn't confrontational; I just approached things from different angles, questioning norms and seeking to innovate. However, this was often misconstrued. "Why do you seem to find problems where there are none? Why complicate the straightforward?" they'd ask. A few even cautioned, "People with your mindset might struggle in life if you are not careful."

Meanwhile, they did not see that life should only sometimes be accepted how it is presented. That is what gave emergence and metamorphosis that happen in Life and Science. Some people say that some things could be changed, and they start the process of changing them, while some see that some things could be reduced or added to. They started the process of doing that, and today, we have a more sophisticated world with technological developments everywhere in health, and other aspects, even in Arts (even though I have a shadowy knowledge about it). I learned some scraps of it from my brother, who spent some of his time reading novels and articles, which I found as one of the boring things. I used to hear him say that Literature has advanced over the years, referencing the age of Reasoning, Romance, and Metaphorical poetry and referring to poets like John Doe, Percy B. Shirley, and Shakespeare, among others.

My curiosity is that "if people in the Art and Humanities felt that there should be room for development and they went on to bring the changes, which stemmed from not accepting life as it was before they started their journey to enlightenment, then why should people always see me as a rebel? Do I have freedom of thought and speech like those people I listed and many of their likes? I first thought that it was because I was a girl, but I later realized that it might just be a fragment of the limitations that my society wanted to place on me."

"That girl? She is just too critical for a sane society" was one of the phrases that made up my growing experiences. I heard it almost every time from people around, and I kept wondering what I was doing wrong. Am I, not a human that is free to experience herself? How rigid could the world we live in be that anyone who tries to change some things, especially in the view I advocated, should be seen as someone with a psychiatric condition? I laughed back into reality.

Chapter 3

The Religious Neighbor

Some moment after, I noticed the comings and goings – visitors came to visit their loved ones, new patients, and bustling staff, but I hadn't been given time to explore the place to my satisfaction.

My curiosity peaked and asked a nurse, "When can I explore this place?"

The nurse's face hardened, her voice sharp and echoed like a stone striking a hollow drum.

"Soon, after you've had your breakfast, and perhaps even after lunch, you'll be accompanied by someone for a tour around the hospital premises. This is an excellent opportunity for you to ask any questions you might have about your condition or any other related matters."

"Can't I go round to see things alone?"

"No, we don't allow our patients to do so because it might be dangerous."

"Dangerous as how?"

She replied again in an unfriendly manner.

"You have to understand that this isn't a usual hospital for everyday illnesses. This is a psychiatric facility where we prioritize the close monitoring of our patients. Besides, all our activities are under the scrutiny of the government" (She pointed out the CCTV cameras mounted on the walls that I hadn't noticed since my arrival). "We cannot afford any lapses. If anything goes wrong, there may be severe legal consequences, particularly for high-risk patients like you."

"What makes me dangerous?"

"Could you refrain from bombarding me with irrelevant questions? Isn't it clear to everyone that you're a threat to yourself, or should we let you destabilize an already challenging situation?"

"I'm not sure what you're implying." "You know exactly what I mean!"

"Regardless, can you please answer my questions?"

"Do they refer people who are normal here?" I questioned the nurse.

"No. The staff members who tend to the patients with psychiatric disorders are the only self-described 'normal' people here. Besides, not all cases are severe; other mental health issues, such as depression or psychosomatic diseases, may be prevalent. But every patient at this facility except for the visiting family members is dealing with a medical condition or is under investigation for some kind of mental health issues."

"Medical condition?", I probed.

"Yes, though with various levels of mental challenges, including cases like yours. Given your demeanour, you appear like someone who could heal quickly with treatment."

"What if I'm not ill and this is all for nothing?"

"That decision lies with your designated physician and the further evaluations they will perform," she answered, her voice rising slightly in irritation.

When I got back to my room, I decided not to ask her any more questions. I noticed that breakfast and my meds were all nicely organised on the table, and my cover had been changed. Before leaving, the nurse who had escorted me earlier gave me some encouraging words. Shortly thereafter, a woman I presumed had delivered my meal arrived, accompanied by another nurse, to oversee my medication intake. After consuming a portion of my meal, they reminded me to take my medications and only departed once they were certain I had ingested them. With time, the overwhelming anxieties I initially felt began to diminish. I was more confident than the first time I came, filled with fears and many obscurities.

When the judge first delivered his verdict, it felt like an insurmountable challenge. My mother, Adam, our son Alexander, our daughter Anna, and my husband Robert's unwavering support brought me comfort. But their absence from this facility made me feel disturbed and unstable.

"Perhaps the institution's regulations have prevented my family from visiting since my arrival. I really hope there's a designated visiting hour; I long to see my children and other relatives. I have missed them. My daughter, Anna, is especially on my mind. I can only imagine her concern, especially since I'm unable to contact her without phone access. Moreover, I'm not given the choice of selecting which nurse to accompany me on hospital tours. If given a choice, I'd opt for the nurse who was here yesterday; she bears a striking resemblance to Anna."

I leaned against the wall after my meal, waiting for Dr. James to show up for the day's medical cross-examination.

A moment later, Dr. James came into the room.

He was wearing a slightly long white tie with a blue shirt underneath. His black shoes and recommended eyeglasses completed his appearance. He was joined by a nurse in traditional white attire, complete with a cap, holding a patient file. He had a much colder attitude than when we had last spoken. He looked less receptive when I tried to give him the same courtesy I had given him yesterday. I pondered whether he was facing personal difficulties or was just running out of time.

"Madam…", he called me.

"Yes, Doctor James."

"I believe we need to conduct some lab tests on you to ascertain the state of your mental health fully. From our conversation yesterday, I'm optimistic that your condition might be less severe than initially assumed. You responded coherently to my queries, which is a promising sign."

"I've been trying to say to you that I'm all right."

"I'd appreciate it if you let me handle the diagnostics. I'm a board-certified psychiatrist with over a decade of experience. I've dealt with a myriad of intricate mental health cases. Often, patients might appear well-adjusted on the surface, but underlying issues could be lurking beneath."

"Well, you're the expert here. However, I'm confident in my state of mind. You questioned me about my children, and my answers were consistent and accurate. If any of my family members were consulted, I'm sure they'd corroborate my story. We'll see what the test results reveal, as long as they're accurate. It's not the individual's fault, but rather the overarching systems — laws that might not always account for the intricacies of human experience. These regulations sometimes cast a shadow, influencing people's perceptions and judgments."

Dr. James straightened up, arms folded, regarding me intently. The nurse beside him fixed a neutral gaze on me, her expression seemingly conveying. My primary concern was ensuring I wasn't unjustly labelled — I did not want to be wrongly identified as someone with a psychiatric disorder.

I was clear-headed and completely aware of my surroundings and my state of mind. If it were up to me, I'd have them interview my family to affirm my well-being. It wasn't about obstinance, but rather the freedom to perceive the world in my unique way, even if it diverged from the mainstream view.

He asked some more questions, and then he and the nurse left the room. I started to feel anxious. Hands on my hips, I paced agitatedly after getting out of bed. The light in the room was golden as the sun's rays flooded in. After some time, I took a seat and leaned in intently, as though mentally recording every detail.

However, I felt a wave of intense rage and leapt to my feet, slamming my fists on the table.

"Oh my God, what is going on?" My voice trembled, a mix of desperation and disbelief. "How could everything fall apart?"

"I stood up again and paced the length of her room. My steps are quick and purposeful. My mind raced, a tempest of thoughts and possibilities churning within me. After a moment of contemplation, with a resolved expression, I approached the window, desperately seeking something, anything, that could serve as an assistant to me, something that would give me hope within the sudden rush of emotional imbalance that I had within me that sprung up without any prior notifications. The incessant beeping of memories came again, and it did nothing but serve as a cruel reminder that I was left to confront this predicament alone. I had always been a lone fighter, even though I had people around me. Yes, they were people only in physical things, but our minds were very far apart! We never shared the same views on almost everything. I did not want to dominate their world with my views, but I wanted a justifiable ground where two truths could co-exist without conflict.

My God! I wanted to scream and catch the attention of everyone around me and see them probably scampering for safety or rushing towards my room to see what had happened.

"Stay calm, Vicky. Just breathe," I murmured to myself, the mantra serving as a lifeline amidst the rising tide of turmoil. As I inhaled deeply, trying to centre myself, my thoughts raced, yearning for the comfort of my mother and close family. Imagined voices seemed to taunt me from the window, whispering reminders like, "Didn't we warn you about this reckless pursuit of unfettered thinking?"

I moved towards the vain imagination as if to squeeze it off my face and throw it inside the dustbin by the corner of the room! With renewed determination, I confronted these mental spectres, declaring firmly, "You won't intimidate me! I have the freedom to live my life and make my choices. I won't be shackled by society's expectations!" The voice struck me sharply, like an arrow from a skilled archer aiming to fall his target. "Wait and see, Vicky. Just wait and see!" it sneered, before fading to a chilling silence. I hesitated, attempting to process the encounter. "Wait and see?" I echoed, trying to confront the elusive phantom.

Though I hoped for a response, the voice remained maddeningly absent. "Vanished into thin air," I muttered with a chuckle.

As I wrestled with my inner demons, a nurse entered unexpectedly. She glanced around, clearly concerned. "Is everything alright?" she inquired; her voice tinged with unease.

"Absolutely," I reassured her.

"But who were you speaking to?" she pressed. "Pardon?"

"I thought I heard voices when I approached," she admitted, casting a suspicious glance around the room.

"You must have imagined it," I responded coolly.

She looked dubious but finally said, "Perhaps you were just deep in thought."

"I was simply reflecting and conversing with my thoughts," I clarified, hoping to ease her concerns.

She sent me a suspicious look, and I could feel her anxiety rising. The room was chilly, yet I could still see beads of sweat accumulating on her forehead. She appeared immobile, her movements stopped, and her eyes narrowed as she stared at me. I felt uneasy staring at her with such intensity, as though she was attempting to read my innermost soul.

I asked, "Is everything alright?" as my anxiety increased.

She said nothing, her face showing a look of both surprise and fear, as though she had come upon something strange and unexpected. She seemed to be debating something inside herself, maybe even doubting my mental state or conjecturing about a supernatural force.

She responded with an agitated "Never mind." "When am I going to the laboratory for the test?"

"That's why I'm here," she replied, rolling each word slowly like a child learning her alphabet.

"Mrs. Vicky, I will be back soon."

As she turned to exit the room, I noticed the back of her white uniform damp with sweat, a clear trail leading down her neck. Even the exposed parts of her legs glistened with moisture. "Perhaps she needs a moment to compose herself," I mused.

After she departed, I replayed the recent events in my mind. "What was she thinking? That I was conversing with spirits? Do they even entertain such beliefs in a psychiatric facility, or is it just attributed to hallucinations?" I pondered.

"There's no need for undue concern. However, science can occasionally yield unexpected results. If that happens, I'll have to convince them of my sanity. But if everything turns out fine, I look forward to reuniting with my family."

Suddenly, the door swung open, revealing the same nurse. Her demeanor had shifted; she appeared more assertive, almost as if preparing for a confrontation. Regardless of her current demeanour, I wasn't particularly concerned about her opinions. Her expression was stern, hinting at a readiness to address any potential resistance from my end.

"Mrs. Vicky, we need to leave now."

I stood up quietly and saw her stealthily looking about the room. Though she exuded confidence, there was a hint of fear beneath the surface. She seemed vulnerable to me, and under her seeming calm, there was obvious anxiety.

As I followed her without any resistance, she appeared to regain her confidence. I thought about asking her a question but decided against it so as not to add to her discomfort. Leading the way, I noticed that once we entered the facility's public spaces, her newly developed boldness increased.

She walked ahead of me, her posture suggesting, "Now we're in public; misbehave and you'll face consequences." I surmised her confidence stemmed from the idea that should anything happen, others would intervene.

She kept her distance from me as if she was afraid I would suddenly attack her from behind. Her actions since the moment she approached me seemed almost ludicrous to me, it was so dramatic that it would easily pass for a good comedy show. When she got to the corner of the horizon ward, we entered a room with the inscription "Laboratory", she summoned me inside and ordered me to sit down. She moved to a part of the room that I hadn't realised was occupied when I sat down.

I ignored what she went there to do. My attention was drawn to the room's decor. It shared the same white hue as the ward I'd been in. Two rows of metal chairs were lined up neatly with handles for people to lean on. A large cabinet filled with files stood next to them. The room was equipped with various medical instruments and two windows draped with sky-blue curtains. One wall featured, a water dispenser and a TV, while the opposite side housed what looked like a testing area beside the bathroom. I was awestruck with the equipment that was inside. Despite the room's ample lighting, I could only see half of the room.

To pass the time, I tried to eavesdrop on the conversation taking place in the other room. "Why did you keep so late?" an unfamiliar voice inquired of the nurse who came to call me.

"I didn't feel so well and I took a short break", she replied. "Are you better now?" Mr. Wales asked.

"Mr. Wales, my heart raced and I was gasping for breath", she emphasized.

"You should consider taking it easier with work," Mr. Wales continued. "Where is our new patient?" The male voice asked.

"She's sitting inside. I told her to wait for you", she responded.

Soon, the two of them approached me. "Good day," the man greeted, introducing himself as Dr. Wales and instructing me to enter the adjacent area.

I went to the room and I was surrounded by medical equipment, much of which was foreign to me. A series of tests were conducted on me, including blood tests. After nearly an hour, I was told to leave and expect the results the next day. I almost asked what the results looked like out of curiosity but the countenance of the man and the other nurse was inscrutable.

Walking back to my room, I mused aloud, "I hope the tests come out in my favour. I don't want foul play here because I do not truly trust those people. But, can I trust them? Manipulation is possible. Still, their professional integrity is at stake, and here in America, the law reigns supreme, they could bag a jail term."

Glancing at the wall clock, I eagerly anticipated my upcoming opportunity to explore the hospital grounds because I had never been allowed to see outside since I was admitted. The prospect of fresh air was invigorating, a welcome break from the stifling confinement.

At 12:30, a man dressed in black long-sleeve shirt and trousers entered my room. "Are you Mrs. Vicky?" he asked formally.

"That's me," I confirmed.

"I'll be taking you for a walk around the facility since this is your first time," he explained.

Curiosity took over, "Why do I need to be accompanied?"

He elaborated, "It's standard procedure for new patients, especially those admitted on legal grounds. Until we can confirm your mental state, staff will oversee your activities. By then, we would be sure of the safety of both parties."

Taken aback, "What are you insinuating, Mr… What is your name?" I inquired about his name, then hesitated, wary of pressing too much.

"Never mind. You can state your reasons first."

I swallowed hard, and my throat developed a sudden lump. I wanted to talk, but I wanted to know if my questions would irk him.

He urged me on, "What do you want to ask? Let me know."

"I was curious… Why the emphasis on 'safety for both parties'?" I repeated his words.

He responded firmly: "Until we determine your mental health status, we can't take any risks. So, do you want us to jump protocols because of you? What if you are not mentally okay and pose a threat to your chaperone?" He threw those words at me like a volcano that suddenly erupted and brought everything it came around to the ground level.

"...Hmmm… So, just because I have strong convictions, I'm labelled as unstable?", I challenged.

"We never said that; We're just following the orders," he countered.

"In any case, I have the hope that by the conclusion of this tumultuous period, I'll demonstrate you all to be mistaken. I'll prove your claims wrong and show you I'm not the mistaken one," I declared defiantly.

"You can't prove us wrong; you can only show whether you are mentally fit or not, and life goes on. That's not our call," he retorted. "Our job is to assess your mental state. The law brought you here, and we must ensure you're safe before returning you to society."

He swiftly interjected before I could say another word "Let's get moving. Your dilly-dallying is eating into your time, and it won't affect me one bit!", he said assertively as we left the room. We stepped out into the hallway, passing anxious and distressed faces, some teenagers grappling with drug addiction, others battling depression, and various other psychosomatic challenges. I felt an unspoken judgment from some staff members, they treated me with a high level of disdain as if my situation were unique.

Stepping outside, I felt a kind of angelic aura and radiance crystalizing on my skin, sinking deeper into my hollow heart. The atmosphere contrasts starkly with the stifling atmosphere inside. "When did I last breathe such open air, unburdened by the suffocating walls of this place?" I mused. "Right in there is a cruel environment that seems to wall your spirit soul, and body until you shrink". I sighed deeply.

He gestured around, pointing out various sights while discreetly gauging my reactions and mental clarity. I couldn't help but chuckle internally, thinking, "You're not as clever as you think, sir." After a pause, I ventured, "What's your name?" I didn't get a response at first. I asked again, this time in a firm voice, unlike the other time that I was trembling.

"My name is Evans…" He replied.

"That's a nice name," I responded, to which he acknowledged with a casual thank you.

After we meandered around for almost forty-five minutes, I noticed other patients. Some appeared dejected, while others seemed relatively calm. While we were strolling, Evans, perhaps trying to build rapport, gestured to a man and recounted his tragic story of losing his children in a fire. The man had been haunted by that trauma, but thankfully, was on the path to recovery.

"Is he now feeling better?"

"I think he is", Mr. Evans replied to me.

Moved by his story, I changed the subject, "You might not know this, but I'm a married woman".

"That's nice…", he replied, looking more interested in my story.

"Yes, I am an architect, a daughter, a wife, and a mother of two wonderful children," I said with a tone of pride of gaiety beaming my once dejected countenance. There was a momentary gleam of surprise in Evans' eyes.

"Then what happened to you that brought you here on the count of being mentally unstable?". He was more curious, and I could see a thousand questions lined up in his mind, rolling out like a torrent of water cascading a hill from a waterfall.

Before diving into my story, I noted, "You seem unusually interested. Hoping to fill some void with my story?"

He nodded. So, I began, sharing about my father's battle with sickle cell anaemia, the pains he went through and how his struggles shaped my worldview. I revealed my different confrontations with societal norms that wanted to box my ideas and silence them forever. I told him I stood vehemently, immovable, and combative against all religious counter-opinions.

"One of the ones I remember vividly was with a neighbour, Mrs. Veneta, who tried to suppress my beliefs with her religious fervour.

She had often told me, "God gave you this life, and He will be the One to take it from you. However, if you choose death, you are not just a sinner who harms yourself and disgraces God, but you will harm your family, friends and those who care about you. How selfish can you be and turn your face away from God? He says in 1 Corinthians 3:17 that <<if anyone destroys God's temple, God will destroy that person; for God's temple is sacred and you together are that temple.>> He created your body as His temple that you should cherish. He put you into this world, and you should not take God's grace for granted. You are going to suffer like Juda! And don't forget that you will be judged for your actions just like the Bible says in Hebrews 9:27 <<And just as people are appointed to die once, and then to face judgment>>.

She was trying to make it look like I never had any encounter with the Bible or my parents were never Christians even though we were normal Christians, unlike those who over-explain things with religious, moral standards eroding common sense."

I continued. "I've studied the Bible, and nowhere does it say that suicide leads to eternal damnation. And when we talk about Judah- yes, he committed suicide and went to hell, but it was because he betrayed Jesus. After all, he did believe in Him. And yes, I would face my judgment on the Judgment Day. If I were an unbeliever, there would be no way out for me, and neither would I get a second chance. My heart is pure and clean. I meant no harm to anyone; all I wanted for everyone was a life filled with joy and happiness without pain… And if there is a God, He shall understand my thoughts and actions. Plus, if I may add, all sins except one are forgivable, and murder/suicide is not one of them as it's indicated in the Bible in Matthew 12:31-32: <<So I tell you, every sin and blasphemy can be forgiven—except blasphemy against the Holy Spirit, which will never be forgiven. Anyone who speaks against the Son of Man can be forgiven, but anyone who speaks against the Holy Spirit will never be forgiven, either in this world or the world to come.>> But Mrs. Veneta was relentless, she wanted to show that I did not know much about God as I proclaimed. She got me really frustrated with her theories and talks about things. She would always quote scriptures upon scriptures, trying to water down my ideas and make me look ridiculously foolish with my claims.

One day she visited, bearing an apple pie, and began her lecture on gratitude. The gratitude of being alive. "For you to exist," she began, "you needed generations of ancestors; two parents, four grandparents, eight great-grandparents, 16 great-great-grandparents and so on… so if you think about it, the last eleven generations for the past 300 years need 4094 ancestors for us to be born."

"We need to have gratitude", she continued. "Think of the destinies, the stories, the battles fought... all leading to your existence. You should be grateful."

As Evans listened, I wondered if he could truly understand the weight of my words, the depth of my experiences, or the complexity of my beliefs.

Chapter 4

Witnessing Trauma at the Psychiatric Hospital

As we continued our conversation, Mr. Evans seemed more engaged than before. Finding a picturesque spot, he gestured towards a rock enveloped by blooming flowers, inviting me to sit. The setting stirred something within me, prompting a question, "What do you observe with this place, Mr. Evans?"

He looked puzzled. "Observe?"

"Yes, don't you observe anything, Mr. Evans?"

"Nothing. Just the rock and flowers". He said convincingly. "Exactly," I said, with a knowing smile. "But isn't there more to it?"

Mr. Evans scrunched his brows, searching the surroundings for any hidden clue. "I've been visiting this place for years and always appreciated its simple beauty, nothing more. What else is there?"

"It is beyond that", I said.

"Then tell me something different that you have observed about it", Mr. Evans replied.

"Look closely, "I prodded. "These distinct entities, the rock and the flowers, exist in harmony. The rock stands in the middle and the flowers grow around it. Each has its essence, neither trying to dominate the other."

Mr. Evans rested his head on his chin, he pondered, his gaze dilated in a restive mood as he seemed to sink my words in gobbles down his throat. I could see the wheels turning in his head. At first, he wanted to interrupt me, but I waved my left hand to him to calm down and allow me to finish my speech.

So, I elaborated, "Nature thrives on a balance, Mr. Evans. If the flowers choose not to bloom, the rock remains unfazed. Similarly, if the rock didn't offer its sturdy perch, the flowers wouldn't be perturbed."

"But...but...Mrs. Vicky, can you explain more what you mean? I don't seem to connect to what you are trying to say." He seemed momentarily lost for words as we locked eyes, both realizing that amidst this tranquil setting, profound lessons awaited discovery.

"My point, Mr. Evans, is that if rocks and flowers can coexist with such freedom, shouldn't humans enjoy the same?"

Mr. Evans looked thoughtful. "But these are non-human entities, they are elements of nature without emotions and thoughts. How do you equate them with people?"

"True", I conceded, "They're not human, but they coexist harmoniously, don't they?"

His eyes twinkling with a hint of challenge, he paused for a moment, then countered, "Even nature, like life, has rules, Mrs. Vicky. Why, for instance, don't flowers sprout directly from this rock?"

His question caught me off-guard. For a moment, I hesitated, searching for a fitting response. Mr. Evans, perceiving my momentary uncertainty, took on a triumphant stance, arms folded, clearly feeling he'd presented an unbeatable argument. He waited for my answer, probably prepared for another counter argument to water down my claims.

Gathering my thoughts and drawing a deep breath, I responded, "While you're not wrong, haven't we seen plants taking root on mountain cliffs and between rocky terrains? Their world isn't as separate as we think."

His face changed, slightly taken aback. His stance faltered a bit. "That might be so, but it contradicts your point of non-interference."

"Interference, yes, but also coexistence. Even if nature's elements overlap, they don't necessarily harm each other. Do you agree with that?"

That assertion knocked him out, it made him momentarily at a loss for words with his lips trembling and waiting to defend himself. After collecting himself, he said, "Nature is programmed and operates on a certain equilibrium. Humans, given our complex nature, can think, decide, and act within the confines of the laws. We are not at liberty to behave anyhow thus we need rules to prevent chaos."

I shot back, "But isn't our society already riddled with chaos? Wars, famine, pestilence, genocides, natural calamities. Many victims would choose life over death if given the opportunity, but circumstances decide otherwise. Only those who end their lives do so out of their own will, and no one arrests them for self-determination. How am I any different if I'm led by my convictions?"

He sighed, "Those who commit suicide are different. Suicide is often a result of anguish, despair, or devotion to certain beliefs."

"But what makes mine different? Isn't that just being true to one's thoughts and feelings?", I persisted.

He sighed, a hint of exasperation in his voice. "Mrs. Vicky, your actions, if allowed, could set dangerous precedents. The world is more complicated and fragile than you think. Before you know it, countries might start entrenching it into their constitutions. Do you want to imagine what happens next when nations endorse individual choices? We live in sensitive times. The world isn't as resilient as we'd like to believe. There are only a few places where people are truly afraid to die. They would rather cut corners and escape death."

I was quiet for some minutes, I picked up a few flower petals and tore them into tiny pieces. I watched them dance with the breeze before drifting away. "Mr. Evans," I said, turning to face him, "You know we live in a superficial dominant world where we're chained by society's precepts. I want people to live and enjoy life as much as I want to choose my way of living. I yearn for the freedom to live on my terms. Why should I fight for ideals I don't value?"

He pondered. "Hmmm… Mrs. Vicky, we all inhabit a world governed by certain standards, this is not the world fashioned by you and not just your perception. Still, there is always a universal law that guides human existence unless otherwise."

"You are right about that but I believe that laws and rules must be bent to accommodate other beliefs."

He smiled, a mix of patience and mild irritation. "I know you are an erudite woman, and you understand how things work. Consider your home, Mrs. Vicky. Even there, with loved ones, boundaries exist. You lock your door during private conversations with your husband, am I right? Just like the bathroom door is closed when in use?"

Caught off-guard, I nodded.

"As much as you love your children, these boundaries, however trivial, are there for a reason. Similarly, society has its 'boundaries' that no one should trespass for the collective good."

"Mr. Evans, but..."

"That is how things work outside your home too. No matter the freedom and love your children enjoy, there are still hallowed things they are not given the freedom to do."

Seeing the earnestness in his eyes, I sought to lighten the mood because I could see some peaches of anger in his voice though it was subtle. I tried doing a cunning U-turn to cushion the effects of arguments and the building anger that I noticed in his tone of communication.

"Do you love reading books?" I asked him. He raised an eyebrow, "Books in general?"

"Any book that inspires, challenges or broadens your perspective."

He hesitated, "My job keeps me busy, but I've enjoyed 'Native Son' and 'Black Boy' by Richard Wright. They are African Novels. I've also read the likes of 'Jude the Obscure' and 'The Mayor of Casterbridge' by Thomas Hardy, as well as classics like 'Wuthering Heights' by Emily Bronte and 'Pride and Prejudice' by Jane Austen. John Grisham is also a favourite; he authored 'The Firm', 'A Time to Kill', 'The Whistler', and 'The Client', among others. Have you read them?"

I smiled, "Absolutely! That's impressive! Grisham's narratives are gripping. He's a good writer and I love his style of writing."

"When did you last read any book?", He asked with mixed feelings, which I sensed as doubts and fear.

"Oh...I still read a novel while my trial was ongoing". I replied gleefully.

He was shocked, and as quickly as he was trying to hide it, I knew that he was stunned because I could see his heart moving faster, like a chauffeur who was drunk and driving in a car with a damaged brake.

The fleeting look of surprise on his face was unmistakable. "Were you? That's...unexpected."

Seeing the intrigue in his eyes, I teased, "I bet you're wondering about my mental state now." He paused, and lowered his head for some seconds, searching for words before answering my question.

"Not at all but... (He paused for a moment); I am just thinking in diversification."

"Don't worry. I already know what's going on in your mind." (I reached my middle finger to write an invisible line on his chest). I can read the lines already. I laughed.

"But you cannot still prove otherwise." He tried defending himself.

"Anyway, I am sane, my mind is functioning right, and I know what I am and want."

"Actually, your words seem to show that you know what is going on around you and I think I am having a clearer observation about you since we came here to talk." He spoke.

"Shall we go back to the discussion of books?" "Sure, because I find it more interesting."

Books became my sanctuary, a place where I felt safe from the severity of the outside world. But to truly cherish them, it's crucial to form a deep bond, to sense a tingling connection as you flip the pages and breathe in their unique scent. With each line, you're both eager for the revelations ahead and dreading the final page. For a book to truly resonate, it should feel like a parting every time you put it down. It's a bond, a chemistry between me and the written pages. While education mandates reading, genuine appreciation comes when a particular piece profoundly touches your soul. For me, it was one word, one fateful day, that forever intertwined my fate with literature. Words became an elixir, transforming me from within.

In today's world, dominated by fleeting images and superficiality, projecting authenticity is crucial. Wisdom isn't about adorning the latest trends but preserving your inner voice amidst the din. In moments of total despair, in underground solitude, when we feel the swamp of the self, crushed by worries and destroyed by failures, literature often serves as the anchor.

Last night I was saved by Oscar Wilde's book – 'The Portrait of Dorian Gray'- after an unsettling encounter in the entertainment room.

I overheard a woman, presumably grappling with schizophrenia confessing her thoughts. She described her haunting reflection: an azure-tinted version of herself, reminiscent of her prime years, her lips mouthing words. "Before I left the conjugal apartment, I looked in the mirror, I saw a blue woman with a cut on her throat, but no blood. She was beautiful, looking like my older self. Her hair was tied back tightly.

Her lips were moving as if she wanted to tell me something. I didn't tell anyone about it because in psychiatric language it's called an illusion, and I knew that if they had taken me to the doctor, they would have given me pills again or hospitalized me. I got angry and turned my head towards the window. I looked at the leaves on the trees and said to myself <what the hell, I'm just normal>, then I looked in the mirror again. The woman was sad. Then I saw some Hindu entities and myself besides, with a rejuvenated face, with a red-orange circle between the eyebrows. I started feeling calmer because the first time I saw myself old, covered in demonic blood.

I talked to someone in my mind who told me that soul mates would communicate telepathically for many years, but it's important not to tell anyone what I know. I will witness what it will be and tell you exactly what its words meant later because it was speaking to me in code. A virgin will be born, but not in the traditional Biblical sense. It will be like an evolution of the soul. She will be sentient and very strong, able to take any form. I had then a unique experience: my soul came out of my body and went to It. All my life, I wanted to die. I was visualizing my death. I could see myself banging my head against the walls and bleeding. Do you realize they want to keep me for a year or two? It depends on what they think, but I no longer dispute their decisions. Before I left the hospital last time, they called me to speak to the students. I told them that I had suffered from depression since I was little, if you can call it the need to be loved and that I have the purple flame. To doctors, we are paranoid maniacs. They told me I was going through a psychotic episode with schizoid and cyclothymic tendencies and that I was bipolar-manic. When I read the main diagnosis, it says mania with psychotic symptoms. In their language, it is true, but for example, yogis who enter a trance and reach a high spiritual level of communication, doctors take them as psychotic. We can all come to perceive divine messages but don't believe them, so we go crazy.

When I first entered the hospital, I lost my faith and said in my mind that there was nothing. Some who remained in history went mad because they were getting so far from the real world, being led by divine powers, that when they woke up, they felt confused. After all, I've seen, felt and heard, I don't want to fall anymore because I'll take revenge on myself and think very negatively. Karma exists. This is the cross of many. Some of us are at the end, dying out for good. The voice seems indifferent, arrogant, shallow and smoky, but it knows a lot. It sure has a sensitive soul.

I know I won't be able to meet it because I have an ego problem. If I'm not physically close to perfect, I can't be serene and shut out the pure love in my soul. It knows me, but It pretends not to know who I am. When you were away, I went to talk to you because I wanted you to get out sooner from this dark place. It told me I was reading Its mind and that It wanted to talk to me about you too. Then I hurt It with scratches. It admitted to me that I was scared. After 24 hours, I started screaming, beating it until I fell. I was writhing on the floor. I couldn't feel my body, even though I had cut my hand. I felt alone, but you were in my thoughts, and I was praying. When I was talking to It about you, I admitted that I could feel you very close and that an immaterial body can reach the person it wants close. It gave you a blue rose because it saw you as the most beautiful and saddest girl. When I heard the voice, I wanted to die and wished I had the chance to put a bullet in my head. I was sitting, seeing its shadow, feeling its touch, cursing it in my mind, doing black-and-white magic simultaneously. I saw my past lives. It told me that IT was in love with you and that you will never be together because you are like a fallen angel, but you rose through love.

After many months of searching for my soulmate, I remembered that's exactly what it called me. The same vocal timbre as I squirmed on the floor in the small back room. It was telling me: wake up! I was begging It to forgive me, to help me. It slapped me awake, pulled me out and threw a bucket of cold water on me. It hides a pain so strong that it would not be able to cry. It's missing half of it.

Then It told me its secret and advised me to think about what it said when I'm sad. I need help. I wanted to be where you are. It said I can if I want to help you leave this abandoned, forgotten place. I had to go down some steps. I wanted to; I wanted to cry. I froze when I saw a shadow with hands folded as if in prayer. You know that I pray for you. Trust me because I love you. Don't be afraid. I know how you feel because I've always been there for you. I know you are suffering. I am. See you. I'll be with you before I see the blue woman.

A distant past binds us. A few months before, I heard Its voice. I was holding a test tube which was a deep blue substance. It told me that it knew what I wanted to do but was there to warn me and that the decision was mine. Suddenly it yelled: STOP! Don't drink that substance because there will be no way back. I received a letter shortly without a sender. It was written: may your life be eternal, free from longing, may your heart be filled with love, may the good look upon you eternally, may sincere love live with you."

I just froze, hearing incomprehensible words, and after a while, I hurried to my room, took the first book from the shelf, and started reading. I am sad that I witnessed her regression during her stay at the institute, being aware that we are powerless in the face of such problems.

He connected more to me beyond the physical level while I was talking. His mouth was opened, and he gaped out his tongue, looking at me like a movie showing characters on the screen, and the imagery of the world that I painted before him with my world seemed to have transferred him beyond the world level into a magical realm. He listened with all his attention and gazed like a serpent ready to strike its victim. He nodded his head at intervals in agreement.

After all those words had poured from my mouth, he told me he would reply to them next time because our time was up. I stood up reluctantly because I was already enjoying our conversation. The most painful part was that Time was against us and could not reply to my words. We sat up and proceeded to the main hospital ward, discussing the patients' concerns along the way.

"I hope that you would be the one to accompany me tomorrow?"

"I am not sure. It depends on the timetable and I have not checked the one for tomorrow."

"Is it pasted daily?"

"No, it is weekly but sometimes, they reschedule it if some of our patients are proving difficult for some of our guardians."

"Oh truly?"

"Hmmm… Some try beating their guardians, especially the new ones unmedicated."

"Can't you curtail them with your skills and physical strength?" Haha...he laughed for a while before replying to me.

"Do you think this is an easy scenario to figure out? We admitted an eighteen-year-old who was brought in by his concerned parents just two weeks ago. Overindulged in drugs, he caused chaos in his neighbourhood. His hands were bound by his aggression; it was a mad dash to get him here. He had shot his mother in a fit of passion over a disagreement over a computer game. She spent days in the intensive care unit, barely evading the merciless grasp of death. That young man was one of the hardest cases we've ever dealt with. Three attendants kept a careful eye on him whenever he was outside in case he had a violent outburst. We made sure he never went near any kind of weaponry, not even a regular stone. He wouldn't be held liable for murder given his mental state."

People around me looked at me curiously as my footsteps resounded loudly. They were challenging my mental acuity and calling me 'insane', a designation the court had unfairly placed on me. I could practically hear their thoughts. I asked if family visits were allowed after admission to the hospital.

"They do, in fact. It's strange, though; none of your relatives have appeared. May I ask you something?"

"Go ahead," I said.

"Why haven't any of your family members come to see you since your arrival?"

That question made me sigh profoundly, almost to tears. I made a hasty attempt to suppress it. But then a knot formed in my throat and, like a cloud bearing down on rain and thunderstorms, it sent a harbinger to announce its approach. My hands trembled uncontrollably. I swallowed hard as I tried to hold back my tears. My teary eyes were a sign of my heart's misery. While heading back to my room with Mr. Evans, I was relieved that he was not fully focused on the personal struggles I was going through. I tried to assure him they would be here before the end of the week, but I remained composed. Perhaps they had to wait for instructions from my lawyers before coming. You are aware that time and law govern everything in this place. I laughed mockingly to mask the tears that were on the verge of welling up in my right eye.

"I am sure that they will come this week to see how you are responding to treatment and how your improvement is going."

"Improvement?" Unconsciously, I had wanted to say something different to dispute his statement, but I said that unintentionally.

"Yes, improvement, you are fast reacting well and you seem to be more stable than when you were first brought in."

"I had always been stable!" I defended myself.

"If you perceived stable, the court would not have transferred you here, do you agree?"

"And do you also agree that the law is not perfect, and it can make mistakes?"

"Of course, since it was made by people who are not consistent as well."

My voice wavered, "So, what are you getting at?"

"Mrs. Vicky, perhaps we should continue this chat another time?"

He raced off before I could reply, as though he had sat on a seat with burning coals under it.

"Always in a rush with rules and time", I mused aloud.

I paused at the entrance, taking a moment to absorb the surroundings. The hallway was crowded, yet no one seemed to give me a second glance. Were they merely too engrossed in their activities or were they apathetic? I was lost in my thoughts when I suddenly realized: "Why didn't I ask Mr. Evans if someone could reach out to my family for my books? It'd certainly help break the monotony." I sighed, regretting my oversight.

"And that is true. I should have done that but you know, I had completely forgotten."

"Then you are not bored!" The voice screamed at me as if we were in physical combat, trying to fight over a piece of cake. I would ask whosoever is coming to take me out tomorrow. When I went back to my room, I noticed everything was immaculate: clean sheets and a fresh, pleasant-smelling space. My mood was suddenly lifted by the scents, which made my worries seem minimal. My stomach growled noisily as I walked around the room.

The conversation with Mr. Evans must have stimulated my appetite. "Oh my, I'm really hungry!" I glanced at the clock while I thought.

Suddenly, raised voices interrupted my thoughts. I raced to the door and threw it open without thinking twice. I saw a disturbing scene: hospital staff struggled to restrain a young boy, his distraught parents trailing behind them. All my attention was drawn to the boy's situation, overshadowing my own. His distress echoed the story Mr. Evans had shared earlier.

"What could have happened to the young man? Could it be a drug-related issue or a normal mental health breakdown?" I felt so connected to the pains of his mother, who was crying as loud as she could. I wanted to gather information about him and looked around to see if anyone could tell me what was going on.

Absorbed in the unfolding drama, my attention shifted when I noticed an approaching figure. A nurse, distinct in her blue uniform approached. Her stark white glasses did her no favours, adding an eerie touch to her visage, reminiscent of a vampire movie character. Her hair was styled in a ponytail with a blue ribbon used as a guard to keep it from falling off her shoulders. She walked with resounding footsteps towards where I stood with a grimaced look. I was afraid of asking her about anything. What if she later came to treat me and mistakenly remembered seeing me, it was going to be something else…

"Good afternoon", I greeted her.

"Good afternoon!", she said in a very deep and resonant voice that caught me off guard.

"Who is this person?" I asked. "Such a commanding presence must be overwhelming for her patients, especially in the dim evening hours. I hope she attends to her clients, wearing a nose mask. Her striking appearance could be intimidating, to say the least. She possesses an almost otherworldly appearance. I hope her image doesn't haunt me tonight!"

Chapter 5

Relocation Experiences

In the quiet repose of my room, I found myself restless, tumbling between the sheets, my thoughts entwined with memories as I thought back on my afternoon outing with Mr. Evans. I had already eaten my lunch and taken the prescribed drugs. My heart ached for the warm, comforting embrace of my family despite the differences we had. I yearned for my daughter Anna's consoling presence, whose touch had always kept me rooted. I wanted to feel the presence of my mother, and the reassuring smile of Robert, my ever-supportive husband. It felt like distant memories. Adam, who had distanced himself from the family turmoil, was a ghostly figure in my memories. Although he had stayed away during the court hearings, claiming my emotional state was overwhelming, his absence was a gaping void. My heart ached for Alexander, my son. I was certain he missed me as much as I missed him. Honestly, I could not lie that I needed all of them beside me. The nostalgic feeling of missing people who are dear to your heart is second to none!

One more thing that I ached for dearly was my collection of books. Reflecting on my conversation with Mr. Evans, my longing for them intensified. My passion for reading was voracious. My interests ranged from business to science, motivational books to ancient histories, arts and lots more. Novels allowed me to travel, absorbing cultures and traditions, ranging from the tragic to the comedic, slave narratives to romance, and delving into the richness of international literature. Poems were part of my days in my low moments. I was in love with Baudelaire, Ion Minulescu, Lucian Blaga, William Shakespeare, Rabindranath Tagore, and so many more… Poem echoes in my mind:

"From childhood's hour, I have not been, As others were—I have not seen As others saw—I could not bring My passions from a common spring— From the same source, I have not taken My sorrow—I could not awaken (…)" The sting of unfinished novels on my shelf pricked at my heart. They were neatly stacked on my bookshelf. My kids were not around, even though they were in college and only occasionally present during my trial, they kept in touch, especially with calls and chats.

My beloved flowers were yet another thing I missed. My love for flowers was unmatched. They were all around our house, each one lovingly maintained as though they were living things. I had many such as Peace Lilly, Rose, Gerbera daisy, and Lavender, my favourite ones.

I missed the easy pleasures that had once been within reach, and the weight of their absence weighed hard on my chest. It felt paradoxical - How could the society I believed would champion my freedom now seem to choke my voice and stifle my rights?

"How much longer will this confinement last?" I pondered aloud. Are these people intentionally punishing me; by now they must acknowledge my mental clarity. I've undergone countless tests; the lab results should speak for themselves. "I had all my expectations of Doctor James, and I was looking forward to our next meeting. It felt depressing to think about staying another week, especially without family visits. Even though they supported the judgement that was pronounced by the judge. To them, it was like a good riddance to whatever I might have been conceiving secretly and if I am treated, my mind would function better and by then, I would be received again into the society with a sane mind and body. What a belief!", I screamed.

I sat back trying to console myself, staring up at the spotless white ceiling. With the sun still controlling the day, the unlit bulbs appeared to be at rest. Whispers and footsteps drifted outside, but I was unmoved, wanting only the comfort of my thoughts.

A bright and clear recollection suddenly surfaced, taking me back to my early years in Stockholm after moving from the United Kingdom before our family finally moved to the US. That July day, the sun shined brightly, matched only in warmth by the brightness of my mother's happiness as she entered the house.

My brother and I had already returned home from school. We sat at the dining table doing our assignment. My father sat on the biggest couch, watching a documentary. Suddenly, my mother came in and shouted, "David! Guess what?" My father quickly left us and rushed towards her, trying to figure out what my mother was trying to say. My mother kept dancing to imaginary music, and we tapped her fingers. My parents were naturally funny people, and dancing was one of their favourite things whenever they had something interesting to tell us.

I can vividly recall the playfulness that often-accompanied big announcements in our family, thanks to my father's whimsical mannerisms. One of the most memorable instances was when he decided to theatrically announce our first vacation to the UK where we originally came from, dancing around with glee. Over the years, we'd mastered some of these eccentric displays which we sometimes mimicked too.

On this particular day, my father stood grandly, reminiscent of the Statue of Liberty, a mischievous twinkle in his eye, trying to guess right what the good news was by moving his head around in a suggestive manner. My mother continued, "Well, since my ever-observant and handsome David hasn't figured it out yet... should I spill the beans?"

"Tell us!" The excitement in the room was palpable and we all screamed in ecstasy.

"Okay, errrmmm... (she dramatically cleared her throat). Here's the big news! I am glad to tell you that we're relocating to the US this December, our paperwork has been completed!"

For a split second, my father feigned surprise, as if he'd been out of the loop and wasn't aware of the processes from the onset. We clamoured for him to confirm, the anticipation unbearable.

"Mom, can you please repeat what you just said?" We shouted.

Repeating the thrilling announcement, my mother couldn't contain her joy. She playfully wrapped herself around my father, showering him with affectionate nicknames and kisses. This move was her dream. Employed by an airline, she consistently believed that the United States offered more potential than Sweden. After many discussions and a bit of persuasion from my mother, they decided to make the leap together.

Watching my brother, Adam, gleefully hurling cushions about and seeing the sheer delight on my father's face are memories that will be forever etched into my heart.

I had never seen my mother act so recklessly as she did on that day. She had always wished to move to the US for a permanent stay, and she was the one who first orchestrated it because of her flight company job. My father had previously proposed that she travel to the United States on her own, with the option for us to visit during holiday breaks. Still, my mother persuaded him to allow us to move at once since her company would be responsible for the relocation.

While the move was instigated by my mother's career, it held special significance for me. I had been dreading the prospect of her living overseas while we remained in Sweden. Now, the whole family was taking this exciting step together.

The excitement of moving across continents can be overwhelming. My brother was already navigating his second year of high school, while I was on the brink of my freshman year. It's strange how quickly the mind shifts gears. As we sat down after supper, from the comfort of my home in Sweden, I was suddenly visualizing the brand-new chapter that awaited us in the US; being in a new environment and meeting a new set of people who might be different and difficult at first. Still, in the long run, we would blend in and co-exist peacefully without friction.

Not many at my age would be thrilled about such a move, but I have always been an explorer at heart. I looked forward to my school life too, meeting new teachers and making new friends.

I started counting down to the days and nights of our departure. December came too slowly. I was always curious about seeing America the same way I had always seen it in movies. America, as I'd seen in countless movies, beckoned with its mysteries and adventures. Each day, I kept records of what I would do when we got there. The imagination started building in my head to the extent that sometimes, I'd stand before our home's large mirror, acting out scenes of my imagined life. One such day, lost in my dramatics, I never knew my mother had been spying and laughing from the corner of her eye. I suddenly turned back and saw her laughing hard.

I screamed: "Mummy! Stop laughing at me!"

That made her laugh more, and I felt so embarrassed that I had been caught. I rushed to my bed and hid under my duvet. My mother ran inside and pulled the bedspread over me. I was shouting, admitting with laughter that she should leave me alone. Our playful scuffle continued as she started singing to me, "American girl, why were you hiding?"

Fast forward, and we found ourselves in sunny California, San Diego. Every nook and corner echoed a different lifestyle. My father, now a Physics teacher at a local high school, decided it best for my brother and me to attend the same institution. This not only made our commute easier – bundled up in his car, riding to and from school – but also eased the family's financial strains. With time, I settled in easily and mingled with other students from different parts of the U.S.

Walking into a new school is like opening a book, each faces a new story waiting to unfold. Many of them who had come before me stared curiously at me the first day. My class teacher introduced me as "the new British girl from Sweden". I could read the curiosity in their minds. Their eyes mirrored the intrigue mine probably did, days earlier. "A Swedish girl from England?" or vice-versa, they seemed to wonder. As I took my seat, a girl next to me, with a constant smile, caught my eye. "Perhaps, my first American friend," I thought, looking forward to countless tales we'd soon share.

During the break, I eagerly sought out my brother to exchange our first impressions and experiences. With a grin, he told of the friendship he'd already established with the boys. Eagerly, I relayed my morning, spotlighting the girl with an infectious smile. As if summoned, she saw and ran towards us.

"Hi, I am Loretta". She smiled at us.

My brother was the first to reply to her. "I am Adam, nice to meet you."

After the introduction, my brother excused himself, leaving Loretta and me to unravel each other's stories as we got to know each other better. We sat on the bench in the flower garden where students often relaxed. As the discussion continued, we discovered we were only a month apart in age – me born in August and her in July. It was the dawn of a fast friendship.

As days morphed into weeks, my circle expanded, and I started having more friends among the students. One connection that stood out distinctly– was my bond with Mrs. Sophie. She was one of my teachers. She was tall and had an elegant figure. Her husband was working in the US Army. Mrs. Sophie taught me philosophy and she was one of my favourites. She was such a good person and her class became the highlight of my day. Whether it was her captivating method or the subject itself, I couldn't discern. Every lesson was an invitation to think differently, to see beyond the usual, and to question the conventional. She ignited a curiosity in me that turned into an insatiable hunger for knowledge. At that point, my heart started exploring what had been inside of me.

Sometimes I mull over, "So, what can be explored further?" I often asked questions during her class, wanting to know more. The more she took her time in explaining them diligently, the more I wanted to know! My mind was already on fire, wanting to grab as much knowledge as possible to satisfy my ever-yearning young mind.

Each time she gave us homework, I felt extremely eager because it meant I had more research to do. However, many parents conflicted with her kind of homework because she was pushing us to think outside the norm. It was not easy to find balance when you got into conflict with reduced-minded people who still lived under the dominance of traditions.

While some of my peers found her teachings tedious and boring, I was magnetically drawn to them because they seemed to secretly fan the embers that had already kindled in my mind since inception.

Each time she taught us, I grew and nurtured my fantasy to know more profound things, and I loved the way my innocent mind started exploding in leaps and bounds to know more. With time, I was captured by the stories and works of great philosophers like Plato, Aristotle, and Rene Descartes– the father of modern philosophy with all his works on scepticism, and dualism, especially his famous phrase "Cogito, ergo sum" "I think, therefore I am". Also, Immanuel Kant, Friedrich Nietzsche, Martin Heidegger, Fyodor Dostoevsky, Mikhail Bakunin and many more, embracing every lesson, and every idea.

I remember one of my most cherished essays was inspired by Jean-Paul Sartre, the prominent existentialist philosopher who wrote on human freedom, responsibility, and authenticity.

Often, when I needed some breaks from the various books I read, in quiet contemplation, I'd lean on our window sill, basking in the golden glow of the sun, with shadows playfully chasing my face. I relished the sensation of something from the distant past resonating in the present, forming memories for the future. The philosophical giants I studied seemed to surround me, their legacies urging me towards intellectual evolution and inspiring me to become a better version of myself.

Once, my parents kept some of my school things that they thought were important in a box. In an unexpected moment of nostalgia, I came across an old essay from school stashed away by my parents in one of my important boxes – "The Authenticity of Existence: Embracing Freedom in a Nihilistic World." A testament to the profound influence Mrs. Sophie and her teachings had on my young mind.

With excitement coursing through my veins, I'd often sneak off to read a clandestine text I'd discovered. I sometimes excused myself from Loretta and my other friends to read a few pages during break time. After reading, nothing quite stoked the fire of my curiosity like the days Philosophy was on the timetable, and I would have piles of questions for her during the class.

One author I read his books more about was Jean-Paul Sartre. His thoughts particularly intrigued me. He was another comprehensive turnaround in my quest for knowledge. I dedicated more time to reading about his ideas and knowing the similarities between his ideas and other philosophers.

J.P. Sartre's ideas continue to resonate to date, challenging individuals to confront the daunting reality of their existence. By embracing our freedom and acknowledging our role as creators of meaning, we can forge our path towards a fulfilled existence. Sartre understood that nihilism, the belief in the inherent meaninglessness of existence, permeates our modern world. The erosion of traditional values and the crumbling of religious certainties have left many adrift in a vast void. Sartre's existentialism confronts this nihilistic predicament head-on, asserting that we are free to define our own without a pre-determined purpose. For him, authenticity is the pinnacle of human existence. It is the state where individuals fully embrace their freedom and take responsibility for their choices.

Authenticity requires an honest acknowledgement of our freedom, accepting that we are not merely products of circumstance but active agents in shaping our lives. By recognizing our power to create meaning, we liberate ourselves from the constraints of external determinism. He emphasizes the inherent anguish of existence, a feeling of unease arising from the weight of our autonomy. The responsibility to make choices and the fear of making the wrong ones can be paralyzing. However, Sartre argues that the anguish of freedom is necessary for authentic existence. By confronting this anguish and embracing responsibility, we transcend our limited selves and create our values. What I found fascinating was that, in contrast to authenticity, Sartre identifies bad faith as a pervasive condition that impedes our freedom. Bad faith is deceiving oneself into believing that we are not free and that external factors dictate our actions. By surrendering our work and succumbing to societal expectations, we deny ourselves the opportunity to shape our lives. Sartre warns against this self-deception, urging us to confront the discomfort of our freedom and embrace our role as self-determining individuals.

He argues that we are tasked with creating our significance in a world stripped of inherent meaning. By embracing our freedom and acknowledging our responsibility, we have the power to forge a meaningful existence. There was something that I also questioned.

Why should it have a meaning? I felt him sometimes like other philosophers trying to reason unreasonable things.

This act of creation is not limited to individual pursuits but extends to our relationships with others and our engagement with the world. By engaging in genuine interactions and acts of compassion, we can transcend the nihilistic void and imbue our lives with purpose.

Jean-Paul Sartre's philosophy offered me and those who read him a profound perspective on the human condition and provided a framework for navigating the complexities of a nihilistic world. By embracing our freedom and taking responsibility for our choices, we can transcend the anguish of existence and create an expressive life. Authenticity becomes the guiding principle, urging us to confront the void with courage and resilience. In doing so, we discover our purpose and contribute to the collective endeavour of constructing a more meaningful and authentic world. I felt from time to time that I needed to question even his arguments.

Why do I need to be essential or do something that has an impact? Maybe I prefer to be like the wind, never seeing Its beginning or Its end... You often feel this gentle and refreshing feeling, but it can also become powerful and tumultuous. I want to be a tactile experience- a soft, caressing touch or a more forceful and invigorating sensation that flows and sweeps through the environment. I can gently influence people's lives just like it sways leaves on trees, creates ripples on bodies of water, or even stirs up dust particles. I can be a light breeze that whispers through the trees, while a strong gust can howl and roar, creating a symphony of sound. I want my existence to be insignificant but evoke a sense of Freedom, Liberation, and Openness, as it can traverse vast distances and is not confined by boundaries. I want my existence to evoke a sense of nostalgia for those who cared, reminding them of past experiences or distant places.

I want to be compared to the feeling of the wind, encompassing physical sensations, movement, sound, and symbolic and emotional resonances. It is a dynamic force of nature that can range from gentle and soothing to wild and exhilarating, leaving a lasting impression on our senses and emotions.

I want to be feeling but not more than that... At times, my contemplative nature drew curious glances from classmates. Some of them, as they listened to my analytical discussions during philosophy and other classes, viewed me as a little witch who was fast becoming rebellious. Some, deeply entrenched in their religious beliefs, even distanced themselves, labelling me an oddity. In their eyes, religion was the bedrock of morality, and my questions threatened this sacred foundation. Whereas religion is a cage that conforms people to a set of laws and bends them to a pattern of thought and action, thereby making them slaves to certain beliefs without thinking if there is a divergence somewhere.

Ironically, I believed in the harmony of diverging truths. Why couldn't multiple truths coexist? The divergent does not necessarily mean an antagonism or opposite, it could be something that blends in the long run, but religion completely shuts its ears and eyes against it because it threatens their laid down rules and regulations, and one of the things that I have come to notice is that even though society tries to deny that religion is not the bane that drives it; it is not entirely true. Despite technology and other developments, societies would still find ways around religion to justify certain things against common sense (regardless of whatever you serve). That is why I concluded that religion is not almost dynamic; it only finds its way around things to still stand on the laws of "thou shall not do this and that", which is against Sartre's proposition.

Humans are created independently and should therefore have the right to do what they feel is right (provided they are not hurting other people).

That was my stance whenever I argued in class or at home, and my mother, out of annoyance, always told me to shut up! My mother often remarked, somewhat exasperatedly, "You're brilliant, but your way of questioning adults can get you in trouble. You can't question everything and everyone!"

Yet her words, oft-repeated, began to lose their edge. Those were the usual lines my mother read any time we argued over anything at home, and as time went on, those words were like beating drums into the ears of a dead man. They no longer sounded like a threat to me because it was almost like my mother had memorized every line and that she only read them out to me like a creed that churches recited after each service to show allegiance to their maker.

To my mother and others around me, I was a storm in a teacup, a rebellious child who did not want to conform to the laws that guarded humanity. However, it was not true. I was only trying to strike a balance based on the philosopher's views and see a melting point. After all, two truths can coexist peacefully without infringing on the other.

But I wasn't all philosophy and no play. I had been interested in various things since childhood, and that might have triggered that fire in me which had won me many accolades. Mrs. Sophie kept getting closer to me, and I was soon referred to as her bonus daughter - the tag I wore with pride.

During the winter house sports, I was among the most popular backbenchers. I was always watching my brother participate in many sports to the admiration of my father, who always clapped for him. Adam basked in the glory of his athletic achievements. My father always asked me why I failed to learn any sporting activity.

"I don't think I can perform better in it. You know that Adam loves physical exercises and much of fancy things but I prefer to stick to what I want", I told him.

"But you can still try. I saw your friend, Loretta, running the other day and she came second. I was thinking about you at that point that my dear Vicky should be able to do this."

Adam, with a twinkle in his eye, would often jest, "Dad, leave Vicky. She probably thinks sports are beneath philosophers!" We'd laugh, and I'd retort, "I'm not aiming for the Olympics, am I?"

Although I had my blend of physical pursuits, even if they didn't shine in the limelight. I did not have a significant problem not being able to cope with sporting activities. My mind was more preoccupied with other things more important than that. However, I found joy in my own small, private escapades - be it a game of football with Adam, a swim, or some good old skipping rope.

"That should be enough." I always defended myself whenever they laughed at me for being too lazy.

Fortunately, my parents never tried to impose any predefined expectations. They recognized my gifts, even if they came with quirks. And while they sometimes wondered at my musings, they always knew there was one person who truly got me: Mrs. Sophie. She wasn't just a teacher; she was a mentor, a guiding star. As time went by, her influence became even more pronounced, moulding my thoughts and dreams in ways I had never imagined.

Chapter 6

Youth Period

I've always felt that I was thinking and acting ahead of others, and one of the reasons was that I detest defeat and humiliation. This prompted me to carefully cross all of my "Ts" and dot all of my "Is", creating a life where my motto, "Never be caught off guard", stood firmly. My careful nature was mirrored in everything around me. I trod with caution, yet critically analyzed every step I took; wanting to delve into things higher than I was and gaining more knowledge was paramount. I never hesitated to invest my time in this pursuit. Especially during our holidays, my room turned into a haven for reading in seclusion.

My mother would frequently knock on my door to know what I was doing. I've never liked being watched... but with parents, you can't avoid it; they are always around.

There were days that I would borrow some books from Mrs. Sophie to read. I'd become so engrossed that I'd mistakenly underline passages that struck my nerve, forgetting for a moment that it wasn't my place to do so.

I committed to Mrs. Sophie's instructions, not to mark the pages and started writing fascinating passages into a large diary that my mother had given me for my birthday. These paragraphs developed over time into a repository of knowledge that I frequently referenced, especially during heated school debates.

In school, I became a beacon, attracting attention and admiration alike. Sometimes, students and teachers pointed at me "That's Vicky, the sharp girl!" Such validation simply stoked my thirst for knowledge even more.

A rare privilege is having parents who are educated. They were significantly responsible for igniting and fostering my love of reading. I was often urged to read, especially over the holidays, by my mother in particular. She kept a close eye on both Adam's and my reading development whenever she was present. Their propensity for purchasing books was evidence of their desire to see us succeed to the fullest extent. "Vicky - Adam, I saw this book and I felt that you guys would like it." Those were the common statements in our home.

My thoughts were constantly occupied with one thing or the other. I felt entertained having intellectual arguments with people around me because it made me crave more information. Not only that, I love to put my opponents to flight and trembling. My mind became like a fertile land where all kinds of knowledge grew, and I gave time to nurture them with sheer jealousy and utmost carefulness.

I'm constantly filled with ideas, as unyielding as my past obsession with chess. There's something electrifying about the strategic dance across the 64-square board, each move a calculated challenge. Seeing my opponent almost sweating and breathing anxiously, I was in love with that timeless pursuit of strategy and tactics. Those pre-tournament nights, with visions of the board and hypothetical moves, would consume my thoughts. Every piece was an extension of me; the aim was always to dominate the board's centre and create avenues of attack. It was exhilarating, predicting opponents' next moves, like a soothsayer peering into the future. My father would jest about my intense fascination, but the drive to win was undeniable.

Debate, too, was another arena I revelled in. I'd dive deep into opponents' minds, with a mirror of my projections and could pick their next move or words one after the other and punch them to pieces with my lines whenever it came to arguments or debates. My rebuttals were always sharp and ready, tearing their points apart.

Sometimes, thunderous claps followed my points because people would always be thrilled. My ability to anticipate earned me the affectionate nickname "the clever witch". Peers would often seek my insights for debates or lean on me during heated intellectual arguments. With those qualities, I had something - a compelling mindset.

Yet, beneath these talents lay an insatiable hunger for autonomy—a thirst to break free from the constraints of conventional thought. I was a sociopath who broke the law willingly. I was compassionate and logical to the core. I would always want to present my points on logical reasoning that often conflicts with other people's ideologies and legalism. However, I did not always feel down when they tried to label me as being rebellious.

One of my most cherished memories from school revolves around a debate that turned into a memorable showdown between my father and me. Debates were my passion, the pinnacle of my extracurricular activities. When I threw myself into them, it almost felt like I was possessed. This particular debate was special; it wasn't the usual intra-school affair. Instead, it was a high-stakes inter-school competition against Astra College.

Being the primary debater, I carried the majority of the responsibility. While I had three teammates to provide support, I couldn't help but shoulder most of the task myself. Ever since I was a child, I'd nurtured a trait of self-reliance, always wary of depending too much on others for fear they might not meet my expectations. So, in anticipation of this debate, I mapped out strategies, and assigned roles, but also prepared extensively, ready to step in if needed.

During my preparations, I enlisted my father as a practice opponent. "Dad," I'd begun, "I've got this debate against Astra College in two weeks. I'd really value your insights on my arguments."

Far from seeing it as a chore, my father wholeheartedly embraced the challenge. Despite his hectic schedule, he always found time for me, remarking, "Vicky's competing against a formidable school. We have to ensure she brings home the trophy and the accolades." Our rigorous prep sessions began one Friday evening over supper. It was I who had to jog his memory about our earlier conversation, setting the stage for a memorable bonding experience.

 "Dad, you haven't forgotten our discussions from yesterday, have you?" I inquired hopefully.

He chuckled, "Of course not, Vicky. When would you like us to start?"

"Hmmm..."

I was about to reply when Adam, ever the stickler for propriety, interjected, "Table manners! it is bad to talk while eating and eat while talking."

"Don't be absurd! I just wanted to remind Dad about our talk", I retorted.

"Don't be so harsh Adam. It's family time so we should be able to talk our mind." Dad replied in support.

Adam's intervention aside, my father reassured me, "Vicky-baby, let's pick up after dinner, alright?" He gave me a gentle pat on the back, signalling it was alright.

Eager to commence our training, I finished my meal quickly, left the table, and grabbed my notebook and pen, ready to take notes. As soon as Dad was done, he came over, settling next to me. "Alright, Vicky, let's dive in. What's the debate topic?"

"Should there be a death penalty?" I replied.

My mother, overhearing the topic, looked alarmed. "That's a very weird topic for a school debate. What kind of people come up with such bizarre topics?"

Adam, sensing a teaching moment, chimed in, "Mom, all topics have value. Today's school discussion could be tomorrow's national debate, especially in the Western World where almost anything is up for discussion."

Mother's eyebrows raised: "Adam, will you shut your mouth? Since when did you start defending weird things in this house?"

Adam defended, "It's not about supporting odd things, Mom. It's recognizing that educators probably have their reasons for introducing them. Topics like this might very well become central discussions in the future."

Mother, still concerned, turned to my father, "Robert, don't you think it's a bit heavy for teenagers?"

Dad nodded thoughtfully, "It's indeed complicated. However, I feel, if we frame it as an academic exercise rather than a personal standpoint, it should be manageable."

Mother sighed, "If you think so..." Dad smiled reassuringly, "I really do."

My mother remained sceptical, glancing between Dad and me, seemingly searching for any shred of doubt to bolster her concerns.

"Can't Vicky just focus on winning the best student award? It's more in line with the other accolades she's earned."

At that, my mother seemed somewhat appeased, shifting her focus to a movie playing on the television. Adam, engrossed in the film, had already cosied up beside her, eyes fixed on the screen.

Breaking our momentary silence, Dad inquired, "So, which side are you debating? For or against the penalty?"

"I'm arguing against it, Dad. The death penalty debate has raged for ages. While some see it as a necessary tool for justice, others decry it as cruel and a breach of basic human rights. I'm aiming to make a compelling case for its abolishment in this country."

Dad nodded thoughtfully. "How about we try a roleplay where you take the opposing stance? For the sake of argument?"

I hesitated for a moment, considering the challenge. "Alright. Who goes first?"

He grinned, "You lead the way."

Taking a deep breath, I began, "…I stand before you today to argue against the topic, 'Should death be a penalty?'…"

"We all know that the issue of using death to curb crimes in human society did not start today. It has existed since the Ancient Laws of China, and the death penalty has been established as a punishment for crimes. In the 18th Century BC, the Code of King Hammurabi of Babylon codified the death penalty for twenty-five different crimes, although we know that murder was not part of them. The first death sentence historically recorded took place in the 16th Century BC in Egypt, and it happened when the wrongdoer, who was a member of the nobility, was accused of magic and ordered to take his own life. During this period, non-nobility individuals were typically executed using an axe. Since that time, the death penalty started spreading as fast as possible in human society, and that was to curb the fast rise of crimes and to put sanity into society. Another example was the Hittite code established in the 14th Century BC that prescribed the death penalty. Also, in the 7th Century BC Draconian Code of Athens made death the penalty for every crime committed. In the 5th Century BC, the Roman Law of the Twelve Tablets codified the death penalty using different degrees of death to punish offenders.

It does not end there; even the Mosaic law supported death for capital crimes. On many occasions, the Jews carried out many gruesome killings of offenders, such as stoning, hanging, beheading and other terrible means to eliminate the offenders. Jesus Christ was one of the victims of such deaths through crucifixion until almost 300 years later; the great Emperor Constantine abolished crucifixion and other terrible punishments for crime after his conversion to Christianity. However, as time passed, many societies re-enacted those laws, and Britain was one of them. Britain and its colonies multiplied the execution of offenders in different degrees of death. However, between 1832 and 1837, reforms started taking place, and many capital offences were swept away; that continued until more were abolished not only in Britain but also in Europe entirely till today.

One of the factors that brought the abolition of the death sentence was civilization. For example, in the Age of Enlightenment, which was in the 18th and 19th centuries, there were many discussions about Human rights, primarily sponsored by factors such as the abolition of the slave trade. There were many uprisings on the death sentence, and voices started rising against the death penalty for crimes. People started seeing it as a cruel way of dealing with offenders, especially those offences that were not as weighty as they were seen. It was like killing a fly with a sledgehammer and not giving room for repentance and reformation, especially in the places that spearheaded the movement: Europe and North America.

In places like Europe, Philosophers like Cesare Beccaria argued heavily against the use of capital punishment; they proposed a more humane alternative that was flexible to allow for regard for human lives, which struck out the death penalty.

Furthermore, in modern times, the 20th century also holds the same views about the death penalty, making it widely accepted in many places. An example is Europe, which abolished or significantly restricted its use.

Another platform that helps to uphold its functionality is international organizations like the United Nations, which have played a significant role in promoting the abolition of capital punishment. The Universal Declaration of Human Rights (1948) calls for the right to life and the abolition of cruel and inhumane punishments. This has led to a surge in the adoption of sparing offenders from the death penalty. By September 2021, over two-thirds of the nations have adopted flexible ways of dealing with offenders other than condemning them to death.

However, some countries continue to employ the death penalty for certain crimes. These include countries like the United States, China, Iran, Saudi Arabia and Japan.

Although in the contemporary perspectives, there are still some arguments for or against on death penalty whereby the supporters of issuing the death penalty on gross offenders take a stand on retribution, deterrence, and the severity of certain crimes as justifications, especially when the offence involves the life of the victims or cause them severe pains.

However, the opponents may see it differently that sentencing offenders to such a cruel payback denies them the opportunity to live and probably denies them the ability to change and be reformed. In some instances, many notorious offenders later change after being punished, and they become good citizens, bringing others to become better like they are. What if they had been killed and not given another opportunity to change?

My opponents argued that the death penalty violates the right to life and fails to deter crime effectively because, on many occasions, many offenders go to prison to become more hardened, thereby unleashing more terror in society after their release. Therefore, in such cases, death would have been the best way to eliminate them and save society from future dangers.

Boycotting the death penalty, as argued by my opponent, fails to deter crime effectively, is irreversible and prone to errors, and is often applied disproportionately based on factors like race or socioeconomic status, which means that judgment on the death sentence could be partial, thereby favouring some and punishing some. There is an ongoing global debate about the merits, ethics, and efficacy of the death penalty, with discussions focusing on issues of human rights, justice, and punishment and how it should be administered.

It's worth noting that views on the death penalty can differ significantly among individuals within countries and that the information provided here is a general overview of academic discourse.

What am I trying to convey? It's simply that society has progressed from archaic practices to a more reformed approach, allowing room for the forgiveness of offenders and providing them with the chance to reform through milder punishments like fines or imprisonment. This gives them an opportunity to learn better ways of coexisting with others before being reintegrated into society."

After delivering my arguments, the conviction and strength of my points left my father astounded. His applause resonated in the room, and genuine admiration was evident in his eyes.

Clearing his throat, he began, "It's my turn now." As I attentively listened, he dove in, "The death penalty is justice for heinous crimes; it's the ultimate retribution to balance the scale of justice. It not only acts as a powerful deterrent against severe crimes but also offers a semblance of closure to the grieving families of victims, giving them the justice, they seek. Another reason we should agree with the death penalty is because it is cost-effective; there is no need to invest more in housing, feeding or providing medical care throughout their lives. These expenses are useless when we think this person got life imprisonment without parole. The death penalty has been in human existence for time immemorial, just as my opponent stated, and it has helped to create fears in the minds of individuals who knew that if they did something that was against the moral ethics of that time, the penalty would be death. This fear helped to establish a sane and safe society and helped many people become responsible."

As he wrapped up, I eagerly jumped back in, "My opponent was trying to appeal to the emotions of the victims of crimes by stating that the death penalty for offenders should be encouraged because it provides relief to the victims' families. He might be right about that but sometimes have we asked ourselves that if everyone is killed for stealing, and other terrible offences, it might not truly bring a sane society? Criminals might devise more sophisticated and subtle ways of carrying out their execution without being easily caught, which endangers our society the more. Again, what about the irreversibility of risking the life of the innocent? Numerous cases of wrongful convictions have been documented, raising concerns about the potential for executing an innocent person. What about them?

Can anyone guarantee that not even one person will be wrongly accused? We all make mistakes; if an innocent person is wrongfully convicted and executed, there is no way to rectify the mistake.

Another argument is the fundamental human right. Regardless of the crime committed, we have seen documented cases where people have changed their lives radically, not all but a few. Some mentally sick people must be held in psychiatric facilities instead of prisons. We cannot ask those who have, for example, schizophrenia not to have it and behave properly. People who are sick need to be helped by doctors, not thrown into prisons and let rot because they will not be healthier if neglected. If you break a bone and do not fix it with the doctor and just lay in bed and do not go out, it will still not heal properly. Another argument is that the existence of the death penalty has not been proven to prevent individuals from committing violent acts. Studies have shown inconsistent evidence on whether capital punishment is an effective deterrent."

After my father's exposition on the intricacies of the law, I quizzically looked at him, asking, "Can you elaborate on the real-world implementation of these laws?"

Pondering for a moment, he responded, "Well, envision laws as boundary lines, signalling 'Do not cross; Don't do this; Don't do that'. These boundaries exist universally, proclaiming, 'Avoid this action or face repercussions.' But here's food for thought: if humans were inherently violent, would such laws even make a difference? No! Because they wouldn't be able to control the whole world. Everybody has knives, forks or other so-called home-weapons that they never use. Because most people are kind, tolerant and understanding. People are harmless. This is the base of a human. Otherwise, even if the law would say 'do not harm', people could potentially take to the streets with household items as weapons and cause destruction. But that's not the case. It's the few, not the majority of the world who are going against our fundamental behaviour, which is harmony and balance. If we think of more examples, there are even people who in extreme situations couldn't harm others.

So, humans by nature are good, whether laws exist or not. For those who cross over the human rights, of course law should intervene, but not with the mindset to harm such individuals, but instead, to treat them, and reset their minds, because those people are not themselves and they need medical support to become better."

"I've never quite thought of it that way, Dad," I answered, intrigued.

My dad was thrilled, and he continued to help me with other points. "Another argument that you could add is the discrimination and inherent bias."

"How's that?" I asked him again.

He elucidated, "Capital punishment (death penalty for example) isn't uniformly meted out. Disparities exist based on race, economic standing, or even the quality of one's legal defence. But there's more."

I added to what my father was trying to explain to me.

"Isn't that a general fact? People are subjective, even if they try not to be. We cannot deny that each person holds a unique set of beliefs and values that influence their perception of right and wrong, as well as their preferences and priorities. These personal beliefs and values shape their subjective views on various topics and their emotional influence. Sometimes, feelings are biased, watering down facts and what should be done properly. In the end, feelings play a significant role in shaping subjective perspectives. Emotions can impact how people perceive and interpret events, leading to prejudices and subjectivity. For example, in the cause of executing justice, negative feelings or bias about someone or a group of people based on a negative experience with that group of people may lead to holding biased views towards that group. Cognitive partialities are inherent shortcuts and patterns in human thinking that can lead to systematic deviations from rational judgment.

People's subjective views can also stem from limited knowledge or exposure to different perspectives. Lack of information or exposure to diverse ideas can result in narrower viewpoints and subjective thinking. When things are approached from the standpoint of subjective reasoning, it is the proper way of doing things. In some aspects, many people have become victims of these subjective views about life, and they cannot get proper justice unless on rare occasions.

Another thing that can make capital punishment unfair is cultural and societal norms, values, and traditions that can also shape personal views. People are often influenced by the prevailing attitudes and beliefs of their cultural or social environment, leading to subjectivity in their perspectives. Laws should promote open-mindedness, empathy, and critical thinking that could help navigate partiality and foster a better understanding of diverse viewpoints. But to get back to our death penalty conclusion, it should be abolished due to its lack of effectiveness, discriminatory application, and risk of wrongful conviction and execution.

Religion is another thing. I have read about Sharia law. The same concept is found in the Old Testament in the book of Exodus. Laws that don't forgive offenders. It is an eye-for-eye approach. However, this stand has no place in the New Testament, where exclusive forgiveness is preached with punishment outside death. In a situation like this, cultural beliefs and religion might also play a major role, and it could be biased based on the prevailing situation, whether in favour or against the offender."

My father could not hold back his awe. He shouted in disbelief where I got the mastery and accuracy from. He got closer to me and gave me a warm hug.

"Diana, can you hear how eloquent your daughter was in speech?"

"I was following you guys and I can say that it was an excellent performance."

"You are smart and wonderful. I would not want to be in the opposite team in this debate."

"Vicky had always been the shine-on girl! Even her classmates testify to it!", Adam added.

"Vicky, darling, if your team wins this debate, I've got a special surprise waiting for you," my mom promised with a twinkle in her eye.

I was taken aback. Mom had often teased me about overthinking things, so her sudden enthusiasm was unexpected and heartening.

Our opponents weren't just any school but one renowned for their outstanding debating prowess. And somehow, it felt like the weight of our school's expectations rested squarely on my shoulders. My tactic? Daily practice sessions with Mrs. Sophie, our debate coach, during every break. Her patience and guidance were invaluable. "I won't let you down," I vowed to her after one such session.

A few days before the debate, our team - Wilson, Brad, Marietta, and myself - huddled together to strategize. As the lead speaker, I was impressed with their arguments. To refine our approach, we consulted our teacher, who provided valuable insights on structuring our points effectively.

"Victoria, Wilson," she said with emphasis, "you both are at the forefront of this challenge. This might be your first external competition, but the school's hopes are pinned on you."

Her words, meant to motivate, only intensified my anxiety. Sleep evaded me for the next two nights. By Sunday, however, after endless hours practising in front of any reflective surface or inanimate audience member I could find, my confidence began to surge. I was ready.

Monday dawned bright and early. Dad, sensing my urgency, drove faster than usual, and we reached school well before the scheduled time. As we approached the school, I noticed our principal already awaiting our arrival by the gates. I hopped out of the car and darted towards Mrs. Sophie, who stood next to him. Her warm embrace greeted me, "You're absolutely radiant today," she remarked. "Thank you", I replied, then turned to our principal, my curiosity about our debate preparations.

"Ready to go, or do you need a few moments with Mrs. Sophie? What do you think?" he inquired.

"A final run-through would be great," I responded.

Mrs. Sophie led me and my fellow debaters to her office for one last practice session. Soon after, we made our exit, heads held high, and climbed into the awaiting car amidst admiring glances.

Upon arriving at the venue, the sight of our competitors left some of my teammates feeling apprehensive. The opposing students appeared noticeably older, casting doubt on whether we were even in the same grade.

"Remember," I rallied the team, "this isn't a contest of age or height. We're here to prove our intellectual prowess. We've got this."

That word seemed to sink into them like a huge stone thrown into a big river. They assured me of their confidence. We walked into the venue that had been arranged, and without much delay, the programme started. The lead speakers belled the cat and the three other supporting speakers. We engaged in a series of arguments and counterarguments.

At last, it was time to add some points to the already discussed ones. As I scanned the audience, familiar faces from our school met my gaze, their thumbs raised high in encouragement and pride. The judges meticulously evaluated each debater based on eloquence, composure, points raised, accuracy, and overall confidence. The suspense in the room was palpable as they tallied the scores.

Out of a possible 50, for individual performance, my team had earned an impressive 45, while my opponent stood at 40. When the team scores were combined, our school emerged triumphant with 48.5 points to the opposing school's 42.

The announcement of our victory electrified the hall. In recognition of our efforts, we were awarded a $500 prize, a plaque for being the standout speaker, and the honour of being on the winning team. Our school received an additional $1000 and a trophy.

The evening's celebration with my family was one for the books, an unforgettable moment that remains etched in my heart to this day.

Chapter 7

A Step Further

After making a mark in the first interschool debate, I became the face of my school at various competitions. This newfound fame turned even my harshest critics into admirers. My father swelled with pride at every one of my academic achievements. Simultaneously, my brother was making waves in sports, frequently clinching awards for his efforts.

Like a flash of light, I was in my final year of high school. But it wasn't all smooth sailing. Those years were punctuated with academic highs and lows and the constant worry about my father's fragile health.

Although his condition wasn't always critical, each time he fell ill, it took an emotional toll on me. Balancing my rigorous science coursework, representing the school in debates, and managing other responsibilities was a Herculean task. Many even questioned my choice of pursuing science, suggesting the Arts might be a better fit given my debating prowess.

But my commitment to science was unwavering. It wasn't that I had an aversion to the Arts; in fact, it served as a calming escape from my demanding science regimen. But I was hungry for challenges, yearning to push my intellectual boundaries. Mrs. Sophie recognized this hunger in me, constantly pushing me to delve deeper. To me, the world of science was like a siren's call, it was a demon that instigated my hollow heart to keep asking for more!

In the blink of an eye, my final month of high school was upon me. My elder brother, Adam, was already two years into his journey at the University of Oregon. With him away at college, our once frequent in-person conversations had shifted to phone and video calls. At first, the house felt eerily silent without him, but soon the impending final examinations consumed my every thought. I was fervently preparing to earn a spot at Columbia University to study Architecture, my dream discipline.

Many raised eyebrows at my choice. In the eyes of many, I was defying conventions. "Architecture is a male-dominated field. The fierce competition might overshadow your efforts," they cautioned. Even Adam, who always had my best interests at heart, expressed his reservations, not out of doubt, but out of concern for the challenges I'd face.

To them, embarking on a career in architecture as a woman was akin to diving into treacherous waters teeming with sharks. Yes, surviving as a female architect is as demanding and pressure-filled as swimming in a large body of water filled with competitors. It is a matter of striving to get to the shore where people are waiting either to congratulate you genuinely or to fake it but having a different thought in their minds.

However, I was prepared for the challenges, competition, jealousy, envy, and side talks to delve into the men-infested world. I first tested the depth of the water and I was sure I could swim to the other end. All I needed was to find people who would encourage and love me, and that I constantly had in my family!

Entering the realm of university life, was like embarking on a thrilling adventure. It is a path filled with creative challenges, endless hours of drafting, and the pursuit of architectural excellence. However, little did I know that within my university's bustling corridors and studios, destiny had woven a love story that would forever change my life. As I stepped onto the campus grounds, my heart brimmed with excitement and anticipation. This department bustled with passionate individuals, each eager to leave their unique imprint on the design world. Studios became our second homes, and the smell of graphite and the sound of pens scratching against drafting paper filled the air. We bonded over sleepless nights and shared aspirations, forming friendships that would last a lifetime among who was my roommate.

I still vividly recall my first night at the University, feeling like a tiny fish in a vast ocean. There I was, lying on my bunk, swallowed by the unfamiliar surroundings and the weight of being away from home.

That day was the first time I ever felt a more acute loneliness as a teenager. I had finished my registration, and the lectures would start fully by that Monday. I rolled from side to side with a deep hollow of solitude. I had never been away from home in this manner. However, this type of loneliness hit differently. I felt like seeing my family members around to keep me company. The light was off and the silence was almost tangible, only broken by the soft breaths of my roommate, Isabella, deep in sleep.

Isabella, having arrived a week prior, had already settled into the rhythms of college life. She was studying social sciences and had opted for a notoriously demanding major, the specifics of which eluded me at that moment. We'd barely spoken, just the necessary introductions and small talk that roommates do when they first meet.

The room was spacious enough to keep our personal belongings and thoughtfully laid out, with distinct spaces for each of us, eliminating the potential for territorial disputes. Against the muted grey walls stood two wardrobes, a reading table, a pair of chairs, a decorative vase that added a splash of colour to the room and a ceiling fan.

I opened my wardrobe to start checking for a novel out of the many I brought to read when I was less busy. The first one that caught my attention was "Wuthering Heights" by Emily Bronte. It was one of the books my mother gave me as a present for one of my secondary school years, and I have been unable to finish it. So, I picked interest in it immediately. It's Friday. I have to finish this book this weekend. I can read later tonight and continue the rest tomorrow." Those were the words that escaped from my mouth secretly. I had no fear about my classes because I knew a senior in my school who gained admission into the same University. He had already given me many of his books and materials to read ahead. So, even without attending lectures, I had covered some grounds ahead.

I picked the novel and went back to bed. I could still remember the last page, even after many months. I quickly opened the page, eager to read, but I felt a kind of blankness in my head. I suddenly grew uninterested. Nothing around me interested me; I wanted to be with my family badly. I remember how sad my father and mother felt the day I was leaving. My mother could not go with me. She was busy with work. It was only my father that accompanied me.

I had been very excited about coming to school, but I did not know why that passion dropped that first night and why I felt alone. Even the presence of my roommate did not enthusiast me. I wanted to see my family. Although my parents had called me that night, I wanted something more. I closed the pages and threw the book beside my pillow.

Lost in my thoughts, I didn't realize when sleep had overtaken me. I blinked open my eyes the next morning, the room bathed in sunlight. A glance at the ornate gold wall clock revealed it was already 11 AM. Startled, I sat up, greeted by my roommate's smile.

"Good morning, Vicky," Isabella greeted warmly. "Morning, Bella," I responded, stretching out my limbs.

"Before you arrived, this room felt so empty. Your presence is honestly a welcome change to me, a sign of relief," she confessed.

Laughing lightly, I replied, "Ahh! I can relate. My first night away from home was overwhelming."

Bella nodded knowingly. "It's typical for newcomers. Give it some time; you'll adjust."

"I hope so," I replied.

"Vicky, have you seen the milieu of the University?" she asked.

"No, I haven't had the chance to explore the campus. With all the registration chaos and settling in, I missed out."

Isabella's eyes lit up. "How about a tour later today? We could use the time to get to know each other better."

"That sounds great! 2 PM work for you?" "Perfect," she confirmed.

Post our chat, I rang up my family, filling them in on my new life. Their voices warmed my heart, they were excited to hear my voice and how I was fairing as a new bird in the University. I felt so proud and playfully reminded Dad that I was an adult, fully capable of navigating this new phase.

Our afternoon tour was both fun and enlightening. As Isabella and I wandered around, we shared stories about our backgrounds, hobbies, dreams, likes and dislikes. I also told her many things about myself, but I noticed she started seeing me as a kind of 'special' being after our discussions. Recognizing her unease, I reassured her, "I might seem unconventional, Bella, but I'm just me, nothing more." The day marked the beginning of a deep bond, one that transcended our individual quirks.

My academic journey was thriving. It wasn't long before I began integrating into the university's social fabric. Beyond the familiar confines of my room and Isabella's company, I ventured out, mingling with a diverse group of students. My circle expanded, especially within the aspiring architects' community.

Amongst these bright minds, one individual caught my attention—Robert. There was an enigmatic aura surrounding him, fueled by his unmistakable passion for architecture. Fate played its part during a studio session when we were paired up for a collaborative project.

This unforeseen pairing sparked the beginning of a beautiful alliance. Working together, we became each other's sounding boards, challenging ideas and mutually pushing our boundaries. Our dialogues flowed effortlessly, oscillating between the complex world of architectural principles to the simpler nuances of university life. Hours became mere minutes when Robert was around, and our camaraderie became the talk of the studio. The seeds of a deep-rooted bond were unmistakably sown.

Outside the studio walls, our bond continued to grow stronger. We explored the campus together, discovering hidden spots that sparked our creativity. We attended architecture-related events and lectures, immersing ourselves in the rich tapestry of architectural discourse. Our shared passion for design became the foundation of our friendship as we ventured beyond the confines of academia and explored the world around us. Months turned into years, and our relationship evolved into something more profound. Once a sanctuary for creativity, the architecture studio transformed into the backdrop of a love story. Late nights were no longer solely dedicated to design but also stolen glances and lingering conversations. Each project we undertook became a testament to our growing bond as we merged our visions into collaborative masterpieces.

Robert was one of the most brilliant guys in our set. He has a magnetic power to draw positivity to himself. He wore trimmed hair and styled his moustache in a lovely way. He always wore a white spectacle on his usual shirt that he used to fold up to his elbows. He walked in graceful steps, and his deep voice added to the radiance of his personality. Robert, who first appeared as the quiet type, took me by surprise on our first official outing as friends. I never knew that he was the lively type. I was first fooled by his soft approach and gentle smile whenever we worked together in a group. As we sat down to have our official discussion that cloudy afternoon at a coffee shop, I saw a different side of Robert that left me in awe.

We sat there, sipping our drinks at the table. No one shared it with us. So that gave us the confidence to talk more privately. Robert looked me in the eye while he talked. I was never shy anyway, so it didn't bother me. I had already built my confidence from a younger age.

"I never thought that this day would come." Robert said with a milky smile that spread across his face, beaming with unimaginable joy.

I smiled back, trying to admire his exceptional handsomeness and brilliance. "I can say that we were destined to be together. If not, why would Professor Linton pair the two of us?" I said, smiling while watching his reaction.

"Vicky, do you know that the first time I saw you..." He sipped his drink and continued talking... "I felt just like I like this smart and beautiful girl. You know how intimidating you always are during practicals and in class, and I could not keep my heart from following you. It was only that you did not notice. I was permanently looking around for you during lectures. Sometimes, you would walk in or out with some of your friends, and I would always be mesmerized. I told myself I would get this girl to be my friend at any cost. She's bright, and I have so much to learn from her."

"Thank you, Robert, I never realized you could truly see me this way – as someone worthy of admiration both intellectually and personally."

His friendly smile greeted my words, and soon our conversation delved deeper into tales of our youth and upbringing. There was a genuine kindness in his demeanour, and his gentleness shone brightly in his interactions.

As time unfurled, our understanding of each other matured. We recognized each other's strengths and shortcomings, but what set us apart was our knack for open communication. Robert's maturity and enduring patience often served as an anchor to my occasional impulsiveness. He brought equilibrium to my world, and this emotional anchoring only heightened my affection for him. His gaze always held an unspoken promise, making me feel like I was the centre of his universe. The euphoria of such a sentiment was nothing short of intoxicating.

But among the many beautiful moments we shared, one stood out, crystallized in time forever – his proposal. Our cherished studio, a place that had witnessed the evolution of our relationship, was magically transformed. It was awash with a galaxy of shimmering lights, and meticulously crafted architectural models dotted the space, each symbolizing a pivotal moment from our journey together. When I entered, the breathtaking panorama left my heart racing in a dance of joy and surprise.

With trembling hands and sincere eyes, Robert professed his love and commitment, recounting our shared moments and expressing his desire to embark on a lifelong journey together. Overwhelmed by emotion, I could barely find the words to respond. Tears of joy streamed down my face as I nodded, signalling my wholehearted acceptance of his proposal. At that moment, our love intertwined with our passion for architecture, merging two worlds into one harmonious symphony.

My roommate could not believe what happened. She was very happy for me even though she had experienced heartbreaks before. Isabella, like me, never got involved in any social vices; she was brilliant and was among the best students in her class, quiet and wise. She was a Catholic and always prayed with her rosary, but her failure to find a responsible guy was one of her serious concerns. However, she did not allow her bad relationship experiences to affect her happiness.

"Indeed Vicky, Robert seems like a catch. From our brief interactions, I could sense the depth of his character," Bella remarked, brushing a stray hair behind her ear.

Chuckling, I replied, "Honestly, I always pictured him as the eternal bachelor. You know, the kind who's so engrossed in his work that he'd only think of settling down when he's old and grey."

Bella smiled, squeezing my hand. "The best relationships are often those that begin with a genuine bond, evolve organically, and are cemented by choices that look towards a lasting future." Her embrace was warm and comforting.

Proudly, I wore the ring Robert had given me. It wasn't just a piece of jewellery, but a testament to our journey and commitment. The news of our engagement was shared with my family, and during one of their visits to the university, they had the chance to meet him.

Adam, having finished his education and now working in Texas, was always a phone call away, offering insights from his own experiences.

The final stretch of my university journey was demanding. With the last semester in full swing, the weight of academic expectations grew heavy. While the glow of my engagement was heartwarming, I was determined not to let it distract me from my academic pursuits. Yes, having a partner was fulfilling, but achieving academic excellence was just as vital. As the days dwindled down to our final exams, Robert and I found ourselves buried in books and notes, often sacrificing our time together to chase our individual dreams. But it was a mutual understanding – a sacrifice today for a brighter, shared future.

Amidst the whirlwind of exam preparations, our relationship was limited to chatting. We were very busy crossing the "T"s and dotting the "I"s to remain on top of the class. These fleeting moments of connection became our lifeline during the gruelling three-week stretch of final exams.

As I stepped out of the lecture hall after my last exam, a wave of relief washed over me. There stood Robert, his eyes gleaming with pride and relief. Without a word, he wrapped me in a warm embrace, declaring, "We made it!"

"I'm overwhelmed," I confessed, my eyes shining. "Let's celebrate. How about a little outing?"

"Sounds perfect," he replied. But before we could decide on a venue, I remembered I had to check in with my family. Fishing out my phone from my bag, I dialled home. "Hey, Mom..."

Robert distractedly plucked petals from a nearby flower, waiting for my call to wrap up. As our chat concluded, I handed the phone to him, letting him exchange a few words with my parents. When he handed it back, he wore a triumphant grin.

He leaned in, his voice barely above a whisper. "Truth be told, you're the most incredible thing that ever happened to me." We both broke into soft laughter.

As the sun set, our conversation flowed - from dreams of the future to reflections on our time at the university. Eventually, we stood up, hand in hand, ready to step into the next chapter of our lives, fueled by ambition and the promise of a shared future.

Chapter 8

The Excellent Family

Lost in the labyrinth of my thoughts, I didn't know how time had gone. I was startled to realize that dusk had fallen. I could not say that I was lucky that day because nobody came to disturb me in my psychiatrist's wardroom; this had not happened before. I was left alone, deeply immersed in my thoughts and soliloquies. I woke up from my reverie and decided to explore my surroundings in an attempt to make some contact with the outside world beyond my introspections. But as soon as I approached the doorway, a familiar nurse's voice laced with disdain halted me, "Mrs. Vicky, can you explain what are you doing here? I hope you are not planning any mischief with your outlandish?"

Her open disapproval since my admission to the ward was evident. "Perhaps she had witnessed the court proceedings that led to my stay here, it could be the reason for her acidic reactions to everything I did", I thought. It baffled me: why did my personal choices so deeply disturb her? We each carve our paths, and as long as they don't harm others, why should they bother anyone else? Everyone chooses whatever they feel is good for themselves. I still couldn't understand why I was being disliked for what did not concern anyone.

Undeterred, she roared again like a wounded lion, her voice rising, "Mrs. Vicky, leave that door now and return to your room! Now isn't the time for exploration. You had your time this afternoon; tomorrow is another day." Rather than fuel the fire, I quietly retreated to my room. I felt a twinge of regret for interrupting my sweet moment of reminiscence. That, at least, had made my stay in the psychiatrist ward less boring. Leaning back in my chair and resting my head on the wall, memories soon whisked me away again. This time, I allowed myself to explore more funny and beautiful memories. The first wave of memory that flashed back to me was the lovely moment of my wedding day with Robert. My wedding was one of the moments that I cherish so much. Love is truly a beautiful thing.

Our wedding wasn't just an event; it was a celebration of love and design, a narrative of two architectural souls merging. University had not only given me an academic pursuit but also a lifelong companion in Robert. Within the studio walls, I found my calling and a husband who shares my dreams and aspirations. I could say that Robert was a partnership made in heaven because we share almost the same views on everything except some critical exceptions on theories on which we have divergent opinions. Robert, who hardly loves argument the way I do, has quickly devised a method of availing himself of further arguments. Anytime we talked about critical things, he would rather excuse himself or bring up another topic to ease the mood. I also understood him and would quickly accept at that point, but I would still bring it up sometimes.

One memory stood out during my university days, some of my colleagues got into one of those critical debates. I did not know the genesis of the arguments, but it captivated me. Stumbling upon a group of peers, their passionate discussion revolved around suicide and its moral implications. I sat and listened to their debate while I learnt a thing or two. The most vocal, a Jewish classmate, argued fervently, saying "Committing suicide or being assisted is forbidden and a sinful act upon both souls", citing Leviticus 19:14, "Do not put a stumbling block before the blind."

At first, I chose to observe and not get involved in the arguments, but at a point, the intensity and critical nature of the argument drew me in. "Life, while precious, should be a personal choice. To live or to end one's suffering should be one's own will," I interjected.

At that point, they looked at me with bewilderment, especially those advocating the sanctity of life. Another peer, siding with me, posed a poignant question, "If suicide or assisted death is a sin, then why do many still advocate for abortion?"

The room was thick with tension, the kind only profound debates bring. Life, with all its intricacies, was indeed a complex puzzle.

Engulfed in the intensity of the debate, I pressed on: "I once had an enlightening conversation with a Jewish priest. To say suicide is universally condemned within Judaism is to overlook key nuances because there is no explicit proof that suicide is prohibited. You might advocate for life preservation as a paramount duty, but it's essential to realize that not everyone perceives life through the same lens.

Moreover, my body, mind, and thoughts are my sins, and regarding what you say, I've done my part. Remember the tale of the mass suicide at Masada? Didn't you and your people celebrate the Jewish mass suicide at the fortress? Those brave souls chose death over capture, but you can call them sinful as I am. Were they not heroes in some eyes? Every individual has their motives, their pain, and their reasons. Who are we to judge?"

The question hung heavily in the air: Who indeed are we to judge? Society's judgments run deep, from religious people branding suicide as a sin or labelling those who choose it as weak. While others call them selfish or cowards. I hope that the world will grow in recognizing these mental health issues and shift towards more compassionate attitudes. I yearned for a world with greater empathy, where understanding would eclipse judgment, and everything would be much easier, even for those with restrictive cultural and religious beliefs. What if we all cultivated a bit more compassion? What if, instead of harbouring resentment, we embraced love? This world constantly throws inequality our way, from economic disparities to imbalances in opportunity. It's disheartening how societal structures can be disproportionately burdensome, amplifying their mental struggles. Intolerant, judgmental, unfairly heartless world. Sad, but understanding those who are depressed. In which world do they live in? Inequality is everywhere, from economic and social to unequal distribution of wealth and opportunities where power leads to marginalization. God forbid one to be born into a low-income family because it can hinder one's potential, increasing mental health issues such as stress, anxiety, and depression. After all, they need to work multiple times more than the average person with a better life start. This world creates individualists who are obsessed with material possessions and overconsumption. We are degrading the environment and forgetting about the negative consequences. We are destroying our communities by disconnecting us from each other.

Some nodded in agreement with what I said because I told them that life should not be forced on people. People who feel that life is not worth it would have a million reasons to have come to such a conclusion, and they should be respected for their decisions and not be castigated for any reason. Life comes in different phases, and someone's nine could be my six, and nothing should make one party force their opinion of either six or nine on others. By the time the argument ended, it felt as if some walls had come down, there was more enlightenment, and we dispersed in peace without anyone feeling bad.

This spirited discussion took me back to my school days. I was often in hot water due to my candid expressions, free spirit and mind, plus my uncensored way of talking. My dad told my teachers that I had this behaviour and I needed to be controlled so that others wouldn't feel uncomfortable around me. One such episode had my father defending my outspoken nature. He paused by taking a noisy breath, then pointed out the inconsistency in the school's stance – they promoted free expression, they told parents not to impose any rules on the children, yet when a child was too forthright, the blame was shifted to the parents. "Children need guidance to grow into grounded adults", he'd argued. "If we don't set boundaries, we risk raising aimless adults ill-equipped to navigate societal norms."

My father was always candid about the challenges of freely expressing oneself. Yet, he emphasized respectful discourse. That day, as he firmly discussed my behaviour with the teacher, his words echoed the importance of mutual respect. "They should have their own opinions but must be confronted when wrong. The system tries to brainwash and robotize the conduct, and I disapprove." He continued, "If children lack guidelines, they become ungrounded adults, who will later trouble society. We cannot expect children without any guidelines or restrictions to be mature enough to act as we wish.

Children explore but need to have limits until adulthood. Until then, they learn about themselves, others, and life so they can make responsible decisions as grown-ups. How could they be integrated into a society without a compass? Parents should put the borders supported by the teachers, system or whatever. Without parents who know to say so or stop, children become confused adults", he continued.

He had difficulties being open about his views on school conduct. He always reminded us whenever we had dinner that most time, people talk freely and get into trouble because they cannot withstand other opinions. Still, we should always be respectful and open-minded. He told us that we should all have freedom of speech and that words should not be offensive as long as we talk respectfully.

My memories were abruptly snapped by the arrival of the nurse, carrying my dinner. "Mrs. Vicky, here's your meal. The doctor will visit tomorrow to assess your progress." I nearly chuckled at her words. Their belief in my imagined ailment was almost comical. "Their perception is so skewed", I thought. "In their eyes, I might be the patient, but in truth, I feel I see the world more clearly than they ever could. I have never shown any act of mental disorder, yet you keep deceiving yourselves. Anyway, I am aware that you will let me return home when you are through with your drama. I understand that each of you is aware that I am well, and your actions are merely an attempt to appease the court and uphold society's laws."

With her face flushed with fury, she stormed out without saying anything, the door echoing her anger with a dramatic slam. I shrugged off her outrage, my attention quickly shifting to the hunger gnawing at my belly. After relishing my meal with an eagerness reminiscent of a starved creature, I settled into a moment of post-meal relaxation.

Crawling into bed, my mind wandered to the magical day I first became a mother. It hadn't happened immediately after marrying Robert. It wasn't until I turned twenty-eight that I experienced the miracle of childbirth.

That profound moment was heightened by the presence of our parents, their words of encouragement bolstering my spirits. My contractions had started late at night, and I was driven to the hospital by Robert, the nervous soon-to-be father. My water had broken and the baby would be delivered anytime soon. I remember that while I was in the hallway waiting for the doctor to take me to the delivery room, a peculiar sight caught my attention. Amid this life-altering event, a bookshelf in the hallway displayed a work by Emil Cioran. Why, I pondered, would the writings of this famed pessimist find a place in a setting teeming with the optimism of new life? Why would his book be somewhere in a hospital? Perhaps someone forgot it or just put it there to make fun of those who are here to bring new lives into this world! Cioran's belief in life's inherent meaninglessness seemed at odds with my current reality.

He believed life was fundamentally worthless and filled with suffering to the very end. For him, maybe, but it's nice to give life and the opportunity for humans to decide whether life is worth it. In one of his works, one that I remember clearly, "The Temptation to Exist", he talked about humans longing for meaning in life, examining existential choices that all make and the consequences of these choices. Am I making the right decisions? Sometimes I am doubtful of my own choices… Every now and then I understand his views about the nature of suffering, human despair or our limits of knowledge. It's frustrating, and we don't have any guarantee that the decisions we make are right or not. Life is truly quite challenging, especially as I stood on the brink of motherhood, with doubts clouding my mind.

Do I have the right beliefs and values? Could I nurture this new life without imposing my own beliefs? I hope to be a good mother who's admired and could guide pedagogically.

Most people I had known and related with, had some unpleasant childhood experiences, whether with parents, teachers or others, but they got impacted in a way that, as adults, they grapple with the lingering effects of the juvenile traumas and sometimes couldn't cope. As an adult, it's terrible to struggle to trust others, simply because you were a victim during your youthful age. And as a parent, it's so hard to keep the balance between being absent and neglectful or being overbearing and controlling. At some point, children become adults coping with different issues; most of the time, they live with it because there is no one to help them. It's hard. There's no definitive manual for parenting, and this uncertainty and disturbance can haunt a parent.

Ironically, we are never enough for our children, whatever or how much we do. But, thinking even deeper, why should we all have children?

Come to think of it, society mandates training and certifications for trivial pursuits; education, driving license, medical certifications, and others. You take the lessons, you study, take tests then pass; if you fail, you are to retake the examination. Yet, there's no 'qualification' to become a parent. Shouldn't there be some guidance, some check on emotional and mental readiness before one is entrusted with a new life? Sometimes I think that is pretty strange. If you're an addict, alcoholic, or someone with mental disorders-nobody can stop you from having children. In many countries, it would be best if you had medical testing for everything, even for getting married. But for creating a life, nobody requests psychiatric control, or at least during pregnancy, some lessons on conduct or whatever would be needed to be mentally stable. At least if, during these appointments, the doctors would presume that you are not mentally capable of shouldering this responsibility, then you should be given a choice of having an abortion or keeping the baby where social workers and psychologists would be involved during a period to ensure the well-behaviour as a parent. And those women who cannot care for their children use IUDs (intrauterine devices), so they cannot procreate anymore.

The optimist created the plane and the pessimist the parachute… both are right to do so but would have done wrong if they hadn't taken the step forward to create what they dreamed of. These thoughts make me tired. I need to take this baby out so I can rest awhile.

Despite these musings, the euphoria of seeing the face of my newborn son, Alexander, was unparalleled. Robert's ecstatic proclamation of fatherhood filled the room as he jumped around, shouting, "I am now a father". Our parents were there, showing excitement in different ways. While I, amid the jubilation, pondered deeper philosophical quandaries; I was still pessimistic about the freedom to be born rather than the freedom to choose to live or not. Now, not just a wife but a mother too, my plate was full. The roles had compounded, especially for someone as career-driven as me.

Navigating motherhood and a demanding career is no small feat. I frequently encountered unsolicited advice, especially from well-meaning family members like my mother-in-law. "Perhaps you should slow down", they'd suggest, hinting that my career might hinder my new role as a mother, especially considering that my son was still very young. But in my heart, I knew I was up for the challenge. I believed I was a strong woman who was emotionally and physically prepared for that phase of my life, and I was not going to halt one for the other. I knew how many people in my place of work, out of what I would call 'petty jealousy', saw my journey into motherhood as an automatic stop on my ever-yearning ambition to rise higher daily. However, they were disappointed because I was unstoppable. Yes, I took maternity leave, but I returned with the same fire, juggling fieldwork and liaising with construction companies. My parents looked on with pride. "The societal norms might try to limit you", they'd say, "but you're forging a new path. At the rate you are going, we won't be surprised if your name starts featuring in different business magazines."

My husband was a pillar of strength. He was supportive and I could not have begged for a better spouse. We shared a friendly rivalry, both of us thriving in the same field but with different companies.

Motherhood did bring its challenges: sleepless nights, breastfeeding during work breaks, and toddler messes. But with my mom and a trustworthy maid by my side, I managed.

I was around the age of thirty when I discovered that I was pregnant with my second child. My joy knew no bounds when the scan showed that I was carrying a girl. While I was pregnant, I was still agile with my career, although I had a health routine that I followed based on the advice of our family doctor. My baby Anna arrived a few weeks after my thirtieth birthday, looking so beautiful and healthy. She had my looks from birth, and I hoped she would grow to have my character. I had more challenges and responsibilities with a new baby added to the family because raising one was not easy. This time around, motherhood was a bit trickier. Alexander, our firstborn, had started walking and he was into everything, making messes wherever he went. As a mom, I was prepared to cope, especially with my maid always around. I was still breastfeeding Anna when I went back to work. My father would often drive from home to see me almost every weekend. My mother also came around when she was not at work.

Nothing beats having good family members around.

A significant professional milestone came shortly after Anna's birth. My company was in talks with Mr. Brent about a lucrative building project. As a key player, I was pivotal in the discussions. Impressed with my insights, Mr. Brent singled me out for praise, hinting at more collaborations in the future,"I think I have been going around having different meetings with various companies, but I can say that Vicky surpassed my expectations. This company is blessed to have her, and after we complete this task, I will keep coming and even tell some of my colleagues in the same line of business. We are awarding this contract to your company based on her intellect. She is vast in almost all the human fields, and I can say that the sky is her limit." With that speech, he shook hands with me and others before departing. This project was monumental for the company, and my role was crucial.

After their departure, I sat at my table, trying to fix different staff to different positions so that the project could start on time. They were new clients, and we had to do everything possible to get them spellbound. The US is a big world of competition, and anyone ready to add more to his best would soon be side-tracked. After checking some of the files they brought, I started calling some people through the phone to see me in my office and to designate the jobs. However, the larger part was on me. I was not trying to be selfish, but I did not want any loophole to occur. I had always wanted things done excellently while carrying others along. That project was the largest we have gotten, and I was prepared to see the best we could offer because it would open more doors of opportunities for the company in the future. Apart from that, I would have already built a name and carved a niche if I had decided to continue alone. People would then patronize my brand instead, I thought.

Some colleagues doubted my capability, citing my gender, my recent motherhood and being new in the system, they believed I would fumble and not deliver. However, I defied those rules and limitations to achieve the feat; I proved them wrong. Since that time, many of my colleagues who disapproved of my type of free mind started wagging tongues behind me. Society has its rules and how it has programmed everything, but I also have my rules and a free way of thinking, which the world frowns at. Modern individuals feel that its guidelines are right, while I think that mine are right, and that is where conflict of interest comes in. Many of my colleagues even mock my philosophical stand about death, that since I feel life is not worth the hype, why am I trying so hard to always be successful in my career and other things? I knew the angle they were trying to come from, and that was to ensure that they slowed me down in my career pursuit. However, I always told them how important it is to make an impact in life, even if you are not staying long. In my explanations, I always list many people who died naturally or by self-decision. One of them was Majid, a young Muslim I always met on my frequent trips to supervise our onsite projects in my company. I remember one day we got into an interesting discussion after reading on the internet about a popular person who committed suicide a day before.

"I don't know why the world is fast degenerating into a loss of dignity in human lives. How can someone think mercy killing or suicide is the best way to deal with issues? How on earth?", he said.

I shot back, "Look, don't mock people who opt to commit suicide or undergo induced death. Life is not as perfect as it appears on the surface. Many people you see who laugh, entertain, or live as if they have no hidden battles are the most people prone to depression. Depression may occasionally result from internal factors rather than external ones.

Among the things that could lead to this are economic meltdowns or natural disasters. However, the consequences are always more devastating. Many people have developed close relationships with certain people, and it can be unbearable to see those people struggle or pass away from the hardships life has thrown at them. The realisation that fame and fortune can no longer reverse the situation is even more profound. Troubles do not recognize class, gender or age. If it does, how come some world-famous people choose to leave all the things they have behind? It originates from within. People are readily judged by the world and told, <<No matter what, you could have still kept staying strong>>, as if remaining strong is compulsory, even though some people are carrying unspoken wounds and others have had dysfunctional childhood experiences from which they have not yet fully recovered.

For example, look at many famous people who have died through that process, leaders like Cleopatra who was the queen of the Ptolemaic Kingdom of Egypt (51 - 30 BC). Tell me, who could have thought that someone of that cadre would someday wake up and say she wants death? Another example was Ernest Hemingway who was an American Literary Icon. What about Margot Kidder, an actress and Activist Known for Her Role as 'Lois Lane' in the 'Superman Film Series'. These people, I am sure had reasons for their actions, yet the society would judge them for their decision to die."

He sighed, then replied "Vic, it is deeper than what you are saying. It has been decreed that we are going to be tested with different calamities in life, and how we respond to them, in the long run, will determine if we will perish or go to heaven. No matter what life brings, no one is the owner of his life and no one has the right to take it. I am a Muslim and the teachings of our prophet Mohammad (Pbuh) do not give room for taking the life you did not create. For example, in our holy Quran, chapter 174:7-10 says, <<...and we have given you (humankind) power in the earth, and appointed for you therein a livelihood...>>. This means that mankind only has power over what he has been given power over and not the free will to choose between life or death."

I replied, "Majid, do you realize that all life forms should be able to choose if they want to live or not? I wonder why they choose to impose what they feel is good based on their perspectives and one of the tools they use to drive home their points is culture and religion. Can you see how you quickly used your holy Quran to justify your claims?"

Majid approached me, his eyes reflecting a blend of curiosity and respect, "Vicky, considering your Christian background and your love for reading, I assume you've explored some parts of the Quran as well? Do you know that if religion was wrong, culture would not support it? It means that they both place premium importance on human lives."

I nodded thoughtfully. "We should remember, who crafted the laws of culture? And who penned down the Bible and the Quran? Weren't they all humans, perhaps inspired by a divine force, a Spirit? Indeed, it's possible that human interpretation played a role in shaping these sacred texts."

Majid raised an eyebrow, smiling slightly, he added, "Let's continue with this argument another time. For now, I need to supervise the team out in the field." He gestured toward the bustling construction site, where engineers and workers were engrossed in their tasks, and then walked away, leaving me to ponder our brief yet profound exchange.

Chapter 9

The Separation

The next morning, I woke up feeling lethargic like I had never felt before. After being confined here for a few days, I was getting impatient with all that was going on around and with me. I never imagined spending much time in the hospital—apart from when I came to give birth. I had never had surgery or been hospitalised due to a medical condition. My only frequent hospital visits were on days when I went with my father for check-ups, and those visits were in the distant past. Therefore, I never expected to be kept here and to make matters worse, it wasn't because I was ill but rather because I disagreed with a natural course that had given me the moniker of 'psychiatrist patient', which I don't think is just. They realized that my thoughts and presumptive ideas were starting to become a menace to the 'sane society'. However, the society did not think about giving me a fair hearing. What a world!

"I deserve to see my family", I murmured to myself, "I'm no criminal. I can't be kept here without allowing anyone to see me. This isn't a prison." I felt isolated, like an outcast, deprived of the simple pleasures and connections that had once been my reality. I don't understand why I am here receiving this needless punishment.

I need to speak the piece of my mind to anyone who comes to this room or whenever I go around with Mr. Evans. This is getting out of hand. I do not know why I am getting these cruel reactions and treatments from the hospital and the so-called court of law. I have been led to believe that I am the worst sinner ever, doomed to an eternity in hell, at least since I've been here, I have seen people admitted here who have their relatives visiting. I hope that Dr. James comes around today. I would have to ask questions about everything."

I sat by the side of the bed, waiting. A nurse entered shortly after, grinning broadly. "Mrs. Vicky, how are you today?" I did not respond with enthusiasm since I was not in the mood for dramatic pleasantries.

"Is my doctor coming around to check on me?" I asked in a deep voice and with a firm expression.

"Yes, he'll be here by 10 am."

After the nurse guided me through my morning routine, she reassured me once more about Dr. James's impending visit and left, securing the door behind her. I was so angry that I could not even think about anything. Alone, my thoughts swirled, pulling me further into a pit of despair. I closed up my memories and felt empty inside.

Overwhelmed, I longed for the escape of sleep, a brief respite from the world's weight on my shoulders. If only I had access to a book, the hours might have felt less heavy.

A glimmer of hope washed over me as the door creaked open, revealing Dr. James. There was a noticeable change in his appearance; he looked rejuvenated and as approachable as I remembered. Dressed in a crisp white shirt, black trousers, and a contrasting blue tie, he appeared polished, his recent haircut adding a touch of freshness. As he advanced toward me, I pushed myself up from the bed. We exchanged firm handshakes and he greeted me warmly, "Mrs. Vicky! How have you been?"

I hesitated before replying, "I've been okay, but today feels... different."

He furrowed his brow in concern. "What seems to be the matter?" "It's the isolation...I feel so lonely and needy", I confessed.

"What exactly do you want?", He queried.

"I long for the comfort of my family. Being here, cut off from the outside world, my phone, and even books – it feels suffocating. I feel like I am in a prison and I am not myself anymore. Why are you still keeping me here?" My eyes pleaded with his, akin to a lost child seeking solace.

"Mrs. Vicky, please take a moment to breathe, be calm", Dr. James began, his tone gentle yet firm. "You must understand that our actions are bound by regulations. As unique as your case is, it's also unprecedented in my entire career. It's vital for you to know that we're navigating unfamiliar territory here, and sometimes, we feel just as lost as you do. The onus is on you to assist us, and there may be legal implications for you once you're discharged to ensure we don't revisit this situation."

I looked at him in confusion. "What do you mean by saying I am the only one who can help myself in this situation; are you implying that I can't make decisions for myself?"

He sighed, "That's precisely where the misunderstanding lies, Mrs. Vicky. Our laws hold immense authority. Given your background and level of exposure, I'd expect you to know better. We operate in a modern society where the freedom of thought you speak of isn't as black and white as you portray. Such demands, stemming from a more archaic line of thought, would never be approved universally. The only exceptions might be for genuine medical conditions to alleviate pain. Physically, you're in prime condition. Mentally, you are still under review, while there's room for improvement, you've cleared a significant portion of our medical assessments carried out on you.

That means that you only need a few treatments to make you at least, 90% okay. With a little more time, I believe we can enhance your well-being even further."

His words flowed uninterrupted, and I absorbed each one, weighing them carefully. Once he concluded with his lengthy monologue, I exhaled deeply, gathering my thoughts in silence.

Dr. James noting the change in my demeanour said, "Mrs. Vicky," he began gently, "Is there anything you want to say? You seem distant. What's on your mind?"

I could not talk. Overwhelmed, tears blurred my vision before streaming down my face. Dr. James, taken aback, reached out, resting a comforting hand on my shoulder. "I've never seen you this way. Is there more to your story that's affecting you so deeply?"

Through my sobs, I managed a quiet, "Y-e-s."

His gaze deepened with concern. "Can you share it with me?"

"It's a part of my past I haven't disclosed yet," I said, wiping away my tears, steeling myself for the story ahead.

Dr. James leaned in, he looked at me with curiosity, and I could tell how much he showed genuine interest. "Please, take your time."

Drawing in a shaky breath, I wiped my tears and began, "Dr James, I grew up in a lovely family and I had a wonderful childhood. My bond with my father was special, the kind many daughters cherish. While my elder brother, Adam, shared a similar closeness with our mother. My father was my anchor, shaping much of who I am today. He masked his health battles from us as children. The day I saw the reality of his condition, it shattered my world. I recall him being bundled under a thick duvet, paramedics prepping him for transport. My mother was a whirlwind of anxiety, and Adam and I watched, utterly lost, as the ambulance sped away. Later, only my mother returned home. Trying to comfort us, she assured us, 'He's stable and will be home tomorrow.' Clinging to hope, Adam and I whispered prayers and returned to our games, trying to find a semblance of normalcy in that chaotic moment."

After that, years passed without anything happening. My father was full of life and was enthusiastic about everything around him. He created countless cherished memories, taking us on vacations, and showering us with gifts during special occasions and birthdays. He was a beacon of love and warmth. Yet, there came a time when his health started to deteriorate once more.

As I shared these memories, I sensed Dr. James's empathy. His eyes conveyed understanding, and I felt a comforting closeness between us. If he could remove my pains permanently at that time, he would do something to help. His encouraging nods prompted me to delve deeper into my memories. I started sobbing again, but he pleaded with me to move on.

"I am getting used to it, and this is nothing but a reaction to show how touched I am". I continued my story.

"One particular morning is etched in my mind", I began. "Back when I was eagerly awaiting my transition to high school. I was more mature and experienced; I could feel more connected to people's pains. My father was going through his exercise routine while Adam and I were engrossed in a game when a distressing shout from my mother pierced the calm. 'David! What's wrong?' She rushed out of the kitchen, and we followed her. My mother shouted, 'Adam, get the phone and call the ambulance!'"

The recollection made my voice tremble, "In his panic, Adam fumbled with the phone, dialling the wrong numbers because he wasn't himself before finally getting through to the ambulance. Fear and uneasiness had overtaken his mind."

My father returned home the next day, but the unsettling events of that morning ignited my determination to unearth the truth. I first approached my mother, who, deeply engrossed in her work, hesitated to explain, hoping to shield me from the distressing details. "Victoria, I'll share more later. For now, know that he's stable."

However, my innate curiosity and concern refused to subside, and I continually pestered my mother to no avail. One relaxed weekend, I seized the moment during her favourite TV show to press further. Her surprise was evident, but so was her admiration for my persistent quest for answers. "Mom, I need to know, what happened to Dad?

Why did he fall ill so suddenly?"

Mom never expected my questions, she thought I had gotten over the incident. She was uneasy and paused for some minutes. She looked me in the eyes, and it was just like I was mindreading her admiration towards me about how perspicacious I was.

"Mom, I think I have the right to know why Dad falls sick often."

"Okay...okay, your father has a condition and that is why he falls sick sometimes. You know that he is a workaholic who hardly has enough time to rest. That's why he falls sick sometimes".

"But you are also hardworking, why doesn't it affect you?"

"Yes I am, but we have different bodies and he was born with that in his blood."

Without breathing, I pelted her with questions, needing to understand the enigma that was my father's health. "Were we born with this condition as well? Are we going to be limited by what we are doing in life? Or why is it that my brother and I don't fall sick? Adam - he's never sick! And also, you said those who are workaholics get sick, none of my teachers have it".

"Your teachers might not be as hardworking as your father and they weren't born with your father's disease." She tried to pacify me with explanations, emphasizing the uniqueness of each individual's constitution.

"Then tell daddy to stop being hardworking so that he would not fall sick if he is more fragile than others".

"Okay, I will tell him." The moment felt cathartic when my mother pulled me close, stroking my hair. I sensed her own relief, perhaps in sharing the burden of the truth with me.

Dr. James's attentive nods and scribbles indicated his vested interest in my story. I guessed he was getting some information about my health status and what could have triggered my strange demands which were pitching me against the natural course and the law.

He prompted gently, "What happened next?"

I delved back into the past "Hmmm...I later heard from the horse's mouth. It was during a family evening, engrossed in a Titanic documentary. Dad offhandedly remarked, 'With my health issues, I wouldn't have survived that shipwreck if I was on the ship.' That admission, so candid, took me aback. 'Your health status?' I echoed, needing more."

He laughed warmly, acknowledging the proverbial cat was out of the bag. "Yes, I'm not as healthy as you might think."

The question hung in the air, "What do you mean, Dad?"

With a hint of laughter masking underlying pain, my father began, "I have SCD - Sickle Cell Disease. I was born with it." Though unfamiliar with the full implications of the term, I could piece together its gravity from the glimpses of my father's periodic episodes. It was more serious than the mere sickness my mother explained.

Adam, typically reserved, found his voice, "Daddy, can you explain more about SCD?"

For a fleeting moment, I saw Adam mirroring my concern, forging a connection I hadn't witnessed before.

My father explained, "SCD is a genetic condition affecting red blood cells. These cells contain haemoglobin, a protein responsible for transporting oxygen. Usually, healthy red blood cells are round, easily flowing through our veins carrying oxygen to all areas of our body.

However, with SCD, the haemoglobin is abnormal, which transforms these red blood cells into a 'sickle' shape, resembling a C-shaped farming tool. This alteration makes them sticky and rigid, causing them to clog blood vessels. As a result, they die prematurely, leading to frequent blood shortages. This can trigger pain, infections, complications like acute chest syndrome, and even strokes."

He paused, making sure we were following, then continued, "There are different forms of SCD, determined by the specific genes inherited from parents. People with SCD inherit genes that contain instructions, or code, for abnormal haemoglobin. The causes of SCD are dependent on a genetic condition that is present at birth. It is inherited when a child receives two genes—one from each parent— that code for abnormal haemoglobin, and this means that my parents had the same genotype, AS. In my case, I, unfortunately, inherited two abnormal haemoglobin genes - one from each of my parents, marking me with the SS genotype, which is why I've faced these health challenges."

Connecting the dots, I asked, "Is that why you're often on medication and have regular hospital check-ups, even if you seem well?"

He nodded, "Yes. Those medicines and visits are preventive measures to keep me healthy and prolong my life. But as you've noticed, they don't completely shield me from the disease's episodes."

Hearing my father's revelation left me stunned. All the while he spoke, my mother kept her gaze lowered, her silence heavy with unspoken thoughts. Perhaps she had intended to shield us from this truth for reasons best known to her.

"Is there any cure for this, Dad?" Adam's voice broke the silence.

"I wish, Adam," my father replied with a sigh, "But there isn't. All I can do is manage it."

Despite the brave smile on his face, I felt a pang of pain for what he must have endured over the years. Was he masking a deeper pain for our sake? Moreover, my mother's quietness hinted that the reality might be even graver than how Dad painted it. Memories of his past crises flooded back, making my eyes well up with tears. I remembered those terrifying moments when he seemed to gasp for air, resembling someone having an asthma attack, as he was hurriedly taken to an ambulance.

Though he always presented himself as a strong pillar, this new knowledge deepened my bond with him. This insight shaped my adolescent views on life's fragility and the inevitability of death. It fueled our family's collective efforts to provide the best care for him, efforts that saw him celebrate his 50th birthday. We navigated the highs and lows together, cherishing the moments when he was vibrant and rallying around him during his downturns until he reached the age of 55.

The final days of my father's life were a whirlwind of activity. Fresh from a rejuvenating family vacation at the beach, he'd revelled in ocean swims and spirited volleyball matches with us. Each morning, he'd ventured out for runs, letting the refreshing sea breeze play on his face, even though swimming was always dicey due to his SCD sensitivity to temperature changes. But Dad was never one to let life pass him by. He'd remained steadfast in managing his condition, punctual with his medication and always mindful of his health.

Back home, the rhythm of life resumed. He plunged into work, and seamlessly transitioned from business mogul to an old friend laughing over dinner and drinks with his pals. His unwavering discipline extended to his personal health regime; a balanced diet and rest were non-negotiables.

However, one morning, an unusual fatigue clouded him. He tried to push past it, but it clung on stubbornly. The unexpected happened soon after – a devastating stroke, a consequence of his SCD weakening his blood vessels and restricting oxygen to his brain. We were blindsided. He had seemed to have a grip on his condition.

The gravity of the situation pulled our family closer. My mother, siblings, and I circled him, our collective strength buoying his weakening spirit. My brief respites from work were filled with precious moments by his bedside. Robert, my pillar, held down the fort at home, while our little Anna and Adam, added their innocent presence to the mix. Even Adam, with his young family, made it a point to be there. The last week leading to my father's passing was heart-wrenching. Memories of our times together flitted in and out, as we held on to hope and each other.

The piercing emotional pain I felt watching my father suffer was reminiscent of the agony I endured during my first childbirth. I could still vividly recall how my father had gently patted my back, offering words of encouragement as I shuffled heavily into the labour room, burdened by physical and emotional weight. I was walking in heavy footsteps as if a brick was tied to my legs. I could not say if I were alive or dead because of how I felt. My head ached, my bones contrasted, my body heavy, and all kinds of discomforts were happening to me! That was how I felt. Now, seeing him on the hospital bed, every groan he emitted mirrored the pain I had experienced then. His battle seemed larger than life, especially juxtaposed against his kind, gentle nature. My mother's tears flowed freely, while Adam tried to soothe him with calming words. Robert, always the rock, whispered words of solace, and I felt a turbulent storm of emotions, leading me to pace anxiously back and forth. But as I nestled my father's head onto my lap, he was restless but he was trying to communicate with us. His sporadic smiles amidst his obvious discomfort reassured me, even if just momentarily. I knew he was tired of struggling between life and death. At that point, I could not figure out why my father was singled out for such suffering - a suffering that stood out from his enormous, lovely nature.

I kept repeating, "Daddy, you will be fine", but it seemed that he knew that it was too late and that he would be happier leaving his mortal pains behind. Still, his discomfort seemed relentless, as though it were more powerful than the combined strength of our love and care. Despite this, he began sharing thoughts of heaven and expressing his boundless love for us all. He also reflected on the joys of life and prayed over us. My mother's sudden departure from the room felt ominous, and when she returned with a doctor to check on him, wiping away her tears, my anxiety heightened. My father's simple request for a warm cup of tea, after days of not eating, briefly sparked hope. Adam quickly made tea from the hot water in our flask. But as he took his last sips, a sudden jolt sent me into panic. The cup dropped, spilling its contents. Adam and Robert rushed to him, trying desperately to fend off the encroaching grip of death. After a few harrowing moments, he took his final breath, leaving a silence that was deafening. My heart felt as though it were tearing apart, and Robert held me tight, shielding me from my own anguish. My mother, inconsolable, sobbed loudly, while Adam, always stoic, leaned silently against a wall.

After some time, his body was discharged, and we took him for burial. His funeral was a sea of black, a testament to the many lives he had touched. As the priest eulogized, referencing the transient and often sorrow-filled nature of human life, I couldn't help but think how emblematic my father's life was of that sentiment. As his casket was lowered, my knees threatened to give way, but Robert, ever-present, kept me upright. The days and weeks that followed were a blur, marked by a profound sense of loss and longing for the presence of a man who had meant so much to all of us.

The void left by my father was overwhelming, often casting me into the quiet corners of my room. His battle with the disease had snatched away many cherished moments, especially with his grandchildren. Yet, despite the sorrows, there were times when I felt solace. Memories of his zeal for life, his laughter, and his resistance to let his illness define him, all shone brightly.

In those reflective moments, I thought of his unyielding spirit even during the direst moments of pain. His passing was not just a loss but a stark reminder of the time we need to cherish with loved ones and the ravages of SCD. Inspired by his resilience, our family pledged to elevate awareness about this condition and to support the quest for a cure.

"I feel so lost without him," I often whispered to the walls of my sanctuary, remembering his gentleness. "Everyone says he should've been grateful for his life, but don't they see the limitations he faced?"

"When I took up that he had to avoid basic activities during his lifetime, like swimming because of the temperature difference, which could periclitate his life, I heard complaints about how superficial I see life and that I have no minimal respect for my ancestors.

According to them, ending an existence goes against this fundamental right by ending the life of a patient prematurely, even if it is at their request. The unbreakable bond that I have with my father will never be extinguished. Each day is like an uphill battle, and I need to struggle to be there for the rest of my family. This weight of sorrow clung to me like a constant companion, consuming my thoughts and draining my energy. My mind is plagued with memories of his vibrant presence, now forever absent. This overwhelming feeling eats me alive with an unbearable ache that seems to have no end. There were moments when the burden of grief felt smothering, like a blanket too heavy to push away. The days seemed bleak, but deep down, his voice echoed, providing a glimmer of hope," her mind continues to whisper.

The world outside my door felt distant and unfamiliar, and the company of others became daunting. I withdrew into myself, seeking solace within the confines of my solitude, where I could mourn my father's loss in my private sanctuary. Deep within my soul, I could hear his voice, reminding me of our shared strength. I sought solace in the memories we had created together, finding comfort in the echoes of his love that reverberated through my being. Gradually, the fog of loss began to lift, unveiling moments of clarity and renewed purpose. I realized that, although my father was no longer physically present, his spirit would forever reside within me. Then an idea occurred to me, which was a new beginning for me and the world.

"Stop the world with its existing chaos! I want to get off!"

Even so far, no vaccine has been found against society under the yoke of which we are. We live in a dehumanized world where everyone is stepping over everyone else to make it better. Others use techniques that I don't believe in; by the way, that's why I chose my path. I believe in what I see, in what I live... I'm flipping through the Tibetan Book of the Dead, idly, depressed and bored, and I don't understand what inspired the rest to continue to convey the same sensations.

Some of my acquaintances blend superstition with medicine or tradition with religion. I find it quite hilarious how saviours doctors sit in the operating room dissecting people and doing incantations at the same time, dancing with the scalpel in their hands and spitting all kinds of quasi-magical dust into the open operation, supposing or hoping to save the lives of those on the operating table.

However, every day, more and more people all over the planet indulge in nonsense. It's like there's an unseen virus that takes over their minds.

Chapter 10

The Criticisms

It was a dull Sunday afternoon. There are always fewer activities in the psychiatrist ward on Sundays, and I could not say if that is because many people see it as a sacred day and decide to stay off the hustling and bustling of life. No visits, no doctors attending to patients unless it was an emergency. The people who were usually on duty were the nurses. My day was mostly spent drifting in and out of a peaceful, dreamless sleep. The only time I was disturbed was when a nurse came to check up on me.

I reminded myself, "There's so much time to rest here. This ward seems to slow time down. My days are mostly filled with questions like 'Have you?', 'Did you?' from the doctors or walks with Mr. Evans." Stretching my limbs, I stood up from the bed and shuffled to a chair, rubbing the sleep from my eyes with my left arm.

As I settled in, memories, uninvited, began flooding back, and it was one of the most frightening moments of my life. I had seen people who lost their dear ones, and they could move on gradually, but I could not! I had always believed the old saying was true that 'time heals all wounds', but in my case, it was different! I could not move forward like other people since my father passed away.

Memories of him, especially those of his final days, played on a loop in my mind. His battles, the pain, his resilience, and the hope that maybe, just maybe, he'd pull through like he always had. But he didn't. The vivid image of him struggling, gasping for breath and wriggling like a wounded snake on his deathbed in his last moments, kept repeating in my head, and sometimes, haunted me constantly. I saw him in my imagination at that same time in life. No matter how much I achieved in life, how wonderful my family was, or how comfortable my surroundings became, there was this void, an unspeakable longing. A desire so profound and personal that I feared it might sound absurd if I ever tried to express it. More than once, I've felt the urge to run headfirst into those haunting memories and shatter them.

"Oh, Dad," I often thought, "If only I could give a piece of my life to bring you back, free from all that pain."

Initially, it seemed like no one truly grasped the depth of my inner turmoil. While everyone around me mourned, they eventually began to find their way back to the light. But I remained ensnared in my grief.

Even in a crowd of loved ones, a profound loneliness consumed me. Each day felt like a dark storm cloud looming over me. It was as if I were navigating a pitch-black night, stumbling and falling into muddy pits, with no guiding hand to steady me. The immense weight of my father's passing had, surprisingly, brought me to my knees.

While the memory of my father's loss persisted, I began to discover that I possess an inner strength, a guiding star through my most sombre hours. There were moments when an inner voice whispered: "Embrace the anguish. Let it consume, engulf, and refine you. It should be so overwhelming that it becomes a numbing balm for the soul. This intense agony can be the very catalyst for healing. But during this transformative process, remain aware and accept the pain, much like an unexpected gust of wind – cold, unsettling, but eventually passing, even if it leaves a bit of chaos behind."

At times, when I was alone, these reflections would provoke a wry laugh from me. The proposed remedy seemed so simple, yet the journey from hurt to healing felt like an arduous trek. True healing was a gradual process, and often my mother's words would echo in my ears: "I understand the bond you shared with him, but remember, you're a mother now. You must stay strong for your children. One day, you'll reunite with your father in Heaven. He knows our love for him, but life's tapestry is beyond our control. Begin to find your way forward. Cherish his memories, but don't let them consume you. You have a family to care for and a career to pursue." Those were my mother's words whenever we spoke on the phone or she came to visit.

But, as much as I wanted to take solace in them, I was more drawn back. Robert stood by me. I could remember the first few weeks of my father's demise; he was the one catering to the children and preparing them for school. I was physically okay, but my mind was shrouded in a dark, thick cloud of despair that held me down.

Lying on my hospital bed, his words resonated like a melody, wrapping me in their wisdom: "Every challenge, every mess, is a lesson. It teaches resilience and sharpens discernment. Embracing life's ebbs and flows equips you for those inevitable stumbles. So when life grazes you, remember that even those scratches and bruises heal over time."

Even on some occasions, my pains spoke mysteries into my inner ears, and I could hear those words loud and clear: "Think of me as coffee. To some, I'm an acquired taste; they're put off by my bitterness, my depth. But that's okay. Not everyone needs or wants coffee. And if they do, they can always sweeten it to their liking."

Meanwhile, I was still stuck at that point despite these insights and the comforting gestures of those around me, a heavy inertia weighed me down. The myriad opportunities life unfurled in front of me seemed more daunting than inviting.

After many days of internal struggles, I realized that it was time to share my thoughts with my family.

"They might not see it my way, but I'm clear about my choice. This isn't about surrendering to despair or being weary of life. It's about wanting to exit gracefully, on my terms. How many elders battle ailments in their twilight years, confined to their beds, waiting for death to come? I won't let that be my story. Tonight, I'll discuss it with Robert", I murmured, packing some files from my table to the cabinet, and readying myself for the conversation ahead.

As I drove home that evening, I struggled with thoughts swirling around the weight of my decision and the profound desire for personal freedom. I had been contemplating this for some time, and now it is time to find the courage to express my truth to my family. I weighed the significance of personal autonomy and the freedom to choose one's path. Living life on one's terms resonated deeply with me. I believe every individual should have the right to decide the course of their existence, even concerning matters as profound as life or death. I contemplated how to approach my family and understood the delicate nature of my decision and its impact on them. I wanted to ensure that they understood my choice, which did not reflect their worth or my love for them. It was about my struggle for autonomy and my longing to maintain integrity. I pondered how I could communicate my thoughts and feelings to my family. I knew it wouldn't be easy for them to comprehend, and I anticipated a range of emotions from confusion to anger and heartache. I wanted to convey my decision with compassion, empathy, and unwavering love, hoping they could find solace in the understanding that this was my journey.

My intention was not to hurt or burden them but to pursue a path aligned with my values and desires. I knew that this conversation would be one of the most challenging of my life as I confronted the fear of rejection and the possibility of misunderstanding. I hoped that by sharing my truth, they could ultimately come to a place of understanding and support, even if they may not fully agree with my decision.

Later that evening, Robert and I were in the bedroom after dinner. He flipped through the newspaper pages, checking for something exciting to read. I was in my nightie, preparing to go to bed after a shower. I decided to talk about it at that moment and not delay any longer.

"Robert", I began hesitantly, "There's something I've been grappling with, a decision that's been consuming my thoughts. I want to share it with you, and I hope you'll try to understand."

His attention shifted immediately; a touch of concern evident in his eyes. "Okay, Vic. I'm listening. Tell me."

Inhaling deeply, I dived in, "I've been feeling this intense need to be in control because I am at the peak of my life, I need to make choices on my terms. It's not about being unhappy or ungrateful. It's about a certain clarity, a culmination of my experiences."

"It's difficult to comprehend, but can you elaborate on what you mean by being at the peak of your life?" Robert said, trying to figure out my statement.

"At this point, I feel fulfilled and accomplished in various aspects of my life. I have fought for myself and the freedom of choice, not just for myself but for others as well. I have advocated for personal autonomy and the right to decide our lives. I want to end my life with integrity while life is still celebrated rather than reaching a point where it becomes a burden. I know this is difficult for you to understand, but I would be grateful if you could see things from my perspective.

I'm telling you this because I want us to have an open and honest conversation about my decision."

Robert's face paled, "Vic! I don't understand. What the hell are you talking about? What is this nonsense you're saying? Are you out of your mind?" he answered without breathing.

Holding back tears, I replied, "Robert, please try to understand that this decision is not made lightly. It's not about disregarding the value of life or taking it for granted. It's about having the freedom to choose, even in matters as profound as life and death."

"You can't do that, Victoria", Robert said, anguish evident in his eyes and continued. "We all face challenges and difficulties, but that doesn't mean we should give up. We find strength and purpose in persevering through tough times. I want us to face the future together, no matter what it brings. You need to talk to a doctor. What happened to you?"

"I appreciate your belief in the resilience of the human spirit, Robert. I truly do. But I've thought long and hard about this, and I've reached a point where I feel that I've done my part in this life. I don't want to wait until life becomes a burden, like it did for my father. I want to make this decision while I still have my integrity intact."

His voice was a raw whisper, "Victoria, I can't bear the thought of you leaving me like this. We've built a life together, and I can't fathom it ending prematurely. I don't want to lose you, and I don't want to imagine a future without you. And the CHILDREN! Have you thought about them?"

"I know it's painful to think about, Robert. And I don't want to hurt you or cause any pain. But I can't ignore the feelings of suffocation and despair that have grown within me. I want you to understand that this decision is about my autonomy and right to choose what feels right for me, even if it's difficult for you to accept."

"Vic! You need to seek professional help and talk to experts who can guide us through this. How do you plan to talk to our children about this? How can you justify leaving them behind and burdening them with the knowledge that their mother chose to end her own life? It feels selfish, and I'm deeply concerned about the impact this will have on them."

"Robert, I understand your worries about our children. I want you to know that I have thought long and hard about how to approach this sensitive topic with our children. I do not take their emotions or well-being lightly".

"Vic… they look up to you. How do you expect them to understand such a complex choice? It will undoubtedly have a lasting effect on their lives, their trust, and their emotional well-being. You cannot put them through this pain!"

"I hear your fears, and I share your love and protectiveness for our children. I don't intend to burden them with the full weight of my decision. Instead, I plan to approach this situation with the utmost sensitivity, ensuring they receive appropriate professional guidance and support. It's crucial that they understand that my decision does not reflect a lack of love for them, but rather my personal struggle and desire for autonomy."

"I worry about the long-term effects on our children's mental health, Victoria. It's a heavy burden for them to bear, and I fear it could impact their perceptions of life, trust, and their future relationships. Can you really expose them and me to such pain?"

"I am committed to providing our children with the necessary support and resources to help them navigate this. Professional guidance will be essential in helping them understand and process their emotions. I intend to communicate to them that my decision is a deeply personal one, and it does not diminish the love I have for them or the importance of their own lives."

"I'm struggling to accept this! I urge you to consider the impact it will have on their lives and their future. They will forever carry the weight of this knowledge, and it will shape their perception of the world. I can't comprehend the level of selfishness in your decision. To think that you would choose to leave our children behind and burden them with this pain is beyond my understanding. I need some time alone to process all of this."

"Robert, I understand that this is a difficult situation for you. I never intended to hurt you or our children…"

He left me talking alone. He was shocked and overwhelmed, leaving the room with a deep sadness. The day after, after Saturday's breakfast, I knew it was time to talk to our children. I couldn't wait any longer.

"Alex, Anna, there's something important I need to talk to you about. Please sit down…"

Speechless, they sit down, their eyes filled with confusion and concern. They felt the gravity in my voice. They saw Robert uncomfortable and silent. They felt the tension in the air.

"I know this may be difficult for you to understand, but I want to be open and honest with you. I have made a decision about my own life, and it's important that I share it with you. Please know that my love for you is unwavering, and this decision is not a reflection of how much I care about you."

Robert couldn't help but react: "Victoria, how can you do this? How can you burden our children with such a heavy, painful discussion? This is unfathomable!"

A heavy silence ensued, broken only by Alex and Anna entering the room, sensing the palpable tension.

"Mom, Dad," Alex's voice trembled, "What's going on?"

I didn't answer them. I stared at Robert and answered him: "I know you're angry and hurt right now, but please try to listen. I believe in being honest with our children and want them to hear it from me rather than from someone else. I assure you that we will all receive the necessary support and guidance."

I continued, "Kids, there's something I want to share. It's not easy, but I believe in being open. Know that this comes from a place of deep introspection, not a lack of love."

Robert, voice choked, interjected, "Victoria, I still can't believe you're doing this. This is beyond selfish. You're tearing us apart!"

We started an argument in front of our kids before I could tell them what was happening: "I never intended to hurt any of you, especially not our children. This decision was made carefully. It's important that our children understand that my decision does not reflect their worth or love".

Their expressions were a blend of confusion and pain. Taking a deep breath, I continued, addressing my children directly, "I need you both to know just how much I love you. I've made a challenging decision. You might feel hurt or even angry, but please know I am here for you."

Anna interjected, her voice wavering, "Mom, what are you saying?"

Taking a moment, I replied, "I've decided on something about the trajectory of my life. It could be difficult and filled with pain. We all have unique journeys, and I feel it's essential for me to decide how I want to face its eventual conclusion. I wish to end my life with dignity at a time of my own choosing. I want you to know that it's not your responsibility to carry any guilt or blame."

A heavy silence settled in, punctuated only by the sound of our collective breathing. Their eyes welled up with tears, as they struggled to comprehend my words. "I realize it's a lot to take in, but please understand that this is about me and the life choices I want to make. I don't expect you to fully grasp it now. What's important is that I love you with all my heart."

They struggled to find words.

"Your feelings and emotions are valid, and I encourage you to express them openly," I said, trying to break that heavy feeling in the air.

Tears brimmed in Alex's eyes as he retorted, "But Mom, how could you think of this without considering us? It feels like you're choosing to walk away from us."

Anna, her voice quivering and filled with hurt, added, "You're supposed to be our protector. How can you leave us like this?"

I felt heartbroken. With a heavy heart, I responded, "I understand your pain and confusion. I want you to know that this decision is not about abandoning anyone. It's about my own personal journey and the complexities of life that I'm grappling with. I love you both and your father deeply, and my decision is not a reflection of my love for either of you".

Alex was frustrated, his voice rose, "This decision rips our family apart! Can't you see that?"

"I hear your pain, honey. I never want to cause any harm or distress. Please believe me when I say that my intention is not to tear our family apart."

"You're prioritizing your own needs above our well-being. We need you here with us, not gone!" continued Alex angrily.

Alex, with despair in his eyes, turns to his sister and says: "Mom is abandoning us when we need her the most."

Robert, usually the quiet strength, chimed in with clear anguish, "The children just want our family intact! They need you here, present, with them!" I felt angry at him for not being quiet, at least. He was throwing gasoline on the fire… up. It was so frustrating.

Tears flowed freely from all of us. Robert, overwhelmed, exclaimed, "Vic, I can't bear this. I can't be here right now!"

Overwhelmed with emotions, he left the room, leaving me and the children saddened.

In a soft, almost whisper, I responded, "I'm just seeking clarity and freedom. My decision isn't about hurting anyone but finding peace within." I felt hollow and unhappy. However, I was still interested in carrying out my decision. Not that I was threatening them, but that I wanted something better for myself.

Repeating to myself, I murmured, "It's about the right to choose... Euthanasia. THE FREEDOM TO DIE." I continued repeating those words as I left. At least I had told Robert about my plans, which was the most important thing to do.

The next day was an exercise in walking on eggshells. Robert and I barely exchanged words. He acted like nothing happened and wasn't interested in discussing it. All I was concerned about was that my mind had become clear from the cobwebs of many entanglements engulfed months ago. I left for work thinking about how I would present it to my children.

Robert and I had no physical argument about it when I got home, but I could sense that he was still worried and uneasy. My children also had the same feeling, and I was bothered. Alex had withdrawn from that jolly boy and was wearing a cloudy face. The cheerful atmosphere our home once harboured seemed like a distant memory, replaced by a thick cloud of uncertainty. As for Anna, she did not act very concerned, but I knew she was also unhappy.

I felt pity for my daughter then, and I was helpless as I tried to explain things the following day while we were in the kitchen.

"I still do not understand what you are trying to say…"

She stormed out of the kitchen angrily, and after a few minutes, I heard her loud footsteps walking towards the main door leading to our sitting room.

"Dad! Dad!". I could hear her calling.

I stood at a spot, unable to move. I never knew about whatever they discussed outside until Alex came in to ask again, "Mom, I hope rethink the discussion of yesterday. Please, don't do this to us". While that was ongoing, Anna and Robert came in. Anna was still furious and talked to me with a raised voice, while Alex was trying to make me reconsider my decision.

Robert did not say a word. He stood up from the couch on which he sat and picked up the book he was reading. He came close to me with our chests almost touching each other and whispered to me, "I hope you gain your sanity soon. Mind you, those children are hurt deeply and you need to have a rethink!" (He said that while pointing to his head).

He left me standing there like a statute. I was frozen and could not say how I felt then.

"I have the right to decide my fate!" I said as I flung myself on the couch, my head banging and my strength exhausted with the reaction from my children.

After many years of fighting windmills, I found that our world is compatible with guilt. You go to school, you work honestly, you fight, and you get sick so that, in the end, it turns out that everything is in vain. It is natural for individuals to be critical and empathize with society's victims (or not). Nevertheless, the problem is that sometimes the accused is the victim of an immoral society and a rotten system.

In certain instances, you might find it necessary to turn to the legal system to assert your rights. However, you wonder how things can get so twisted after years wasted in courts and lawsuits. Media coverage in a certain way is essential. You are lost if you are put against the wall, insulted, and called a certain way because of preconceived ideas!

For some, the truth is somewhere in the middle; for me (for each individual), the truth is the one we present without hesitation to anyone. And if the words hide even a little of the truth, then the Divinity will pour His wrath on us as we deserve. In other words, if someone's innocence is real, they have nothing to fear. However, those who judge coldly realize how easily a gullible individual can be manipulated. This naivety can be fatal.

I was thrown into an underground with inhuman cruelty. For them, a psychiatric hospital was the solution to eradicating my mind. From the beginning, the judges were against me, treating me like the most insignificant object. To the judge, the accuser was like a God, and I was the victim, his target. They hastened to offend me with mockery, looking at me with contempt, their opinion already formed. They were brainwashed, and my arguments didn't matter anyway. Not for them, not for anybody!

Justice demands that the judge maintains a fair balance, yet he heavily tilted the scales towards the guilt of the accused, doing so without the slightest hesitation. Who empowered him to mix the quasi-deed and the doer? Because until a trial is completed, no one can say that you are 'guilty' without any doubt. And was I guilty of wanting something different for my life! And what gave him the right not only to condemn the 'perpetrator' (for that is his attribution) but also to take revenge against him?

The judge and prosecutor considered themselves omniscient, and to dispute their perfect knowledge was to unleash all the lightning of their zeal for revenge upon my head. So that only the pretender, the cynic and the decrepit could find mercy before them. How can anyone bow before the judge when he turns a possible victim into a beast? I was the beast of wanted freedom from my or others' deaths. We who choose this! We choose to be free from the burden of life!

Horror stories are sometimes made up for the ears of the listener. It is extremely easy to point fingers, to write immortal stories, but life is not a game. It isn't easy to put into practice the lessons implemented throughout life. It is even more difficult to deceive our own lives than to try to deceive those around us. In an environment where lies are breathed, the best escape is silence. Bullying is not uncommon in toxic environments, but everywhere, there are exceptions. When some tap their feet with dance to certain rhythms, others tan their elbows on countless manuscripts. What's sad is that while some are terrified of reading, others like me are saved by it. Books are a refuge for the soul.

'How does reading help you?' was the question of a person from the psychiatric hospital. I was so flustered by the question as if someone had told me to stop breathing. What is a man without a book? How to acquire wisdom? How to be free? Some believe that life experience is enough to say that you have come to know everything! What about history? Or can we claim with sincerity and without any intention of offending that at the end of the life of a man lacking in study, we can 'gather' wisdom? Of course, one can learn from their mistakes. We are the seedlings that must always 'water' ourselves with learning; otherwise, we risk drying up. How can one explain to a person what the love of the book means and what freedom we get from it? Can love disturb? By reading, I found love, I found myself, I travelled, I made friends, I suffered, I rose, I learned, I escaped and I was free.

On the long, dreary and cold days, I read with the same passion as in the silent and damp nights or just as in the endless summer days when the buzzing of flies never stopped, blackening the big picture, and mosquitoes made you loathe your existence. I would give you all to enjoy from my little, but I can't! I cannot pour feelings into one's soul.

Due to some dramatic events, an acquaintance who became mentally ill experienced the horror, and I watched helplessly, finding that there was no salvation for her. We read horror; others live the terror. Her confessions were as shocking as they could be, but I could understand her through wisdom. Is there anybody who understands my nightmare?

I remember how my husband summoned a priest to our home one evening. It was one of the most dramatic moments I had seen since the battle for my freedom of choice started. Robert, who had become helpless since the first day I stated my mind, had thought that my children could bring me back from the imaginary journey I had embarked on. However, since my children couldn't change my mind, he sought another channel to convince me, and that was to bring a priest to talk to me, using many Bible verses to remind me of how precious each soul is before God and that He frowns at such thoughts. I sat on the opposite couch with my elbow resting on the arm of the chair while my fist was used to support my cheek. I listened to everything he was saying. All his words were like planning an off-key keyboard tune. I heard them, but they did not make any difference; I only sat there to please Robert. After he finished his long sermon, he prayed and promised to come around often to check on me, which he did. However, not even the priest coming around to pray and listen to those in need understood me. Father Michael thought I was a troubled soul on the edge of despair.

He said softly, "I understand that life has become an unbearable weight for you, a labyrinth of darkness and pain. But please, let us explore another path together before you make a decision that cannot be undone. Let me tell you the story of a man standing on the precipe of despair, ready to surrender to the darkness."

I replied: "Father, I don't think life is meaningless and without a purpose for the rest, but for me, it's an unnecessary effort."

"Purpose is not always something that reveals itself instantly. It often emerges gradually through small acts of kindness, self-reflection, and seeking support from those who care about us. It may take time to heal, but remember that you are never alone. There are people who love you, who want to help you through this difficult journey." He replied to me.

I wanted to laugh at his ignorance, but I saw the pity in his eyes, so I continued: "It's not about the purpose or the strength. I do have both. But it's my wish to be free from everything, and this is a permanent mindset without running from problems. I really hope you understand that I'm not depressed, sick or whatever they want to stamp me with. I just feel that life is not worth struggling for any longer. I want to end this with grace and on my own terms!"

"Let us work together to find hope, to rediscover the beauty that still exists within you and the world around us. Your life has meaning, and I am here to walk this path with you every step of the way."

"Father, I hope you won't be judgmental, but others need you more than me. I've decided my path. Not you, your God or anybody else will change my mind!", I continued.

I saw despair in his eyes. I remember the same despair in Robert's eyes when I talked more about euthanasia.

"I have some concerns about your support to this extreme extent for euthanasia", he said.

"I understand that this is a sensitive subject for you, and it's against your personal beliefs and values." I continued.

"I know you feel uneasy about it, that you have a different perspective and that it bothers you. But you agree with me that freedom is what we all believe in, isn't it?"

"Vic, don't distort the subject into something about freedom… that's not what you are talking about…"

"I can understand your concerns, Robert!"

"Do you? What about the children? How could you even speak about this when you have brought them into this world?"

"This is even more reason to fight for all of us to choose when to die! I believe in the autonomy of individuals and their right to make decisions about their lives. It's all about Compassion!"

"Compassion? Yes, for those cases of unbearable suffering, not for you or other healthy people. Are you out of your mind? That's sickness! We have our precious children, and you would want them as adults to intentionally end their lives legally because they choose to? How can you think that's normal?" shouts Robert.

"I can understand your frustration, but…"

"But what, Vic??? Your judgement is clouded by depression or some other mental illness, and I will ensure that this is not going to happen because you are impulsive and not considering any treatment! You need mental health professionals to be involved in this process. I can't believe you're talking about this with such apathy!"

"Do you think I dreamt about this one night and the day after, I just said 'I want to end my life?' I just don't see the reason for all this!"

"You need to seek therapy! I'm trying to understand you, but losing you is not an option. I love you; our children love you; our families love you. We can't bear the thought of life without you. Why are you so selfish??? Why can't you cope with the misery you're talking about for our sake?"

In the dim glow of the living room, I looked into his eyes, seeing a depth of despair I'd never witnessed before. But my own conviction burned bright. "Robert," I began, tears streaming, "I've always valued your feelings. I do care about your input. This isn't about shutting you out. It's about ensuring I live - and leave - on my own terms. I need you and the kids to understand, even if you don't agree. My love for you, for Adam, and the rest, remains unwavering. But this decision transcends all I've ever known."

He choked back tears, his voice shaking with emotion, "We're supposed to be partners in this marriage, that was our vow. To consider and respect each other's feelings. I just want to help you. Can't you see the toll this is taking on us? On our children? Your stance feels so baseless."

 I exhaled slowly, trying to find the right words, "Robert, how can I make you understand, euthanasia, to me, represents compassion, dignity, autonomy, and yes, FREEDOM OF CHOICE! I'm not out to harm anyone, not even myself. It's about life's inevitability and choosing how I face it. I want to choose when is my time…"

His eyes, glistening with tears, conveyed a tumult of emotions - anger, sorrow, powerlessness. He might have understood my perspective, but acceptance was another battle.

The days that followed saw many attempts from our children to bridge the divide. They reached out with heartfelt messages, hoping to sway my decision. But despite their genuine affection, I felt strangely distant, numb to their pain.

I was in my wondering moment when a nurse told me that it was time for my medications and my supper.

Chapter 11

Family Apart

Every day felt like a relentless loop, it became burdensome and I craved an escape. My spirit, once free and untamed, now felt trapped and muted. This life of confinement was stifling, and I longed to break free from these unseen shackles of the law that kept me static in a position!

After undergoing my third test in the lab, I faced another interview session with Doctor James. This time, a new face accompanied him, a middle-aged female doctor whom I wasn't familiar with. I thought she was transferred recently. Curious, I later asked the nurse who attended to me that evening about her, only to learn she'd been around for some time – our paths had just never crossed.

That doctor was one of those who could make you implicate yourself if you were to be in the law court. Her interrogation style was intense, almost relentless. Her questions came rapid-fire, and she seemed determined to catch me off guard. But I prided myself on staying composed. Upon concluding our session, she recommended an additional examination. She believed, as she worded it, that while I displayed 'an iota of mental stability', there remained undiagnosed complexities in my psyche. So, despite her recognizing some clarity in my mind, it was determined that I would remain under their care for further evaluations.

The note Dr. James had taken during our previous meeting where I narrated my story seemed valuable for his profile assessment. He assured me that we'd reconvene next week for another session. Once he left, a surge of excitement washed over me. My upcoming tour with Mr. Evans was moments away, and I eagerly watched the clock, anticipating each passing minute. Suddenly, a soft knock interrupted my reverie. Hastily, I made my way to the door, opening it to find Mr. Evans peeking through. His greeting was warm, "Mrs. Vicky, how have you been?"

With enthusiasm, I replied, "Just as well as last time. It's time to go, right?"

He nodded, "Indeed. I'll await you outside." "Okay, I will join you soon", I replied.

With a sense of urgency, I slipped into my shoes and stepped into the hallway. I noticed Mr. Evans by the iron railing, engrossed in a phone call. Patiently, I waited for him to finish, eager to embark on our adventure.

"Mrs. Vicky, I trust you're feeling better since your arrival?", Mr. Evans inquired, his tone gentle.

"I've mentioned before, Mr. Evans, that I feel perfectly fine. There's nothing wrong with me," I responded with a hint of frustration.

"Understand this, Mrs. Vicky," he began earnestly, "psychiatric hospitals aren't solely for those grappling with severe mental challenges. They're also spaces that help one recognize and value the mental wellness gifted to us by God."

I chuckled, "What lessons could I possibly draw from a place like this? My sole wish for euthanasia was born from wanting control over my exit from life, not from any ailment. I've been gravely misunderstood."

He frowned slightly, "But don't you think that it is weird voicing such desire?"

"It's not," I retorted with conviction. "It's about not wanting to endure the inevitable suffering that comes with age. I've seen countless elderly suffer from numerous ailments. My wish is to depart while I'm still vibrant and in control. That's all."

His voice firm, he replied, "That might not be feasible." I sighed, "Well, it is what it is!"

As we continued our walk and approached the exit, Dr. James, on his way to his car, greeted us.

He called me, "Mrs. Vicky, I'll see you tomorrow."

I nodded in acknowledgement, thinking to myself how futile all of this felt.

I paused, taking in the scene as Dr. James settled into his car, its engine humming to life. Only when he reversed out and offered a friendly wave did I let out the breath I didn't realize I was holding.

"Dr. James seems like a kind-hearted professional, don't you think?", I remarked.

"He's one of the best", Mr. Evans nodded with respect. "I've been here for years, and he stands out as one of the most compassionate figures in this place. Speaking of, has your family come around to see you?"

His question darkened my mood instantly. "No, they haven't!" The weight of their absence felt heavier than ever, I was helpless.

"Do you think that's one of the court's directives?", he asked gently. Uncertainty filled me, "I'm not entirely sure."

He replied, "That is one of the things that baffles me because we have many patients here whose families frequent here. Anyway, your case is a different one and they might have been instructed not to come check on you."

The thought pierced deeper than I cared to admit. "I don't know why I am beginning to think it is not about the court injunctions, they might be punishing me, who knows? I know that they never supported the idea of euthanasia in the first place and they might deliberately withdraw from me to make me see how they feel about me. I have been missing them…" At that point, my eyes grew moist with unshed tears.

"Mrs. Vicky, everything is going to turn out fine." Mr. Evans started, his voice laden with empathy, "I get your perspective, but remember: your family's apprehension comes from a place of love. I am positive that if you were in their shoes, you would feel the same. If your daughter approached you with a similar request, wouldn't you be worried, you would rebuke her and make her realize the danger in her request, regardless of understanding her rights?"

I hesitated, "I... I…I…, Mr. Evans, I will be but I will understand that it is her right and..."

He gently interrupted, "It'd be heart-wrenching, wouldn't it? You wouldn't be as calm as this if you were to be in their position too. Seeing someone you love make such a choice?"

I sighed, lost in thought, when an old memory floated back. "Speaking of my family, my son Alex, was not comfortable with it from onset. One day, he came back home with his sister, excited about a new friend he made."

His eyes shining, Alex exclaimed, "Mom, I made a new friend!" I'd teased him, "Oh? What's he like?"

With a chuckle, Alex had corrected, "It's a 'she', not a 'he', Mom!"

"Alright, so what's so intriguing about her?" I probed Alex with a playful grin.

"It's her religion, mom!" His eyes lit up.

Raising an eyebrow, I nudged, "Alright, spill it. What about her religion is so fascinating?"

"You can't guess?" He teased.

"Enlighten me," I responded with a slight roll of my eyes. "She's a Buddhist!" Alex exclaimed with excitement.

"A Buddhist?" I echoed; my curiosity piqued. I had met people of various faiths, but seldom a Buddhist. Especially with my thoughts often circling the themes of life and death, I wondered how Alex perceived their beliefs. We'd had heated debates about subjects like suicide before, so I trod carefully, allowing him to lead the conversation.

As I delved into the story, I noticed Mr. Evans listening intently, absorbing every word. The topic seemed to intrigue him, especially as it involved my son's perspective on mortality.

"You wouldn't believe the depth of our conversation, Mr. Evans," I continued. "It was as if I was watching a thought-provoking film unfold. I was surprised though it was interactive between us."

"Mom," Alex had started, his tone earnest, "I know you are tired of arguments, but I want to tell you about Elinor. I had a deep chat about her Buddhist beliefs, particularly around the theme of suicide."

"Go on," I had urged, genuinely interested.

"She explained that even though it's a sensitive topic, generally, Buddhists value life and believe taking one's own life disrupts the natural progression. But they also approach such topics with deep empathy and understanding. Did you know, Mom, that under certain oppressive circumstances, Buddhists believe it's honourable to choose to end one's life? Elinor posed a question: 'Why shouldn't someone be able to transition to their next life and possibly have a more fulfilling experience?' Nobody can guarantee that in the new body and new life situations, I will not have more satisfactory experiences, be more enlightened, and get to Nirvana."

"She also shared that suffering, while an inherent part of life in Buddhism, isn't the end-all. Their teachings stress the potential to overcome pain through mindfulness, compassion, and wisdom. She told me about the importance of seeking support from family, trusted friends or professionals and how ending one's life prematurely robs them of potential growth, healing, and happiness. She even mentioned the power of meditation."

My voice softened, Alex then looked at me and said, "Mom, have you ever tried meditation?"

Laughing gently, I queried, "Why would I, when you know my stance isn't driven by emotion?"

His earnest eyes met mine, "Maybe it is not emotional. But Mom, to Buddhists, meditation can unlock solutions to many of life's challenges."

"Alex dear," I began, trying to explain, "I understand the value of meditation and respect Buddhist beliefs. But I am not a Buddhist and I approach my decisions from a logical standpoint, not emotional.

Can't you understand what I have been saying?"

But he countered with fervour, "In Hinduism too, taking one's own life is equated to committing murder. It's seen as a grave sin."

I replied, exasperated, "So, I should suffer just to avoid being labelled sinful?" I punched his point again, and you won't believe how it was becoming interesting though intense at that point.

His expression was one of disbelief. "Mom, what do you mean? You have a good job, and a loving family—us. What 'suffering' are you talking about?" My son asked again.

I countered again, "In Hinduism, if one deprives himself of food and water and starves himself to death, it's seen as a noble sacrifice. So why is it okay to torment the body but not the soul?"

"Mom, I'm not suggesting you torture your body like the Hindus believe. I'm pointing out the reverence for life in these religions, and how sacred death is, hoping it might make you reconsider what you are advocating for," Alex replied.

"We all understand the sanctity of life, Alex. But should that limit our choice in matters of life and death?", I queried.

He looked anguished. "I can't understand why you'd want to do this to us," he said, voice shaking.

He was red with anger, but I replied calmly, "Alex, life is about evolving. One day you'll leave home, charting your own course," I reasoned.

"But leaving home when you're grown is natural! I'll reach that point in my life, ready to embrace new challenges and become more responsible and independent." He replied again.

"You see, that's what I mean. You are going to make a decision that is best for you because it's the natural thing to do". I told him point blank.

"Common… you cannot compare dying, ending your life with my moving out!" He said loudly.

"It's the idea of making life changes, making decisions for our well-being. I appreciate your concern, but you won't be needing me anymore as I continue my life without my father… I still have a strong bond, even if he's not here. The physical distance doesn't matter…" I told him in a pitiful but firm way.

"I can understand that memories last forever, but the emptiness and the thought of you not being here. Who will I share my stories with? Who will cook from time to time my favourite meals? Who will confront me or make me laugh when I need it? You have your part, and Dad has his". Alex tried to counter me.

"This situation is demanding for all of us, but it's crucial for everyone's personal growth. You might not understand now, but as you grow up, you will." I answered him.

However, I could see that my son was not still satisfied with my submission. He rose slowly from the couch, walked to the back of the couch and leaned on it. After a long pause, he blurted out: "You leave me speechless. I don't know if I should cry, shout at you, despise you, ignore you... I really don't know!" continued Alex breathing heavily.

At that point, my daughter walked in, I did not know if she had been listening to our conversation or not, but I could sense some funny gestures in her slow movement. As she walked in, Alex blurted past her in intense anger.

"Alex, what's going on?" Anna asked him.

She just came home from school. She was almost 13 years old but smart and perspicacious. We couldn't hide things from her. She wouldn't say so much; she would analyze things, be quiet and explode when it was too much for her.

"Nothing Anna", Alex replied.

Anna didn't see the need to delve deeper when her brother remained silent about what was discussed. I did not either, so I would not heat the already fanned embers. Alex is best at his calm state, but when he's angry, the once calm face could be fierce though he seldom gets angry. So, I allowed everything to slide.

"Anna, my dear, how was school?". I tried asking to avoid further queries from her. My children are brilliant and could raise a million questions in the blink of an eye because they quickly read meanings to the slightest harmless gesture.

"Then you must be lucky then, can't you see?" Mr. Evans said. "Lucky? How?"

"You have intelligent kids, and you are a proud mother!"

"You know that it can be occasionally disturbing especially when they keep quarrelling with you over an issue that you have already resolved."

"Anyway, what happened later?" Mr. Evans cut me short. "Oh, about my kids?" I asked him.

"Yes", he replied.

So I continued my story.

"Mom, what do we have for dinner?" That was the next question my daughter asked.

"Your favourite!", I replied.

Alex gave a look and muttered: "That's what I was talking about… who's going to make our favourite…"

"Let's get ready for dinner before Dad arrives home," I encouraged them.

"You seem like a great mom!" Mr. Evans began with a hint of sadness in his voice. "Did you ever reconsider your choice, especially for your children's sake?"

I met his gaze steadily. "Mr. Evans, why are you making it look like I made a wrong decision? I'm conscious of what I did and I don't want pity or sadness from anyone. My love for my family is immense, but emotional appeals don't overshadow my logical thought process.

They've tried countless times to sway me with emotion, but it hasn't influenced my stance."

Mr. Evans hesitated before saying, "Your detachment is a bit unsettling. Why are you so cold towards people around you? Some might say it's reminiscent of how psychopaths disconnect from their emotions."

I bristled slightly at the implication. "Well, I am not one. Being detached and being a psychopath is vastly different. At least, from what I have read about psychopaths, they do not have a strong bond with people's pains. They don't form meaningful bonds and some go as far as killing people for fun. Do you know that some psychopathic people end up becoming cannibals? This is because they can't feel an emotional attachment to the people around them. I have no such traits. At least from what have told you so far, you can see that I cherish my relationships. The depth of my feelings should assure you that I'm empathetic. My choice is personal, and it shouldn't hurt others."

Hoping to steer the conversation in a less confrontational direction, Mr. Evans asked, "What happened after your children left?"

I took a moment before sharing, "Later that night, everyone went to bed and I sat on the sofa, reflecting. I remember being a teenager, engrossed in 'A Search in Secret India' by Paul Brunton. I was so enchanted by India and its spiritual traditions that I'd drive my parents nuts, talking about moving there. I insisted that I'd relocate in the mountains to do meditation when I was an adult. My parents never took me seriously, but I was as serious as possible at that moment. I started reading Mircea Eliade- 'India' or 'Maitreyi', exploring their culture through Indian writers such as Rabindranath Tagore, Khushwant Singh and many others. I was struck by how they could make such an impact through books when we hadn't even been there and felt what they were talking about. I felt like 'Alice in Wonderland', but this place actually existed.

Would my path have changed if I had gone to India before college? I might have instead experienced spirituality at a different level, having encounters with mystical teachers, yogis and even mediums. I would have meditated, and discussed spiritual awakening, reflecting on the impact I could have had on those around me back home. Those teachings would have enlightened me, but I still don't think I would have become a much different me. I couldn't sleep, so I stayed longer. Lost in these thoughts and memories of my conversation with Alex, I was startled by footsteps. It was Robert, my husband, descending the stairs. He whispered, 'Why are you up so late?'"

"I can't…. I've just been thinking about Alex and our discussion earlier, he confronted me trying to change my mind" I responded, my voice low.

He looked concerned. "Why didn't you mention this to me earlier?"

"Both Alex and Anna were still up, and you looked so drained", I began, looking at Robert's face. "I didn't want to burden you further, and honestly, I needed some solitude to think about everything."

Robert sighed heavily, "Life is full of challenges, Victoria. But when two people face them together, they can weather any storm. I have tried my best. Yet you seem so rigid, unwilling to reconsider. I even brought in a priest to speak to you. What more do you expect of me? I don't know what has come over you. It feels like you're on this relentless mission to hurt not just me but our children with this unyielding stance of yours." Robert continued defiantly.

I took a deep breath. "Robert, this isn't just about the ups and downs of our personal life. My cause extends beyond us—it's for the greater good. This issue we are discussing is deeply rooted. It might seem like I'm championing a minor issue, but the few affected are worth standing up for. It's a call for change that those in authority need to recognize and respect."

Robert shook his head, exasperation clear in his voice, "No sane person would back your demands. They'd see it as too extreme, helping no one."

"It helps me," I replied calmly, "And others like me. Your fears are valid, but my vision is of a world where people are free to make unconventional choices."

His voice grew more strained, "But at what cost, Victoria? I'm struggling to understand you as much as you wish me to. You're so immersed in your feelings and you prioritize your emotional well-being blinding yourself to the pain you're causing us. How can you move ahead without thinking of the void you'll leave? Have you thought about what would happen to those you're leaving behind?"

I find myself caught in a whirlwind of emotions, frustration, and sadness as the arguments at home with my husband and children seem to deepen, and I feel like my thoughts and feelings are not truly understood. When I'm alone with my thoughts, I engage in conversations with myself, seeking solace and clarity amidst the chaos.

Why don't they understand? - I ask myself. I pour my heart out, trying to express my needs, struggles, and desires, yet it feels as if my words fall on deaf ears. I long for understanding, empathy, and a genuine connection that transcends the surface-level disagreements we find ourselves trapped in. I question myself, what if I need to communicate more effectively? Should I be more patient and more composed? Deep down, I know that my feelings are real and valid. In these moments of introspection, I remind myself of the importance of self-compassion. It's crucial to acknowledge my pain and frustrations without dismissing them. It's okay to feel overwhelmed and misunderstood. After all, navigating the complexities of family dynamics is a challenging task. I remind myself that my husband and children also have struggles and perspectives. They carry their burdens, and perhaps their inability to fully comprehend my experiences stems from their limitations or internal battles. It's a delicate balance between seeking understanding and offering empathy to them.

I contemplated seeking outside help, wondering if a professional perspective could shed light on the underlying issues and guide our family. Counselling might offer a safe space to express ourselves, where a trained professional can facilitate understanding and promote healthier communication. I'm worried that the therapist would also not understand my point of view, and it would strengthen everyone's accusing thoughts.

In the midst of the tumult of thoughts and emotions, I've come to understand the importance of enduring and being resilient. Deep down, I hope that we can bridge our differences and truly understand one another. I dream of a household where we respect and support each other's paths even if they diverge from our own beliefs or view of life.

In moments of solitude, I self-reflect, drawing strength and clarity from my innermost feelings. I sought resilience to navigate the so-called 'war at home'. I tried to keep my sense of self intact during the turbulence, clinging to the hope that mutual understanding was on the horizon.

After sharing my heart's journey with Mr. Evans, he paused, "Your husband seems like a good man. Many men might have reacted very differently to all this, Mrs. Vicky."

Curiosity piqued, I inquired, "How would you have reacted in his place?"

"Divorce! I would have divorced you." Mr. Evans stated candidly. "If I and the kids had tried everything, brought in therapists, and still found no compromise, we'd have left. You've rendered your family powerless with this unyielding logic of yours. How do you think that makes them feel? Your actions have served as the metaphorical signing of the divorce papers; you have opted to go your separate ways from them."

"Mr. Evans, I don't wish to hurt anyone. But they're not seeing my perspective, and that leaves me feeling trapped and helpless. My decisions aren't rooted in emotion, so why should theirs be?"

"But don't you see a connection between your feelings and the bond you had with your father? Have you searched your heart and you have been convinced that it is deeper than just logical reaction to things?" he questioned, concern evident in his eyes.

"I'm no child, I know when something is emotional and logical", I responded defensively. "I've studied different books on death extensively, long before my father's passing. My decision is not in any way tied to my father's death. I have grieved him and I understand life flow."

Mr. Evans persisted, "With the way I see things, I think you have not truly moved on. I will suggest that the court schedule you for a therapy session. One thing about depression is that sometimes you think you are okay but empirically, you might not be. You are thinking that your reaction is not tied to something external, but with the way I am seeing it, it started from something external and nurtured itself into something internal."

At that point, I was angered because Mr. Evans kept repeating the same thing, trying to link my reactions and decisions to my father's death and traumatic experiences.

I felt more frustration rising, angered by his insinuations. "Mr. Evans, can you hear me out one more time."

He nodded, giving me his attention.

I continued, "I want to depart life on my terms. I don't want to become frail and powerless. I want to make my choice while fully aware of the world around me. I want my wishes granted when I am fully conscious of life and everything around me! I aspire to be remembered during the peak of my best times in life!"

Mr. Evans cuts in since he realizes I have been saying the same thing, "We should leave. It is almost time."

We walked towards the building silently. Glancing at the looming building and the darkening sky, I remarked, "Looks like rain tonight. Perfect sleeping weather. I want to sleep like never before."

"It's still early in the season, the rain can't be heavy yet." Mr. Evans replied, unexpectedly. "Come mid-year, the rains will be torrential, likely confining us indoors. Who knows, you might be lucky to have gone home by that time." Mr. Evans's response made me a bit relaxed because I thought I had pissed him off earlier because of how he stopped the conversation abruptly.

"I don't expect they'll keep me here that long," I mused.

"Perhaps that will come once you shift your position and refrain from defending something that shouldn't have been discussed in the first place.", he hinted.

"I hope an end comes to this drama soon! I wish that day would come when I could look those nurses and doctors in the face and tell them:

'Screw y'all, I told you I was fine, but your legal routine of doing things wouldn't make you believe me!'", I murmured.

I could picture myself removing their clothes from my body and walking away from that disgusting environment. I could imagine waving at them both the ones who treated me shabbily and those who were gentle with me. I could visualize leaving forever from the dark memories and the torture of loneliness I was subjected to!

Chapter 12

Alone with My Thoughts

The day had been tediously long, with its monotony broken only by my outing with Mr. Evans. That night, the rain brought a crisp chill, amplifying the silence within the ward. The nurse who looked after me did not allocate a substantial amount of time to my care. Her demeanour was stern as she handed me my medications and asked a few questions. The assistant, who brought my dinner, placed the tray on my bedside table wordlessly, eyeing the nurse throughout our brief interaction. After my meal, I slipped into bed, and as sleep approached, my memories engulfed me again.

The journey to where I found myself was not self-inflicted as many saw it. Society, no matter how exposed or civilized it is, would always want to bend you to fit into their narratives, and I was the rebellious one who was hard to mould. I have heard many criticisms flying around me, even before being admitted into the psychiatric hospital. It did not end there. When I came into the clinic, many workers had shown me naked hostility. They never pretended or lied about it. I wore the tag of that 'that stubborn woman'. Especially some nurses, who threw their hate at me at any slight opportunity. I could read boldly what was going on in their minds towards me 'Is this not that woman who was clamouring for death?' That was the question one of them asked the first day we had contact. I sat there and looked at her sitting on the chair behind a table, looking at me with utmost revulsion, which stared at me. 'Madam why this and that?' were the sermons that followed. However, I was less bothered because no matter how they see things, they do not see it through my lens, and I don't blame any of them for it.

How could I fault outsiders for their judgments when even my family continually questioned my choices, despite my numerous attempts to explain? I still vividly remember my mother's reaction when Robert broke the news to her. 'Victoria, what is making you think about this?' she had asked, her voice laden with deep concern. It was a side of her I hadn't witnessed often. She was typically decisive and unwavering, she was the household's chief decision-maker, always with our best interests at heart.

Yet, here she was, not resorting to her usual blend of assertiveness and negotiation. Instead, she seemed to melt in her desperation to understand and convince me otherwise. The sight was almost comically heart-wrenching. Endless phone calls, countless reasons, and numerous visits – she tried everything to dissuade me. But her words, no matter how poignant, simply rolled off me, leaving no impact. Some might say I inherited her steadfastness, and perhaps they're right.

As she realized I wasn't budging, her gentle persuasion gave way to a firmer stance. But as the pressure around me mounted, I became even more resilient. Each wave of criticism, rather than drowning me, taught me to navigate these tumultuous waters more adeptly.

It got to a time when many people who had deeper contact with me started seeing me as 'demonized', especially those religious. To the medically inclined ones, I was battling with mental illness; to the philosophy-tending ones, I needed a mental evaluation. Society was trying to figure out what was wrong with me in many ways.

Nevertheless, I was perfectly fine, yet they doubted my well-being When society saw that I would not give up, I was called a mad person who needed to be taken to the mental hospital as soon as possible.

At first, I did not take it seriously because I thought I had the right to decide my fate, but everyone kept telling me 'No' until I had to do what I felt was the only way to get them off my back.

To counteract the societal pressure, I sought legal aid, hoping the law might be my salvation. But the first three attorneys painted a grim picture, discouraging me at every turn. 'This is what the law says.

This is a no-win scenario; no court will take this up', they chided, suggesting I undergo therapy over legal action.

I could not decipher why they all thought I was opting for euthanasia out of despair. No matter how I told them I was not depressed, they would not want to believe me. I would walk out of their offices, and sometimes, some of them nodded in pity for me. The 'Nos' I got from each of the attorneys made me more adamant in my requests, solidifying my resolve, "I am not going to get tired over this; I know my fundamental rights." Ultimately, I connected with another legal counsel, someone who supported me and with whom I could work closely. As I walked out of his office that day, I told myself, "I am going to win this. It's my right to decide whatever I want over my own life". Further, I presented myself for questioning and I presented relevant information needed to win my cause in the court of law.

The courtroom soon became a battleground of legal rhetoric. Quotes from lawyers on both sides of the 'euthanasia' motion were flying back and forth. I remember the day before I was brought to the psychiatric hospital, my confinement was swift; the judge, believing I might be a danger to myself and society, ordered my incarceration and my papers were immediately prepared for my transfer. The court ordered that I should be monitored pending the time my fate is decided. What a horrible experience!

As I was led through the hollow passage, I saw many staring faces looking through the tiny rooms guarded by thick iron bars to prevent criminals from escaping. Many stood by the metal doors, looking at the 'new convict'. They did not know what my offence was, but they must have been convinced that I was a felon like they were. Finally, I was led to the latter end of the hollow passage, and a door was opened as I was led in.

The big dark metal door closed behind with a thundering noise. The sound made me shiver. Letting myself fall by not making a sound. My eyes didn't want to discover more from the nightmare. But I felt the energy of their staring. I felt how uncomfortable the silence was.

Inquisitive inmates were staring, undoubtedly wondering about my crime. Most of these women were either caught in criminal activities or were victims of societal prejudices. It was pretty hard to classify the category which I was coming from. To them, I was an enigma – was I a psychopath advocating for death's normalization or a humanitarian, tragically misunderstood?

I often think of life's paradoxes. Like the universal appeal of coffee – inherently bitter, yet beloved. I liken myself to black coffee: some people appreciate its unadulterated form, while others are repulsed. The irony? While some add milk and sugar to mask its bitterness, if I remain as I am – dark and intense – I'm seen as problematic. Isn't life's double standard fascinating? Regardless of opinions, all I sought was the freedom to be me, like that cup of black coffee longing to evaporate into the ether.

Life, to me, felt like an in-between stage. Hell existed before my birth, life feels like a purgatory, and liberation to paradise is achieved when I am free from the burden of compulsory existence. Many warned me that rejecting the Spiritual realm, God, The Energy would lead to my downfall. Their penetrating gazes unnerved me, a silent judgment that left me uncomfortable.

Back home, long conversations with Gloria, my neighbour, offered some solace. We'd share our observations about the world's peculiarities, like the strange symbols worn by news anchors and their cryptic gestures and words which are usually evident at the beginning and end of the shows. Yet, Gloria's mental state had deteriorated over time. Her emaciated form and haunted eyes weighed on me. I tried to offer a more grounded perspective, suggesting that every era had its crises, which humanity eventually overcame. But Gloria remained resolute in her beliefs, challenging mine at every turn. In my view, humanity didn't need to adapt to its surroundings; I never saw the world as adversarial.

I had always been a strong and resilient individual who faced life's challenges head-on and never backed down. Nonetheless, the whispers questioning my sanity began to affect me. But, with the help of my lawyer, Filip, I was determined to reclaim my narrative and prove my lucidity.

From our very first meeting, Filip radiated hope. As I unravelled my story, he listened intently, absorbing every nuance. I shared my struggles, explaining how external circumstances had created significant stress in my life. At first, he wanted to understand my points so he could be reasonable in his arguments against the prosecutor. He assured me that he would fight to bring my truth to light. He believed that my mental health was being weaponized against me, and mental health accusations could have severe consequences, tarnishing a person's reputation and impacting their personal and professional life, so, he committed to setting the record straight. We meticulously reviewed my medical records, seeking evidence to support my claim of stability. We also gathered testimonials from friends, family, and colleagues, all attesting to her sound state of mind and the strength I had displayed up to this point. Understanding the importance of presenting a solid case, Filip contacted mental health professionals who could provide expert testimony. He sought renowned psychiatrists and psychologists who could evaluate my mental state objectively and testify to my overall stability.

We couldn't convince the judge to set me free until the trial, fearing for my safety. Through these tumultuous times, Filip remained my steadfast anchor. He kept me informed about every step of the case, explaining the legal strategies and helping me stay calm during a trying time.

In the sombre courtroom, Filip stood before the judge, his voice filled with compassion and understanding. He knew that my request was deeply personal and emotionally charged, as it involved the right to make decisions about one's own life.

The judge initiated the introduction after closely observing us. "Good morning. Today, we convene to address Victoria's plea regarding her right to choose in matters of life and death. Mr. Filip, proceed with your argument."

Filip, understanding the solemnity of the issue, began, "Thank you, Your Honor. I recognize the uniqueness of this request, but I request this court to approach it with open-mindedness. Victoria seeks the liberty to determine her own life's course, emphasizing that such freedom is a bedrock of personal autonomy and human dignity. I'm here to voice Victoria's plea. This isn't a matter we bring lightly. We fully grasp the moral and legal dimensions of euthanasia. But we must navigate this with respect for Victoria's personal sovereignty and her heartfelt wishes."

"Mr. Filip, I must admit, this plea is indeed out of the ordinary. Our legal guidelines primarily address terminal illnesses or unendurable pain. How do you suggest we extend such rights without these qualifying conditions?" the judge asked.

Filip, after a momentary pause, replied, choosing his words carefully, "Your Honor, the magnitude of this isn't lost on me. We aren't seeking carte blanche on euthanasia but rather the acknowledgement of an individual's fundamental right to decide their fate. Victoria, a rational and competent individual who has contemplated her choices carefully, believes her autonomy and right to self-determination should extend to a unique choice—whether to continue living or not."

"But, Mr. Filip, broadening the scope as you suggest might have far-reaching consequences. We've laws and checks to shield the vulnerable from euthanasia misuse. How can we be certain this won't pave the way for unintended outcomes?", the Judge wondered.

"Your Honor, I share your concerns regarding potential risks and the need for safeguards. My proposition is the creation of a robust regulatory framework, similar to the existing protocols for cases involving terminal illnesses. A rigorous evaluation of the framework, involving diverse medical and psychological assessments, can ensure individuals are mentally sound and wholly comprehend the gravity of their choices.", Filip responded.

Judge paused before resuming his response. "Mr. Filip, while your proposal has merit, I'm left pondering: should the judiciary decide on such deeply intimate matters? This traverses beyond legal to ethical, moral, and societal domains. We empathize with those in unbearable pain, with a terminal prognosis and no respite. Their choice of euthanasia is grounded in a bleak reality. But Victoria's plea is unprecedented and leaves me grappling."

Filip, seizing the moment to gauge the judge's reaction, offered a sympathetic nod before continuing, "Your Honor, the cornerstone of our judicial system is recognizing an individual's right to self-determination. She is a rational and autonomous individual, fully capable of making decisions regarding her own life, even in the face of adversity. By granting Victoria's request for euthanasia, we are respecting her autonomy and allowing her to exercise her right to die with dignity. By granting Victoria's plea for euthanasia, you would be demonstrating not only a commitment to the principles of autonomy and compassion but also a profound respect for the sanctity of life, even in its final moments."

"This is a complex and unparalleled case, and I must weigh it with both our legal principles and societal norms.", Judge responded.

"Indeed, Your Honor, I agree that this is a profoundly personal matter. Yet, the heart of the matter is personal autonomy. While this is uncharted territory, it's crucial for the courts to balance individual rights with societal protection. When faced with cases where an individual seeks to exercise their freedom to choose life or death, it is the responsibility of the courts to ensure that the law respects their fundamental rights while also providing necessary safeguards to protect against potential abuses."

"Given the implications of this case, I'll need time to review existing precedents and ponder the arguments shared today before passing my verdict.", the Judge retorted.

"Thank you, Your Honor. We respect and understand your decision. We trust that you will give this matter the careful consideration it deserves, recognizing the importance of personal autonomy and the freedom to make choices about one's own life and death."

"Mr. Filip, considering the gravity of this request and the unique circumstances surrounding Victoria's desire for the freedom to choose, I believe it is necessary to ensure her mental well-being throughout this process. To that end, I am inclined to order Victoria to be taken to a psychiatric hospital for further evaluation of her mental state and to minimize any risk of self-harm during the trial. This will help us gather a comprehensive understanding of her current psychological condition."

"Your Honor, while we share your concern for Victoria's security, we firmly believe that she is of sound mind and not a danger to herself. Nevertheless, we respect the court's authority and are willing to cooperate with the order for a psychiatric evaluation. We'd suggest an in-home assessment by a renowned psychiatric expert to ensure she remains in a familiar setting, minimizing any undue distress."

"Mr. Filip, considering the gravity of this request and the unique circumstances surrounding Victoria's desire for the freedom to choose, I believe it is necessary to ensure her psychological health throughout this process. To that end, I am inclined towards directing that Victoria undergo a thorough psychiatric evaluation at a mental health facility to assess her psychological condition and reduce the potential for self-harm during the trial. This will help us gather a comprehensive and unbiased evaluation of her current psychological condition."

My emotions surged, an overwhelming mix of fear and desperation. I screamed, "Filip, please! Don't let them take me. I can't be locked away. Please help me. I need you to help me stand my ground", I cried out, I was so helpless and felt more vulnerable than I'd ever felt before.

Filip, ever the protector, responded, "Your Honor, I understand the court's concern for Victoria. I implore you to consider our proposal. An in-home evaluation can be just as thorough while preserving her dignity and autonomy. Locking her up in a psychiatric facility, against her will, may only exacerbate her distress and undermine the very principles of personal autonomy she sought. She's made her feelings clear, and her plea should resonate deeply within this court's chambers."

"Mr. Filip, I acknowledge your perspective, but I must emphasize that the court's primary duty is to ensure the safety and mental well-being of the individuals involved. The decision to admit Mrs. Victoria to a psychiatric facility is not meant as a punishment or infringement on her autonomy but rather as a measure to provide the necessary environment for thorough evaluations by qualified professionals. I also appreciate your willingness to cooperate, Mr. Filip. This step is essential to ensure that we proceed with the utmost caution and care as we navigate uncharted territory in terms of the law."

"Your Honor, I propose a compromise that could address both the concerns for Victoria's safety and her freedom. We could allow Victoria to undergo the evaluations on an outpatient basis, where she can remain in her own home or under the supervision of a trusted individual. This would allow her to maintain a sense of normalcy and control over her surroundings while still receiving the necessary psychiatric evaluations."

"I appreciate your efforts to find a middle ground, but I am concerned that an outpatient evaluation may not provide the level of oversight and care needed to ensure the thoroughness and accuracy of the assessments. A controlled and monitored environment is essential to address any potential risks and to gather a comprehensive understanding of Mrs. Victoria's mental state."

"I respect the court's position but wish to emphasize that Mrs. Victoria is neither a risk to herself nor others. Her intentions are clear, and she has sought legal aid to address this intricate issue. Confining her to a psychiatric facility could be perceived as an infringement on her rights and contrary to the autonomy she wishes to uphold."

"Mr. Filip, while I take your concerns into account, it's my responsibility to determine the best action for everyone involved. To ensure an unbiased evaluation and to prioritize Mrs. Victoria's well-being, I deem it necessary for her to be admitted to a psychiatric hospital. I want to assure you that the evaluation will uphold the highest professional and ethical standards."

"Your Honor, although I respectfully disagree with the decision, I will comply with the court's ruling. I request that the court exercise diligence in selecting a reputable psychiatric facility and that Mrs.

Victoria's treatment and evaluation process be monitored closely to safeguard her rights and well-being."

"Rest assured, Mr. Filip. The court will ensure Victoria's rights are upheld throughout this journey. We'll keep both you and your client updated at every step to maintain transparency and alleviate any concerns."

Filip turned to me and whispered: "Stand up, please; Now is your moment to make your point."

Judge began speaking with an intrigued expression: "Mrs. Victoria, you've heard both Mr. Filip's defence and the court's viewpoint. I want you to share your thoughts on this matter."

"Thank you, Your Honor, for allowing me to voice my feelings. My plea for the right to choose stems from a deeply personal space. It's about maintaining control over my destiny and exercising the freedom to decide my life's course. I respect the court's concerns about my well-being, but being institutionalized against my will feels like an infringement on my personal freedom and a negation of my right to decide for myself."

"Mrs. Victoria, I respect the conviction in your words. The essence of personal autonomy is paramount. However, the court's recommendation for a psychiatric assessment in a monitored setting aims to safeguard your well-being. Our priority is to ensure a meticulous evaluation of your mental state to ensure you're making the best decisions for yourself."

"I recognize the court's good intentions, Your Honor. But, feeling like I'm being stripped of my freedom, especially when I've sought legal counsel to champion my rights, deeply troubles me. Being confined goes against the very concept of autonomy I'm fighting for."

"Your sentiments are noted, Mrs. Victoria. It wasn't an easy decision. This evaluation is meant to offer a holistic picture of your mental health and ensure your decisions are well-informed. While the court upholds the value of personal freedom, we're also obligated to safeguard individuals and uphold the judicial system's integrity. These duties guided our decision."

"I appreciate the clarity, Your Honor, but I still fundamentally disagree. I am capable of making my own life choices without being incarcerated. It's disconcerting to feel my rights are curtailed, especially when I've sought legal pathways. I feel like I'm enduring consequences for my choice to follow the legal process instead of taking matters into my own hands."

"I understand your distress, Mrs. Victoria. This wasn't a decision made in haste. I've deliberated over the arguments from both sides extensively. While our views differ, our shared goal is ensuring your welfare. We are committed to upholding your rights and dignity throughout this ordeal."

"I beseech the court, Your Honor, to remain open-minded. I trust that the evaluations will be handled with empathy and equity and that their outcomes will genuinely reflect my capacity to take charge of my life."

"Your request to be heard and your perspective will be taken into account throughout this process. The evaluations will be conducted with the utmost professionalism and sensitivity, and the court will review the results in a fair and impartial manner. It is important that you continue to cooperate with your legal representation and engage in the proceedings to ensure your rights are protected, and your voice is heard."

With his plea concluded, Filip stepped back, allowing the weight of his words to resonate in the courtroom.

The children were not there. I predicted a hard trial, and I didn't want my husband to bring them and witness those moments. Robert was pale, without expression. It was like his soul and mind was out of his body. He was blank.

I turned my face to Filip and nodded: "What the hell just happened, Filip? Locked in a psychiatric hospital?" It was hard to control my voice!

"I understand that you're disappointed with the court's decision, but allow me to elucidate what comes next and outline the forthcoming steps. The court has ordered a psychiatric evaluation to assess your mental state and capacity to make decisions about your own life.

While this evaluation will take place in a psychiatric facility, it is crucial to approach this process with an open mind and trust in the professionalism of the experts involved."

"Your attempt to explain doesn't help Filip. I understood that already! It's hard for me to accept being confined in a mental health institution when all I want is the freedom to make choices about my own life. It feels like my autonomy is being taken away from me!"

"Your worries are valid, Victoria. Feeling constrained in such a situation is natural. But the essence of this evaluation isn't to curtail your autonomy. It's more about gaining a holistic view of your mental state. It provides a platform for a mental health professional to gauge your decision-making abilities and to impartially assess your mental well-being."

"It's easy for you to frame it like that, Filip. You're not the one being scrutinized! If the evaluation validates my mental competence, could the court then potentially alter its stance?"

"An excellent point. If the evaluation underscores your mental stability and decision-making process, we can then leverage those findings. By presenting them to the court, we'd seek a reevaluation of its initial decision. Securing all pertinent evidence and persistently advocating for your rights throughout this intricate process is imperative."

"But I'm teetering on a tightrope of scepticism and fear here, Filip. I'm concerned that psychiatrists, judges, and all involved might bring their own biases to the table, and not genuinely comprehend or honour my perspective and desires. How can I be assured that my viewpoints and desires will be respected and understood?"

"Your doubt, especially considering the circumstances, is completely natural. However, it's pivotal to remember that the legal apparatus is crafted to assure a fair and impartial evaluative process. The professionals implicated, doctors included, are bound by a commitment to uphold ethical norms and contemplate all pertinent facets in their analyses."

"But what if their own prejudices and preconceptions shade their judgments? How can I be sure they won't let their personal opinions sway their objectivity?"

"While no system is entirely immune to biases, our legal structure is robust with checks in place to curb these pitfalls. Medical professionals, especially evaluators, are rigorously trained to maintain objectivity and strictly follow ethical guidelines. As your legal counsel, my primary duty is to champion your rights and guarantee your perspective remains central throughout."

"Your words are comforting, I hope you're right, Filip. But the looming fear remains - that my voice might get lost amid legal jargon and procedures, causing them to overlook the essence of my feelings and beliefs. It saddens me to think that others might dictate my path, perhaps without grasping the essence of who I truly am."

"I get it! And I vow to marshal every resource and tool at my disposal to ensure your voice resonates loud and clear. Our combined efforts will construct a formidable argument, fortified by credible evidence and expert testimonials, underscoring the sanctity of individual liberty and your right to govern your life."

"Your unwavering support offers some solace. My hope rests on the professionals involved. That they demonstrate utmost integrity and lend an attentive ear to my side of the story. They need to truly grasp the gravity of personal freedom and the inherent right to make choices."

"While we can't steer others' actions or thoughts, our strategy will be to craft a narrative so compelling it underscores the paramountcy of your autonomy and choices."

"I wish everyone involved would don their roles armed with the neutrality and compassion this situation warrants. So, how long will this entire ordeal stretch?"

"Hold on tight, Vic. It's hard to pin a timeline on proceedings as unique as yours. But remember, this is your battle, uncharted territory! Stay connected. Reach out anytime you need clarity."

At that moment, my mother, a portrait of bewilderment, waited. Robert stood silently next to me, seemingly lost for words, absorbing our conversation.

Breaking his silence, Robert queried, "What's our next move?"

Summoning optimism, I responded, "It's uncertain for now, but believe this - everything will align for the best in the end."

Chapter 13

Arguments

Embracing the tumultuous chapter of my life, I found myself wrestling with forces beyond my control. The psychiatric hospital, with its oppressive walls inching ever closer each day, could have stripped me of sanity if not for the slivers of humanity shown by a handful of its staff. It felt as if a symbolic albatross was draped around my neck by many nurses there; my plight mirrored the solitude and condemnation Jesus Christ must have felt upon his death sentence by Pilate. Alone and battered, I too was in battle, albeit helplessly, and amidst profound loneliness. The majority deemed my punishment well-deserved, a harsh lesson to be learned laboriously, devoid of swift mercy.

I grappled with my peace of mind on one of the nights. It was one of the hardest nights, and I was struggling to find some meaning to how I found myself in such situations where everyone, including my family, would abandon me to show that they were never in support of my decision and that they had tried all means to stop me but I was adamant and stubborn. They felt I walked with my eyes wide open into the ditch, even in broad daylight.

My decision and steadfastness puzzled many, especially since I had never spiralled into trauma or depression. Though the memories of my father's death and his struggles in his final moments had gradually dimmed, and despite my longing for him, I wasn't shrouded in depression. Still, many erroneously linked my decisions to his passing.

"She needs therapy; we're sure her choice is tethered to her father's death or perhaps something even more profound", was a sentiment that echoed prominently among my peers, despite my affirmations of emotional stability and assurances that my decisions were made independently of such notions.

Seated in the dimness, I intentionally drowned the light early that evening, after supper, aspiring to dive into a peaceful slumber. Yet, sleep, my usual respite from the day's cacophony of doctors, nurses, and discussions with Mr. Evans, betrayed me. My days, monotonous and identical, were momentarily disrupted only by the embrace of sleep.

Turning on the fan – not for its coolness, but as a mechanical companion – I was cast back into reminiscences of my life before this oppressive building imprisoned me away from life's important things.

"SELF LOVE?" I pondered. "People proclaim their zest for life and their battles for it, but at what cost? By smouldering their lungs, drenching their livers, and numbing their emotions?" I found no resonance with the conventional definitions of true satisfaction. Life, in its candidness, laid out a plethora of choices, each to their own. My choice, solely mine, seemed to send societal norms into frenzied disarray as if my existence was inexplicably tethered to theirs. The general incapacity to absorb my reality bewildered me.

Alarmingly, even devout believers condemned me, attributing my decisions to demonic influence. "Perhaps it's spirits, akin to those Jesus expelled from the man of Gennesaret, lurking around her soul, whispering chaos and sowing confusion in her mind", they surmised. I found an unexpected chuckle the day a priest, summoned by my mother, suggested just that. Initially, I sought clarity on his statement, but my mother's stern countenance while explaining morphed my query into laughter. His shock was unmistakable despite his clerical garb, yet he didn't exhibit anger. He would've perhaps stormed out, slamming the door behind him, had he not been a man of such tranquility. Delicately selecting his words and citing Bible verses, he tried to reach me, while my mother, her face a silent plea, sat absorbing our exchange, and I had to comport myself.

"Sister Victoria, may the Angel of the Lord's presence visit you tonight as he did Jacob, guiding you toward the right decision", the priest implored. "Amen", my mother responded fervently. I remained silent, offering only a wave as my mother escorted him out.

"Is my choice truly bad?" I pondered internally. When my mother returned, she launched into another lengthy sermon. I refrained from interrupting her, despite the irritation simmering within me. After she concluded, I grabbed my bag and departed, assuring her we'd speak again soon.

"Victoria, reflect on everything the priest and I have discussed. We'll continue over the phone", she urged.

Driving away from my mother's house, my hands lightly grasped the steering wheel as I mentally replayed the day's events. "I speak of personal freedom, and it unsettles everyone. Yet when I seek a genuine conversation, they feel assailed by my perspectives. They refuse to acknowledge my autonomy, interfering under the guise of concern, but recoil as if I've affronted them when I express my truth. Why is life perceived as an obligatory gift? How can my family selfishly insist on my enduring what feels like an eternal purgatory for their comfort?

They desire my presence but disregard my consent. Don't we permit divorce in a similar vein of personal freedom?"

One particular morning at work, amidst the infancy of my trial on personal autonomy, I greeted my colleagues, mustering as much cordiality as I could: "Good morning, everyone. I trust you all had a pleasant weekend." I exhaled deeply, bracing myself.

The workplace was a battlefield in its own right. Initially, my colleagues remained reticent, each absorbed in their own tasks, none daring to probe. I discerned a universal human trait: reluctance to confront the unconventional until someone courageously breaks the ice. And so, it happened to me.

Eventually, a familiar face from my office circle approached me, one of the few with whom I'd forged a semblance of rapport over a shared admiration for my insights and broad knowledge base.

"Morning, Victoria. Disturbing rumours about you surfaced over the weekend", he disclosed.

"Oh? What might those be?", I inquired.

"It's said you're advocating for euthanasia, championing the controversial right to choose between life and death in court. How true is this?"

"Entirely true. I firmly believe in the significance of individual autonomy, particularly in decisions concerning one's own life or death", I confessed.

"But isn't euthanasia ethically contentious? It challenges life's sanctity", he argued.

"I'm aware of the moral dilemmas surrounding euthanasia, and it certainly rouses deep-seated sentiments", I acknowledged. "Nevertheless, I stand by the conviction that individuals should dictate the courses of their lives, inclusive of how they wish to end them."

"What of the risk of malpractice? The vulnerable could be unduly influenced into choosing death", he pointed out.

"An absolutely legitimate concern", I concurred. "That's why stringent protective measures are imperative to preclude any coercion. Legalizing euthanasia doesn't imply ethical disregard. On the contrary, it mandates established regulations, ensuring the defence of susceptible individuals while honouring their autonomy."

"I'm grappling with understanding your stance on such a contentious issue. To me, it seems baffling, almost comical, and deeply concerning. Euthanasia, from what I understand, isn't for those in perfect health. It is typically reserved for those in severe, unending suffering who have exhausted all other options to no avail. Even when animals face euthanasia, it's often a last resort after exploring other avenues. So, how can someone of your intellect and worldly experience equate euthanasia as if it's as trivial as plucking a piece of cake from a box? Many nations vehemently oppose even discussing it. Are you, perhaps, undergoing some form of depression lately?... But, even if that were the case, euthanasia isn't a solution. One would be directed towards professionals for mental health care because if despair justified euthanasia, we'd be facing a drastically dwindling population given the rampant unhappiness people endure. So, I must ask, what drives your advocacy for something so profound and grave?"

"While I'm grateful for my current state of health, it doesn't negate my capacity to empathize with those in excruciating pain or battling terminal diseases", I responded. "My advocacy is rooted in compassion and respect for individuals confronting intolerable suffering or terminal conditions. They deserve autonomy, dignity, and the right to choose without intervention from any authority provided their choice harms no one else. Why must we be rendered powerless over our own existence? What rationale dictates that another can govern our bodies, minds, and lives?"

"I respect your perspective, truly. But I can't align with your advocacy. It contradicts my core principles and beliefs.", he countered. "Moreover, I'm surprised you're the one championing this cause.

Doesn't your Christian faith speak against taking one's life? How do you reconcile advocating for what essentially boils down to suicide with your religious convictions? While euthanasia and suicide aren't synonymous, promoting it as you do, seems analogous to endorsing suicide. Now, you assert that you're not driven by despair and are mentally stable, yet you're essentially campaigning for a right to end one's life. It's paradoxical. How do these sentiments reconcile? Am I missing something here, please let me know. Is my judgment clouded?"

As the debate intensified, one colleague chimed in, "I have to admit, I'm taken aback. This topic is incredibly polarizing, and encouraging for something so many deem unethical doesn't seem right."

Another nodded in agreement. "That's where it becomes perplexing. Are you aiming to defy societal norms? Are you aware of the serious repercussions of your advocacy? We live in a complex, volatile world. Instigating further controversy is akin to beckoning an all-out conflict. I suggest you reconsider before things spiral out of control."

"I appreciate that we all have diverse opinions", I responded, striving to remain composed as the tension continued to rise. "Fostering open discussions and honouring these differences is essential in a constructive professional setting."

One colleague's expression was laced with dismay. "I'm genuinely disappointed and disheartened, Victoria. I thought I knew you better than this. It's hard for me to accept that you would support such a controversial cause."

"It's not my intention to upset or offend anyone, and if you feel disappointed in my beliefs, then I'm sorry", I replied calmly. "My stance stems from a profound belief in personal autonomy, in individuals' rights to make even the most profound decisions about their lives."

Trying to diffuse the situation, another coworker interjected, "Clearly, we're at an impasse here. Let's respect each other's boundaries and keep personal convictions separate from our professional interactions."

But I could see the simmering anger in their eyes and how they barely controlled themselves. One pointedly said, "Victoria, to me, this is a direct affront to God. It's morally indefensible. If you persist without remorse, I fear for your soul, this could lead to eternal damnation."

The chorus of disapproval continued, "It's shocking, Vic. I can't believe you would support such a sinful cause. How can you contravene the fundamental precepts of our faith?"

"That's precisely the point!" another burst out. "She identifies as a Christian, but there's no scriptural basis for her actions. I challenge you, Vicky, to show us any biblical endorsement for this.

Furthermore, consider the American Constitution, steeped in religious tenets, even reflected in our currency. It underscores the nation's foundational values. You're up against an unwinnable battle. And from a legal standpoint, your position is perilous and seen as disruptive to societal harmony. Imagine the impact on impressionable young minds. Picture children whimsically requesting euthanasia, influenced by peer actions or fleeting life struggles. Absurd, right? Yet, you're promoting this without facing any 'struggles' yourself, as far as we're aware. Ufff.... I rest my case."

Exasperated, he slumped into a chair against the wall, his case seemingly rested yet laden with silent judgment.

"I understand that you hold strong religious beliefs, but it's important to remember that we all have the right to our own beliefs and opinions. I'm not disrespecting or attacking anyone's belief. I simply believe in advocating for personal autonomy and compassion in difficult situations," I replied.

"This isn't about personal beliefs; it's about God's divine will. You're actively working against that, and I can't just stand by silently. God himself is against things like this and you know it!". He retorted.

I responded, attempting to maintain composure, "While I respect your viewpoint, it's inappropriate to use religious sentiments as a tool for judgment or coercion. Everyone is entitled to their convictions and the liberty to champion causes they deem humane."

"It's not about bullying or judgment, Victoria. We're voicing concerns grounded in our faith. We're convinced you're treading a perilous path. Imagine if your own child approached you with such thoughts.

Wouldn't you, as a loving parent, seek understanding by asking a series of questions?"

"I value your genuine concern. However, asserting that I'm defying God and invoking eternal damnation isn't constructive or courteous. Let's engage in a dialogue that promotes mutual respect and understanding."

"Perhaps if you fully grasp our faith's teachings, you'd discern your missteps. But until then, I'll pray for your enlightenment because this is not you. The Victoria I knew years back was different. I'm tempted to alert your family to your current stance, and advise your family to watch on you, fearing you might act impulsively."

Another colleague, interjecting with urgency, remarked, "Are you thinking what I'm also thinking? This might be deeper than what we thought. I pray she grasps the severity soon!" He exited swiftly, his departure as abrupt as a fleeting shadow.

Rising to leave, I replied, albeit with restrained frustration, "Moving ahead, let's prioritize a collegial and deferential workplace."

Later, while settling into my workspace, Yasin whispered, hinting at a brewing conversation, "I've been meaning to discuss something that's been on my mind for a while."

Though not in the mood, I sensed the impending dialogue's inevitability.

"Ufff…. Alright, Yasin, what's on your mind?"

Yasin looked earnestly, "I overheard your conversation regarding religious scriptures and suicide. While you mentioned the absence of explicit prohibitions in some religious texts, the Quran is unequivocal about it. For instance, Sahih Bukhari 78, mentions that '...whoever commits suicide... will be punished... in the Fire.' Another verse, An-Nisa 4:29, states 'Nor kill yourselves: for Allah is indeed Merciful to you.'"

"Yasin, I have never advocated for self-destruction. The stance I have taken on euthanasia is about providing a compassionate choice for individuals who are suffering and for the freedom of choice."

"It doesn't matter what you call it, Victoria. By supporting euthanasia, you are endorsing actions that go against the explicit teachings of any faith. Suicide is forbidden, and we are meant to trust in Allah's plan, even in times of extreme suffering."

"Yasin, I respect your devotion to your faith, but I believe it's important to approach these discussions with understanding and empathy. Euthanasia is not about promoting suicide, but about allowing individuals who are facing unbearable pain and terminal illnesses to make decisions about their own lives while considering ethical guidelines and safeguards. However, it's important to have a nuanced understanding of the Quran's teachings. When I mentioned that there is no explicit scripture that forbids suicide, I meant that the Quran does not specifically address the concept of euthanasia or the ability to choose death. I am advocating for the right of individuals to have the freedom to make decisions about their own lives, including the option to end their suffering in a peaceful and dignified manner."

"You seem to be defending actions that starkly contrast traditional moral or religious tenets", he began.

"In promoting the right to personal decision-making, even as life nears its end, I'm highlighting the value of empathy and individual empowerment. This isn't about sidestepping religious values, but about acknowledging the myriad complexities of individual experiences," I responded.

He shook his head, "I can't align with your stance. It isn't our place to determine our end. We should find solace in Allah's will and navigate the challenges bestowed upon us."

Recognizing the chasm between our viewpoints, I stated, "Our perspectives on this matter differ fundamentally."

Before departing, visibly pensive, he said, "Every choice has its repercussions, both in this world and beyond. I've been devoted to Islam from a young age, and I've immersed myself in the teachings of the Quran. You, as a Christian, must also be well-versed in the Bible's teachings about life and death. Regardless, the decision rests with you. I've no doubt you've contemplated the implications deeply. My prayers will seek guidance for you from Allah."

"Your concerns are noted", I replied.

Once he exited, gently shutting the door, I pondered, "Yasin truly exemplifies grace and respect in discourse. Unlike many colleagues who, even when making valid points, often become confrontational. Their raised voices and condescending tones often eclipse their message."

"Why can't my choices be mine, without all these dramas?", I thought to myself.

The subsequent weekend, my mom requested my presence at her place. From our recent phone call, I anticipated a casual visit, nothing serious. She had been eager to refresh the look of her home with a new coat of paint and wanted my input on colour choices. My brother Adam, preoccupied with his own family, hadn't been visiting our parents as frequently. Mom was showing her age, and with Dad no longer with us, she craved company. So, I made it a point to drop by often. Sometimes, even Robert and the kids would accompany me.

En route, I made a quick pit stop to fetch the groceries mom had asked for. Little did I know, her home wasn't empty.

"Darling! How've you been?" Mom greeted, her face lighting up.

"I'm good, Mom", I replied, wrapping her in a warm embrace. "How about you?"

"Oh, just been waiting for you", she beamed.

Entering the living room, an unfamiliar face greeted me. Exchanging cordial greetings, I didn't press for introductions, choosing instead to set down the groceries. As I made my way to the kitchen, their hushed conversation pricked my ears, but I dismissed it, choosing to focus on grabbing juice and some snacks. Settling into the dining area, I was quite content until my mom beckoned, "Vicky, could you come over here for a moment?"

"Sure, Mom. I assume this is about the paint colour choices?" I responded, trying to keep the atmosphere light.

She shot me a look, "It's not quite about that."

Curiosity piqued, I prodded, "Alright... what's this about?"

Sighing deeply, she began, "Errrmmm...Victoria, you know we've had numerous discussions about the choices you've been making. I felt it was time for a new perspective. This gentleman here is a revered Muslim cleric. I've brought him in the hope that he might offer a fresh insight. I've tried various avenues to get through to you, hoping you'd understand my worries. This Imam, originally from

Egypt, has guided many individuals through their life's tumults, and they've emerged stronger. Often, spiritual counsellors like him are the guiding light in times of dilemma. I truly hope you'd lend him an open ear."

I recognized the familiar strategy in my mother's approach to sensitive topics and chose not to contest it. With a polite smile, I turned my attention to the Imam.

"It's a pleasure to meet you, Sheikh". I nodded my head in acknowledgement, signalling that he could proceed with speaking.

He began, "I am glad you agreed to listen to me." His gentle demeanour was evident. Sheikh Abdulaziz, a seasoned religious figure who had spent substantial time in the U.S., prided himself on his deep understanding of various religious doctrines. "In my years as an Imam, I've interacted with a diverse array of believers. I've learned to appreciate and respect the tenets of various faiths. We, too, hold Jesus Christ, or Prophet Isaiah (PBUH) as he's known to us, in high esteem. We follow God's will as he did. I'm familiar with the teachings of the Bible and other holy scriptures, and I assure you, none advocate for what you're supporting. In the Holy Quran, Surah Ar-Rum chapter 30, verse 40, 'God is he who created you and then sustained you, then causes you to die, then gives life to you again...' Then in chapter 30, verse 54, 'God is He who shaped you out of weakness, then appointed after weakness strength, then after strength, appointed weakness and grey hair. He creates what He wills. He is the Knower, the Mighty.' All these verses I quoted place emphasis on the cycles of life and death, emphasizing God as the sole authority over them." "You see", he continued, "seeking euthanasia is akin to knowingly consuming poison. It's an act of will, a deliberate step towards death.

Should that be considered natural? Consider the profound implications – the eternal consequences, the mourning family left behind, the societal backlash, and potential legal ramifications, even if you believe you have a strong case."

His voice was earnest. "Life is precious, meant to be lived fully, enjoying God's blessings. I implore you, for everyone's sake, to reconsider your stance. Withdraw from this pursuit that shadows your life and the afterlife."

Sheik Abdulaziz filled the room with his passionate discourse, peppering his plea with life stories and scriptural references. After his lengthy monologue, he took his leave. My mother's eyes, laden with unspoken pleas, met mine. To keep the peace, I assured her I'd ponder the Sheikh's words.

However, legal realities awaited my attention and I needed to see my lawyer ASAP. "I'll see you later, Mom", I announced, as I picked up my handbag and phone.

The courtroom atmosphere was filled with tension and anticipation as usual, as the continuation of my case was announced.

The judge, with a piercing gaze, addressed me with clear concern. "Mrs. Victoria", he began, his tone a blend of sternness and empathy, "are you aware of the precarious path you're treading? Legalizing euthanasia is a slippery slope. What begins as a merciful end could spiral into gross misuse. We risk creating a world where people, even those in perfect health, might be terminated without consent or against their wishes. Furthermore, you're challenging the very ethos of the medical community. Doctors and nurses are sworn to heal, not to play arbiters of death. Your stance forces these professionals into a moral quagmire, potentially eroding the sanctity of healthcare."

He continued, "This debate encompasses the core rights: the freedom of choice regarding one's own life versus the overarching sanctity of life. Euthanasia presents an option for those with terminal conditions to exit with dignity. However, it simultaneously harbours the risk of misuse, especially concerning medical professionals."

Taking a deep breath, I responded, "Your Honor, I recognize the potential pitfalls you've outlined. However, I hold a staunch belief that every individual, regardless of their physical or cognitive capacities, has an inherent moral compass. Despite societal biases and misconceptions about disabilities, our ability to discern right from wrong remains intact. I'm not seeking leniency or exceptions. My plea is for autonomy over my life choices, fully cognizant of their ramifications."

"I firmly believe", I continued with emphasis, "that everyone, irrespective of their conditions, can evaluate their options and make informed decisions. Our aim should pivot from limiting rights based on predisposed notions to fostering an environment of equity, dignity, and respect. The emphasis should be on safeguarding all citizens while valuing individual freedoms."

The room was silent for a moment. As the proceedings continued, my mind raced, replaying the day's events. Sleep evaded me for most of the night. By dawn, the house was stirring with faint sounds of activity. I found solace in sleep only as the first light of daybreak filtered through.

Chapter 14

The Dust Keeps Rising

I woke up feeling like a storm cloud, dark and heavy with a mood to match. I was grateful the hospital staff seemed to sense my brooding irritation and kept their distance; I was in no state for small talk. My fears were mounting up. My thoughts were a whirlwind of betrayal. "How could my own family treat me as if I were just some disposable objects?", I brooded. The absence of my husband, in particular, cut deep. "Could the court have barred them from visiting me?", I wondered. Deciding I needed answers, I resolved to speak with Dr. James, who had been in court during the last hearing.

"Hmmm..." A deep, weary sigh escaped me as I recalled the last court session's fiery ordeal. The upcoming court date loomed over me, a constant reminder of the gruelling interrogation I was to endure. Yet, the stake was higher. I found solace in knowing Dr. James would be by my side, ready to attest to the court that my mental faculties remained sharp, dispelling any insinuations of insanity that the court might have preconceived. Nevertheless, the emotional exhaustion was overwhelming, and I clung to the hope that the end was near, with the court's decision hanging in the balance. Though fear gnawed at me, hinting that the judge might rule against my wishes, I tried to keep faith that it would all work out.

The day of the hearing began earlier than usual. Dr. James was present, gently reminding me of the schedule. His calm presence was a slight balm to my frayed nerves. Upon arrival at the courthouse, my lawyer was already waiting. We engaged in a succinct discussion, strategizing and fortifying my resolve before I stepped onto the battlefield.

The courtroom was dense with anticipation, each person present absorbing the weight of what was unfolding. I could barely keep myself together, feeling every ounce of my energy waning as I was ushered inside. Dr. James was there too, ready to take the stand, a pillar of hope for me.

The judge commenced, addressing Dr. James with a seriousness that matched the gravity of the situation, "Dr. James, we are grateful for your presence. Given your thorough evaluation of Victoria during her tenure at the psychiatric facility, we're keenly interested in your professional insights. Specifically, we're wrestling with whether Victoria's desire to have autonomy over her life-or-death decision is morally defensible."

Dr. James nodded, his demeanour the epitome of calm deliberation. "Your Honor", he began, "it's imperative to note that my role hinges on evaluating Victoria's mental competency and the capacity for decision-making, not adjudicating moral values. Nonetheless, I'm prepared to offer an ethical lens on the matters of end-of-life decisions and individual autonomy."

The judge leaned forward slightly, gesturing for him to continue. "Please proceed, Dr. James. Your professional standpoint is vital to our deliberations."

"Ethically speaking", Dr. James continued, his voice clear, "personal autonomy is a cornerstone in medical ethics. It's imperative that individuals, assuming they have the requisite mental clarity, retain the right to make informed decisions about their health and medical treatments. This respect for self-determination is fundamental."

At this juncture, Filip interjected, seeking clarification amidst the complex ethical considerations. "Dr. James, your insights are invaluable. Could you elaborate on whether, during your assessments, you perceived any evidence of external coercion or a compromise in Victoria's ability to make this profound decision?"

Unperturbed, Dr. James responded, "Victoria exhibited a lucid understanding of her situation throughout my evaluation. There was no evidence suggesting coercion or faltering judgment. Her communication was articulate and her reasoning consistent, indicative of a person with a firm grasp on the ramifications of her choices. It is my professional opinion that Victoria's decision is rooted in her deeply held values and beliefs, made independently and with full autonomy."

The judge paused, absorbing Dr. James' expert testimony. "Given your testimony, Dr. James, and acknowledging the lack of evidence pointing to impaired judgment, could you delve a bit deeper into the moral aspect of Victoria's decision from your perspective?"

The room held its collective breath, awaiting what Dr. James would offer next in this delicate balance between life, death, and personal liberty.

In the quiet gravity of the courtroom, Dr. James pondered before responding. "Your Honor, the terrain of morality is vast and often contingent on one's cultural, religious, and personal beliefs. For some, certain religious or personal tenets may negate the choice of euthanasia or personal autonomy in such matters. Conversely, others firmly advocate for an individual's right to make deeply personal decisions about their own lives, emphasizing the importance of self-determination. It's a multifaceted issue, where varying beliefs and values intersect."

The judge nodded appreciatively, "Thank you, Dr. James, we're indebted to your insights, which have illuminated the intricate ethical dimensions of Victoria's request."

Filip then interjected; a fervour evident in his tone. "If I may add, Your Honor. Victoria's plea for freedom is not an impulsive whim but a culmination of deep introspection and reverence for personal liberty. She embodies the essence of self-determination, fully aware of the weight and repercussions of her choice. As such, her request is not just a mere wish, but a powerful testament to her belief in personal self-determination."

The courtroom resonated with the depth of Filip's words, underscoring the gravity of Victoria's decision within the bigger picture of human rights and personal freedom.

In the hallowed silence of the courtroom, the Judge continued, "Mr. Filip, I want to emphasize my recognition of the intricate layers surrounding Victoria's autonomy. Her decisions were clear-minded, and devoid of any bias or external influence. Yet, we're confronted by broader philosophical quandaries here — the pursuit of absolute truth and the repercussions of radical decisions. Both demand our deepest introspection. Our justice system isn't merely about the application of written laws but also the pursuit of authenticity. Yet, what is 'absolute truth'? It remains an ever-shifting mosaic, shaped by perspectives, personal biases, and societal norms. Our aim is to uncover the truth based on the available evidence, but it's important to understand that our individual truths may not align with those of others.

Radical decisions, particularly when they toe the line between life and death, compel us to reconsider our societal benchmarks. These are the decisions that test the very fibre of our ethics and stretch the horizons of our societal understanding. As we tread through the maze of this case, our mission remains twofold: to serve justice in its truest form and to respect the intrinsic rights of every individual. Yet, we must also remain aware of the inherent fallibility of our legal system, one that functions within our ever-evolving societal and ethical landscapes. With such weighty matters before us, I urge everyone present — to consider the gravity of our discussions, sift through the evidence judiciously, and continuously introspect. This case calls for more than just legal insight; it beckons empathy, understanding, and respect for varied perspectives. So, with this foundation laid, Mr. Filip, you may proceed."

Filip took a moment to adjust his stance, ensuring he had the attention of everyone in the courtroom. "Your Honor, before we explore the core of this case, there's a broader context of our modern age I'd like to address. Today, in the vast expanse of the digital realm, the lines between reality and impersonation have blurred. Social media platforms and online spaces allow one to craft and don any identity, often without any tangible repercussions. One might question the relevance of this to our current proceedings. However, it's imperative to understand that this digital dynamic complicates our notions of truth and authenticity."

He continued, "The ease with which identities can be assumed and manipulated online prompts us to reflect on the reliability of the information we consume and the authenticity of intentions behind them. Given these challenges, it is of utmost importance that this court dives deeply into the sincerity of Victoria's intentions. We must move beyond superficial judgments and gauge the depth of her convictions. In a world rife with deception, it becomes vital to rigorously assess Victoria's mental and emotional state and ascertain the genuineness of her desires."

Filip took a breath, emphasizing the weight of his next words. "Empathy should be our compass as we navigate the intricate terrains of personal autonomy and individual rights. Although bold choices can divide public sentiment, our legal system serves as a symbol of impartiality, crafted to safeguard the sanctity of personal liberties. As we proceed, let's be acutely aware of the challenges our digital age poses to discerning truth and remain steadfast in ensuring that our deliberations are both rigorous and empathetic. We owe it to Victoria, and we owe it to the tenets of justice we uphold."

Judge Harmon gazed around the room, pausing to emphasize the weight of his next words. "Thank you, Mr. Filip, for highlighting the nuances of our digital age. It's undeniable that the world of screens, with its myriad of avatars, can cast shadows over genuine identities. Yet, beyond this digital realm, there lies the very tangible, very real world of mental health." He leaned forward slightly, ensuring he reached every ear in the room. "For every individual who may use the online world as a stage, there are countless others genuinely wrestling with profound internal conflicts. They navigate a labyrinth of emotions, often feeling lost and misunderstood. When such personal battles intersect with monumental decisions, like the choice of life or death, it is our responsibility to ensure that such choices aren't being made from a place of fleeting emotion but from one of reasoned clarity."

The judge continued, "It's in these moments that the expertise of professionals like psychiatrists and psychologists becomes crucial.

Their insights delve deeper than surface-level observations. They offer us a window into the individual's mind, helping discern genuine convictions from impulsive sentiments. While we must honour the principle of personal autonomy, we can't forget our collective duty to safeguard an individual's well-being. Striking a balance between these two is no easy task, and that's where our trusted specialists come in.

Their assessments are the fulcrum on which we balance these considerations." Taking a deep breath, he concluded, "In Victoria's situation, we must lean on this expert analysis to illuminate her mental and emotional state, determining the roots of her desires. With a decision as profound as hers, we owe it to her, and to the sanctity of the court, to ensure every facet is examined. Mrs. Victoria, this court lends you its ears. Would you like to say anything?"

Victoria's voice wavered with passion and emotion, each word ringing out with determination. "Every individual's life is a deeply personal journey, one filled with choices and decisions unique to them. And here I stand, pleading for the right to make perhaps the most personal choice of all. Why can't I decide the fate of my own existence? If I feel, with every fibre of my being, that my life has run its course, why am I denied the right to exit it with grace and dignity?"

Her eyes searched the room, attempting to connect with every person present. "When our pets suffer, we grant them the mercy of a painless end. Yet, when it comes to our fellow humans, why do we trap them in a cycle of agony? Why is this paradox where ending needless suffering in animals is kindness, but offering the same to humans is taboo?"

Taking a deep breath, she pressed on, "We have these terms – active and passive euthanasia. In passive euthanasia, we withhold treatment, letting nature take its course. But isn't that a mere semantic detour around the act of actively hastening death? When it's cloaked under 'denying treatment,' society finds it palatable. Yet, when it's direct, it's suddenly controversial."

Victoria's eyes moistened but her resolve was unyielding, "If a medical professional, after evaluating all options, believes that ending a life could be in the patient's best interest, why is that deemed unethical? After all, isn't the underlying intention the same, to spare needless suffering? Our world desperately needs an educated discourse on this issue, understanding both its ethical nuances and the deeply personal stories behind each choice. I only hope that my story can be a catalyst for such a conversation."

She resumes after a brief pause: "For example, the perceptions of those with anorexia who believe they are overweight pose a challenging question: Do we accept their perspective as their reality, or do we intervene? Similarly, if someone identifies as something - someone else or another entity, should that be embraced as their truth? Objectivity and subjectivity are distinct concepts; what we feel is not always in line with what is objectively real. Navigating the waters between personal belief and verifiable fact demands a logical and reasoned approach.

I find myself at odds with the prevailing opinion. Don't we all have inherent rights? Your freedom shouldn't dictate how I live, just as my choices shouldn't infringe upon your liberties. The right to express oneself and make personal life decisions—free from undue external influence—is fundamental. This, of course, pertains to competent adults making informed decisions. The crux of the matter is determining the boundaries within which the law can dictate our life choices.

While differences in viewpoints are inevitable, one's freedom shouldn't curtail another's. It's essential to remember that people globally face struggles and, amidst their pain, need empathy, understanding, and a listening ear.

In his chaotic lonely world, there's a growing concern that society is blurring the lines between sanity and insanity. When those who genuinely grapple with mental illnesses are viewed as the touchstones of objective reality, it breeds confusion. This haziness makes individuals question their own mental well-being, especially if they feel out of place in the prevailing narrative.

If I were diagnosed with schizophrenia, I would expect society to recognize my condition and support my need for appropriate care. A society grounded in objectivity provides its members with a compass, guiding them through the complexities of life. However, if my genuine struggles were dismissed and I was labelled 'normal', not only would my healing be compromised, but others would begin doubting their own mental states. It's unsettling to think that we might be nudged to live by standards that aren't rooted in reality. Why should anyone be coerced into accepting such a narrative?

Weil once noted that death is mankind's most valuable gift, a perspective often dismissed by contemporary society. Such a view doesn't inherently diminish life's value. One can cherish life and yet understand and respect this perspective. Just as my arrival in this world was celebrated, shouldn't I be granted the autonomy to decide its conclusion?"

The Judge pauses me: "Mrs. Victoria, I value your sincere expression of your convictions and your wish for independence in your life. Your speech raises essential questions and challenges societal norms surrounding end-of-life choices and personal autonomy. You argue for the right to die with dignity, comparing how we euthanize animals to prevent their suffering. Your question about the difference between active and passive euthanasia is thought-provoking. It brings to light the ethical considerations and societal perceptions surrounding these practices. You also touch upon the distinction between objective reality and subjective feelings, emphasizing the importance of logical reasoning and the potential confusion when societal norms deviate from objective standards. These are complex and philosophical issues that require careful consideration.

While I cannot provide a definitive answer to all the questions you raised, my heart is confident that your speech has been heard. This court must weigh the principles of individual self-governance, the sanctity of life, and the impact on society when making decisions. Standards and rules create paths for humans to follow, but even those who can navigate them can get lost.

In cases as profound as this, we are responsible for ensuring a fair and just evaluation of the circumstances while considering the implications for both the individual and society. We recognize the immense weight of the decisions at hand and the deep impact they can have on individuals and those around them. Your plea to be treated with decency and allowed to make decisions about your life is valid and deserving of consideration. As we move forward in this case, we will continue to evaluate the legal, ethical, and societal aspects involved to arrive at a just and informed conclusion. Please understand that the court's deliberation does not reflect your worth or your value as a human being. Our responsibility is to navigate the complexities of the law and the values underpinning our society. Your voice and perspective will be considered as we strive for fairness and justice."

Without hesitation, I continued: "While none of us can pick the circumstances of our birth, we should at least have a say in how we conclude our story. If our personal freedom becomes so constrained that it barely resembles freedom at all, then what's its true value? I stress 'freedom' here, ensuring my choices don't impinge upon others.

I would like to elaborate further on the concept of absolute truth and its significance concerning my situation. 'Absolute truth' means a reality that exists no matter what anyone believes. It doesn't change and isn't influenced by personal opinions or experience. It is true, without considering emotions or thoughts.

Yet, when the human experience comes into play, what is 'absolute' may differ based on individual perspectives. People's understanding of truth evolves, moulded by their emotions, experiences, and convictions. Two individuals might perceive the same fact differently. This doesn't necessarily mean one is mistaken. Just because many may challenge my truth doesn't make it any less significant to me, and I, in turn, honour their truths.

My pain, my suffering, constitutes my undeniable truth. It is the bedrock of my decisions and life experiences. To disregard it as mere subjectivity is to invalidate my existence.

While the notion of 'absolute truth' leans towards objectivity, it's worth noting the multifaceted nature of truth. Objective truths, verifiable by evidence or science, exist in the tangible world. In contrast, the arts and literature embrace truths open to interpretation. A literary piece might portray darkness, yet symbolically represent despair. Both interpretations are legitimate, akin to diverse life perceptions.

Discerning between objective and subjective truths becomes pivotal when discussing personal freedoms and choices. The realm of subjective truths is rich with empathy, understanding, and emotional resonance, urging us to honour diverse viewpoints.

My truth, perhaps unconventional by societal standards, embodies my authentic experiences. Its validity doesn't waver based on mainstream acceptance. True 'absolute truth' should be comprehensive, acknowledging the intrinsic value of personal experiences and feelings. Embracing such a definition can foster a society that respects personal autonomy, even in profound discussions of life and death."

With a compassionate expression, the judge proceeds with his speech. "Mrs. Victoria, your viewpoint sheds light on the complexities of human existence and the individual experiences that shape our understanding of reality.

Nonetheless, it is crucial to consider the wider ramifications of individual self-governance and the diversity of experiences within society. As a judge, I uphold the law and ensure fairness and justice for all individuals. In doing so, I must consider the more enormous implications and potential consequences of granting unrestricted freedom in matters as profound as life and death.

While personal autonomy is a fundamental right, it is also necessary to recognize the interplay between individual rights and societal values.

Being human encompasses our desires, beliefs, and responsibilities to the larger community. We exist within a social fabric that requires us to balance our rights with the well-being and interests of others.

Reality is vast and includes various aspects such as experiences, beliefs, and viewpoints. Due to this diversity, society must set boundaries and rules. These measures are implemented to maintain a stable and orderly society while protecting individuals and preserving societal harmony. We understand that there are many views about important things in life, but should we dance to all whims and caprices of anyone who feels they have the right to choose whatever they feel like? We have many people who call bad things good, and should we allow them to misbehave because they have a right to be themselves? No! This world is bonded by many laws that stem from many beliefs and traditions and are systematically woven into the law-bound society's fabric. Your views are right based on how you see it, but before we mark it 'yes', we should see what the law says about it and how far it can influence society. While your emphasis on personal freedom is understandable, it is essential to acknowledge that granting unrestricted autonomy without any safeguards or evaluations may have unintended consequences. The decision to someone's life is a profound and irreversible choice, and it is necessary to assess whether such a decision is made with a clear and rational mind or if transient emotions or temporary circumstances may influence it.

It is not my intention to undermine your suffering or dismiss your perspective. Rather, I must consider the more enormous implications and the responsibility I bear as a judge in ensuring that decisions of this magnitude are made with careful consideration and adequate safeguards to protect the rights and well-being of all individuals involved.

Please understand that the decisions made in this court are made with a thorough understanding of the complexities and moral dilemmas involved. While we may have differing views on the extent of personal freedom, I must carefully evaluate the evidence and arguments presented and arrive at a decision that reflects both the individual's rights and the broader interests of society.

In light of this, I hereby call for adjourning this case until the 23rd of next month."

The court registrar called out, and as the judge and the lawyers left, everyone in the courtroom stood up.

"Mrs. Vicky, you have heard what the judge said. We will have to be back next month, but I hope the next sitting will take us where we want to be. With the presence of Dr. James and his testimony before the court on your mental state, I believe we would come to a reasonable conclusion on the case. All I want is for you to rest your nerves and allow the law to take its full court. Let's hope for the best."

My mother was conspicuously absent from the courtroom that day. Instead, she had visited my elder brother, who was celebrating the birth of his child. Only Robert was there to witness the proceedings. He observed silently from the sidelines, only drawing near when my attorney began discussing the case details with me. As my lawyer spoke, Robert merely watched, his emotions masked.

After that, I was led back into the vehicle that brought me from the hospital to the court. While in the car, one of the nurses who came with said, "I wish you did not put yourself through all these. Can't you see how drained your husband is? I don't know your gain in deliberately humiliating the people around you. You are pushing a dead-on-arrival course, and I do not see you winning this case."

The driver chuckled and said, "I always look at this woman with strange bewilderment and wonder how someone would hate existence. Life is sweet and beautiful, but someone is here thinking of checking out even at the peak of her career. Madam, do you think that those who face death go there with happiness? Death is not easy, even when it comes suddenly, not to talk about someone who wants to walk into demise with her consciousness intact."

I did not respond to him because I did not want to enter another session of arguments with them. It was even inconsequential because they were not my lawyer or the judge. After all, they listened to everything I said in the courtroom, and repeating my arguments would be unnecessary.

A few minutes after returning to the hospital, Mr. Evans arrived to escort me for my usual outing. Initially, I considered expressing my disinterest in going out that day but ultimately joined him without sharing my thoughts with him.

"How time flies! You have spent some time with us here..." Mr. Evans exclaimed "I like your company because you are wise and well-read. Nevertheless, my only problem with you is your insistence on Euthanasia. If you say that you are no longer interested in it today, you will see how people will smile at that statement."

"But I do not think that my agreement to something I want should bring problems to anyone except me, and I am not complaining about it."

"Yes, you cannot know the depth it sank into in the minds of the people who love you, and you will not know the wide difference it would make by renouncing it."

"You made me remember how I tensed my court sitting was the third time. It was a clash of the Titans between my lawyer and the court."

"Tell me about." Mr. Evans said enthusiastically.

"You should have come and seen how intense it was. Besides, it had been adjourned till next month."

"Mrs. Vicky, I got you a novel you asked me to help you with."

"…'The Poor Christ of Bomba' I have never read this book". I replied.

"I'm eagerly anticipating your review of the book and your thoughts on it. I bought it some years back. Mongo Beti is one of the most fantastic African writers. Still, I hope you will not develop another religious philosophy from this book because he is a writer of religious criticism. This novel is among those that delve into the complexities of religion, and I believe these themes align with your interests."

"Let me read it first. I've already perused the book's synopsis, and it appears intriguing. At the very least, it will spare me from the monotonous routine of repeating the same actions consistently."

After some moments of having several discussions, I went back to my room. I just felt so exhausted after the moment of a debate with Mr. Evans. He was the one who led the most significant part of the dialogue. I could have been livelier. I kept longing for something better, and I was beginning to feel the absence of my family, especially my children.

I fell into my bed as soon as it back to the room. I remembered how my family went under further pressure to make me give up. My kids did not want to have it lying low with me. It is always, "Mom, can't you see it this way? My heart is sinking. Mom, I can't afford to lose you." Sometimes, I did not want my children to talk about it because I felt they were too young to understand. Besides that, they were always distracted by that, and I wanted it to be manageable for their educational concentration.

Sometimes, Robert woke me up at night and would talk for hours, but my mind was already made up. He tried talking about me to reconsider it, let the chapter close, and let life continue. "Haven't you stressed everyone enough?"

"Can we just go to bed? You know that I will be going to work tomorrow." That was one of the ways I tried to dismiss Robert's arguments and pleas, whenever he wanted to make me look like I was being selfish.

I paused my thoughts and began to read the book.

Chapter 15

Moving Beyond the Conventional

For years, I've advocated for the right to dictate the course of my life, including how and when I might end it. Euthanasia offers a way to conclude life on one's own terms, sparing the long, gruelling journey of those trapped in an unending cycle of illness or treatments for incurable conditions.

Why should anyone be denied a death filled with dignity? Consider someone terminally ill, imprisoned by ceaseless pain and robbed of life's control. If I were in such dire straits, or even facing a different yet equally challenging scenario, shouldn't I have access to this final solace? Offering individuals the choice to embrace euthanasia can mitigate the overwhelming anxiety and stress that accompany prolonged illness or life's unrelenting burdens. This option provides a serene and dignified exit, instead of an agonizing, drawn-out struggle.

Moreover, it's crucial to recognize the emotional toll on families, constantly wrestling with these dilemmas. For those supporting loved ones with terminal conditions, the physical, emotional, and financial burdens are immense. A peaceful, dignified conclusion, free from extended anguish, is a goal we should universally pursue.

Death is dignity, but of what use is getting to old age and struggling with many illnesses? I have seen many older adults who wished they never grew old to the point of suffering many sicknesses such as loss of memories, arthritis, and many more. Those who have tasted old age rarely see blessings in it as against the commoner. Old age is a 'blessing', meaning we might have been deceived all along. Was it not Job who said that the days appointed unto men are filled with pains? Even Solomon, with all his wealth, stated on many occasions that 'vanities of vanities'. So, what is the fuss about old age and that you will have to become a liability to others and life would be dictated to you?

The body is imprisoned in different fazes from birth until death. That is the only moment of freedom that's hope because nobody returned and assured us that there is no other dimension where we will restart the same spiral and go through the same hell repeatedly. Imagine being finally free but reborn into someone or something else, eternally trapped in different forms. We are helpless in the face of life. And what I sometimes wondered was if life is the authentic underworld, and we try to portray it as the desert so we could all bear to survive. What if everything is a mind game, and the idea is to keep us playing by the rules so nobody would question reality? What if…? What if…?

In the maze of bureaucracy, consent often feels like an illusion. We're thrust into life, and similarly, death's inevitability is determined without our say. Everywhere I turn, I'm met with the echoes of society's judgments: 'Suicide is never the answer', or 'Euthanasia is a word spoken in hushed tones'. I can't help but wonder: who decided these rules for us? Was it the religious underpinnings of our society shaping the laws?

'Why should a society dictate your very existence?', I often ponder. The irony isn't lost on me when I see that the very courts, the supposed guardians of individual freedoms, often entrap people in these unbending rules. It baffles me. We advocate for the fundamental right to live, yet paradoxically deny individuals the right to decide their own exit. Such hypocrisy!

Civilization, like knowledge, is ever-evolving. And my choice, however unconventional, won't crumble its foundations. After all, isn't it the same society that permits abortions? Some of these are undeniably vital, saving the lives of mothers. But what about those who choose to terminate pregnancies out of personal choice? Aren't these doctors and patients a part of our society too?

Yet, here I am, an adult seeking a dignified departure from this world, being vilified, and made an example of. Some confront me with optimistic tales, 'My great grandfather lived till 100 and was spry as someone half his age'. Others argue, 'Why are you dreading an old age that's not even promised?'

They might have a point, but what if my worst fears do manifest with age? Even if I never reach the sunset years, the crux remains the right to determine my destiny is mine. I shouldn't have to reach the point of no return, weakened and powerless, to yearn for a serene journey into the cosmos.

Clear-minded individuals inherently grasp what they desire, making choices that resonate with their innermost convictions. It's a universal truth that while many vigorously cling to life, even though they could let go at any moment, their decisions should be seen as just another aspect of existence, rather than an over-dramatized crossroad.

Laws, interestingly, aren't designed with the majority in mind, but rather for those on the fringes who might challenge them. Otherwise, the strictness of the laws would forbid even more things. For example, in both religion and this, it's forbidden to hurt someone. If humans had this intent in their nature, nothing could stop them when we think we have all the means to hurt those around us; that's the same idea when we think about ending our lives. My life should be in my control, not under everyone' anyone's control. That is the beauty of life, and it's in human nature to fight for their lives, but for the few who prefer to die with integrity, why should they be left to suffer? If we live in a world where society accepts self-harm, self-change, and irreversible actions, why should I not be able to choose to die? Parents and society bury their born children to let someone else be reborn.

Who are we as humans? Nowadays, people can impersonate whom they want without being accused of neurological sickness. Nobody questions their spectrum of reality. They can use which adjectives they choose, but I cannot choose which reality I want. What's the difference between me and others who choose what they wish to do with their lives? Who decides? Where do we draw the line? Who wields the pen?

While guidelines and standards are essential to steer society, they must be flexible enough to accommodate every individual's reality. If someone perceives themselves vastly different from societal norms, whether it's body dysmorphia or identifying as non-human, how should society respond? Do we accept or intervene?

There is helplessness in front of those who are in charge. Are we truly free? Are we in charge of our own lives? Hell no! Never have been and never will be. I feel handcuffed in my own home, living my life, not having the freedom to choose when I want to end the life I never requested.

The beauty in chaos can be likened to a mesmerizing symphony, its appeal often dependent on the beholder. My father, a physics educator, had a unique perspective on the universe. He'd say, 'Darkness is merely an absence of light.' Everything is conceivable if you opt to perceive it that way, and equally, one can decide to be oblivious to it. Through his eyes, life danced as waves, particles, and shades, sometimes fading into the void of darkness.

Conversely, my mother's world thrived on spiritual energy. To her, spirits were real entities, and they defined her reality, a realm she neither wholly affirmed nor denied. In her view, life's very existence testified to the presence of a divine force. For me, existence is more a series of 'whats' rather than 'whys.'

The unseen has always intrigued humanity, sparking countless cosmological, teleological, moral, and ontological debates. Every individual carves their path in search of meaning. Some find solace in the embrace of a higher power, while others, craving tangible evidence, tread paths of scepticism.

Certain philosophies argue for divine existence based on the Universe's very presence, proposing an initiating cause or an eternal being—God—as its architect. Another perspective admires the meticulous order in nature, suggesting an intelligent force behind its creation. Furthermore, our intrinsic moral compass, our innate sense of right and wrong, is believed by some to hint at a supreme moral authority that has set these benchmarks.

At the heart of such discourses lies the concept of a perfect God. As the argument goes, if one can envision a supremely perfect being, then existence itself would be one of its inherent attributes. Hence, by this logic, God undeniably exists.

When I think about what people bring for arguments to support God, I would ask the question if it's possible for there to be a God who is all-powerful, all-knowing, and all-good when there is so much evil and suffering in the world. It challenges the idea that such a God can coexist with the existence of pain and injustice. Isn't enough tangible evidence or scientific proof to support the belief in God or the existence of a higher power? At least not in my view alone; let's think about all religions – can they all be simultaneously true? They have different traditions, beliefs and conflicting claims about God. Do we mean that a hand of people would land in Heaven and the rest in eternal suffering? Religion is one of the hilarious things I grew up to find myself in.

Growing up, my home championed spiritual flexibility over dogmatic rituals. We never felt compelled to chant specific verses before embarking on daily tasks. Some cultures, I've learned, find solace in religion, particularly among the less fortunate. For them, faith compensates for worldly disparities. Sentiments like 'What shall it profit a man if he gains the whole world and loses his soul?' and 'Blessed are the poor in spirit, for theirs is the kingdom of heaven' echo this. Paradoxically, some followers of the same religion assert that prosperity signifies divine favour, further muddying the waters of belief.

Religion offers solace to many, but it has also imprisoned logic and reason. It's perplexing to witness believers of the same God quarrel over their worship methods, with some decreeing damnation for perceived deviations in practice. What a conundrum! For now, I choose to find comfort in concepts like the Big Bang, evolution, or the all-encompassing energy that powers our Universe. Should a Supreme Force truly exist, I trust it will recognize and empathize with my doubts and questions when my time comes. Until then, I'll cheerfully raise a glass to the mysteries of existence. Hail to Whatever! Those who remain quiet and don't dare to speak up will always be in chains and continue participating in this circle of life, forcing others to feel alone and weak. No one wants to sacrifice their comfort to make a change. It requires courage to stand up for your voice or others that don't fit society's standards.

I was sure that some of the people judging me and those who did not might have once nursed the idea of going for euthanasia, whether for themselves or their loved ones. However, the fear of what the law says might have restrained them from doing it, but because I was bold enough to be vocal about mine, they hypocritically joined forces to condemn me. Meanwhile, if I fought the same battle and won, some of them would be the next in line to visit the euthanasia centres to ask for it and the few who would not go there might be afraid to do so because of their beliefs. What two-faced people?! Anyway, I was not bothered about what anyone thought; I had a cause I was fighting for, and those petty distractions might cost me a lot.

While in court, it was my turn for the closing statements: "We have discussed a deeply personal and sensitive matter— the right to choose one's fate. While I understand the court's responsibility to interpret and uphold the law, I firmly believe that personal autonomy and compassion should also be considered. Throughout this case, we have presented numerous arguments highlighting the importance of allowing individuals to choose euthanasia. We have emphasized the need for stringent regulations and safeguards to prevent abuse and protect vulnerable individuals. We have shared stories of those who have also expressed their desire for a peaceful and dignified end.

Despite our arguments, I understand this is a complex legal issue, and the court must consider various factors in its decision. However, I implore the court to acknowledge the value of individual autonomy and the principles of compassion. Thank you."

"Thank you, Mrs. Victoria and Filip, for your passionate arguments. However, after careful consideration of the law, precedents, and the arguments presented, this court finds that euthanasia, as it stands, is not legally permissible under current legislation. The court acknowledges the importance of the issues raised. Still, it is ultimately the role of the legislature to determine the legality and parameters of euthanasia. I understand that this decision may be disappointing for you, Mrs. Victoria, but it is essential to respect the rule of law and the boundaries set by our legal system and I hope you won't resort to personal actions. I encourage you to continue advocating for change through lawful means and engage in the democratic process to influence legislation on this matter. The court is adjourned."

While the judge used his hammer to adjourn the meeting, I felt how my soul left my body. I felt hollow. I felt powerless. I felt unheard. I felt unseen. I felt insignificant. I thought they were unworthy of my time. I felt numb. It was time for me to go home broken and confront my demons.

I stepped out of the courtroom with a heavy heart, my mind still replaying the emotional proceedings that had taken place inside. It had been a gruelling battle, fighting tooth and nail for my justice. While I journeyed back to my residence, I could feel the weight of the day pressing down on me; I longed for the comfort of my sanctuary, hoping that I could find solace within the walls of my home. But little did I know that my troubles were far from over.

Sitting in the car, I remembered that I had gained physical freedom, which was my discharge from the psychiatric hospital. The law had tried all it could to nail me as mentally unstable, but after many critical tests were performed, it was clear that my brain was intact. Though I had been discharged, the mental breakdown was hard to bear.

I remember the lonely days and nights and how everyone disserted me, including my family. As I walked out of the ward on that fateful morning, the memories of the dark days were left at the entrance of the big passage. I decided not to carry any of it along with me. I remember how Mr. Evans shook hands with me with mixed feelings. One factor was his joy over my release, while the other was his strong belief that I would be greatly missed. I hugged him and waved as I walked slowly with Dr. James and my lawyer, who had come to oversee my discharge. I was unaware my family members were outside, standing afar off and waiting for me. I feigned happiness as I laughed a mirthless laughter when my mother approached me to hug me.

Robert stood by the car door, waiting for me. He hugged me and jumped into the car without saying a word.

I was too exhausted to start questioning anyone about not coming to check on me when I was admitted. It was such a long process of going to court from the hospital, and I saw how unhappy my mother was about it. My brother Adam did not show much concern. I thought he had already written me off and decided my fate, which he would have tagged 'the price for stubbornness'. Anyhow, I was not prepared to start any unnecessary conversation about that. I needed rest!

When we got home that day, my children's mood was unwelcoming, but I did not show that I was bothered. 'The court is yet to give a final verdict, but I am not going to back off'. I mumbled as I threw myself on the bed after having my meal and a warm shower. I needed more time to give people feedback about my psychiatrist ward experience. If any of them were interested in knowing about it, they would have come around to see for themselves. So, their absence showed that they did not care about whatever happened there.

It was not long after I came back from the psychiatric hospital that another argument on the issue of euthanasia sprang up in my home. It started one afternoon when my husband heard me talking with my lawyer about the next step.

"But Victoria, I think you should have allowed this matter to rest, why are you still hell-bent on talking about it?"

"I think you are not getting the point, Robert! We can appeal! That means it's not over yet!"

"No problem, but I feel that you should have allowed that to stop. What else do you want?!"

"Robert… let me just talk. I want you to listen, and please don't stop me while I talk my mind. This is not the end of my battle. I want you to know that my essence will linger, being suspended in the ethereal expanse of the universe if I die. Like a beacon of light, my energy will guide you through the vastness of the multiverse until the day when our souls intertwine once more.

The connection we shared, forged in the crucible of love and shared experiences, cannot be extinguished by the physical separation we will endure. It transcends the boundaries of this earthly existence and reaches into the realms where the ethereal and the material converge. You must find solace in the knowledge that my essence remains tangled with yours! And in the depths of my being, I hold onto the belief that when you and our children's journey in this life is completed, the eery bond we share will reunite us in a realm where time holds no sway.

The ethereal realm, the unseen fabric that permeates the cosmos, holds the promise of our reunion. It is a realm where quantum physics and the mysteries of parallel dimensions intertwine, weaving together the threads of our eternal connection. My energy will wait patiently, biding its time until we will be reunited once more.

Why are you afraid of it? In reality, we're not really dying; we're transforming our physical structure into another one, like photons, matter, energy, noise, frequency, sound into an unseen existence."

He answered simply: "You're insane…", as he turned his back and started reading a book.

I could not believe it as I stepped through the front door, and the sound of raised voices greeted me. My heart sank as Alex and Anna engaged in a heated argument. The tension in the air was palpable, and I felt my patience wearing thin. I rushed into the living room, my voice firm but filled with weariness. "That's enough! I've had a difficult day and can't handle any more conflicts right now."

The room grew thick with tension as my children's expressions morphed into masks of anger and exasperation. Alex's eyes bore into mine, resentment and rebellion swirling within them. Suddenly, in a fiery surge of emotion, he lunged at me, pushing me off-balance.

Time seemed to stand still, and the world tilted. I felt gravity pull me back, step by agonizing step until I hit the floor below with a jarring crash. That was the last thing I remembered from that moment onward.

A chilling silence was pierced by the realization of the terrible turn events had taken. The fury in Alex's eyes vanished, replaced by sheer horror and remorse. Anna looked as if the colour had drained from her, and Robert's hands quivered as he made an urgent call for help. Those next few minutes stretched on interminably.

Frozen in place, Alex was trapped in the aftermath of his heated moment, unable to comprehend the consequences of his impulsive action. The weight of his anger had turned into a heavy burden of guilt within seconds. Anna, overwhelmed with emotions, reached out to him, her voice breaking as she whispered, "Alex, what have we come to!?" Meanwhile, Robert, our pillar of strength, showed cracks in his composed facade, pacing anxiously and murmuring prayers.

Soon, the piercing wail of sirens echoed in the distance, drawing nearer. As the medical team burst into the scene, they worked with swift precision to stabilize me. Their gravely serious expressions said more than words ever could. Before they wheeled me away, Alex stepped forward, his voice quivering, a broken reflection of a single, impulsive act.

Stammering through his sobs, Alex managed to say, "It... It wasn't intentional. I never meant for any of this." His plea was desperate, "Please, save her."

The head paramedic paused, giving Alex a firm, yet compassionate look. "We'll do our utmost," he assured with professional calm. "Right now, we need space to operate. Please stand back!"

With a heavy heart, Alex stepped back, watching as they swiftly transported Victoria to the ambulance. The vehicle's blinding lights painted a surreal atmosphere on an already tense scene. Anna, trying to find solace, wrapped her arms around Alex, both seeking and offering solace.

After the ambulance roared away, Robert's emotions bubbled over as he confronted Alex, a blend of fury and fear evident in his voice. "What on earth were you thinking?" he exclaimed, trying to keep his composure. "Listen, don't discuss this with anyone until I return!"

Alex's eyes were filled with remorse. "Everything just spiralled so fast", he whispered, guilt evident in his tone. "I... I couldn't rein in my anger."

As Robert drove from the house to the hospital, his hands gripped the steering wheel tightly, his knuckles turning white. His mind raced with a whirlwind of emotions, struggling to understand what had happened.

Each passing second felt like an eternity as the hospital neared. The journey seemed interminable; the distance stretched indefinitely, amplifying Robert's anxiety.

Finally, the hospital loomed into view, its imposing structure a stark reminder of the battles fought within its walls. Robert manoeuvred the car into a parking spot, his hands trembling as he turned off the engine. He took a deep breath, attempting to steady his nerves, but the chaos within his mind persisted. He hurriedly descended the sliding doors, stepping into a whirlwind of fluorescent lights and bustling medical personnel. The urgency in the air was palpable, setting Robert's heart pounding faster.

He approached the reception desk, where a nurse greeted him professionally. Her eyes held a trace of sympathy as he shared Victoria's name and explained the circumstances. Robert's voice wavered slightly as he conveyed the urgency of the situation.

The nurse nodded, her expression understanding. "Please have a seat in the waiting area," she said softly. "The doctors are attending to her, and they'll update you as soon as they can."

The weight of the silence hung heavy.

Minutes turned into hours, and the weight of the guilt grew heavier with each passing second.

Finally, a weary-looking doctor approached Robert, his eyes filled with exhaustion and sympathy. He held his breath.

"I won't sugarcoat it", the doctor began, his voice gentle yet grave. "Your wife has suffered significant injuries, but she's stable for now. We'll do everything we can to help her recover, but it's going to be a long and challenging road."

Relief mingled with the lingering guilt as he listened to the doctor's words. He thanked him and settled into an uncomfortable waiting period, their minds consumed by the weight of their actions and the uncertainty of Victoria's future.

As Robert sat in the waiting room, grappling with a mix of relief and guilt, he suddenly noticed two uniformed police officers making their way towards him. His heart sank as a wave of apprehension washed over him. He stood up, his legs feeling unsteady beneath him, and braced himself for the impending conversation.

While waiting, he heard a voice: "Excuse me, sir!" It was a police officer. "Are you Mr. Robert, Mrs. Victoria's husband?"

Robert nodded, his throat dry as he managed to utter a hoarse, "Yes, that's me."

The officer extended a hand in introduction. "I'm Officer Stevens, and this is Officer Thompson. We're here to gather information regarding the incident involving Victoria's fall."

Understanding the importance of cooperating with the authorities, Robert smiled weakly and shook their hands. "Of course," he replied, his voice laced with regret and determination.

The officers led Robert to a quieter area of the hospital, away from the bustling activity. They found a secluded corner, and Robert sat, his hands clasped together in his lap, his gaze fixed on the floor.

Officer Stevens began the interview, his tone gentle as he navigated the delicate nature of the situation. "Can you walk us through what happened leading up to Victoria's fall?"

Robert took a deep breath, his voice trembling slightly as he recounted the events, sparing no detail. He described the heated argument that had escalated into a moment of unchecked anger, his voice heavy with remorse.

Officer Thompson listened attentively, occasionally jotting down notes on a notepad. Sensing the guilt and remorse in Robert's voice, he offered a compassionate nod of understanding.

"I understand that this was an unfortunate accident", Officer Thompson interjected, his voice reassuring. "But we still need to conduct a thorough investigation. Do you have any history of violence or prior altercations?"

Robert shook his head emphatically. "No, never", he replied, his voice tinged with sincerity. "I understand the seriousness of the situation."

Officer Stevens leaned forward slightly; his gaze focused on Robert. "We will need to gather statements from other witnesses and examine any evidence", he explained. "This is standard procedure to ensure a comprehensive understanding of the incident."

Robert nodded, his eyes welling up with tears. "I completely understand", he replied, his voice barely above a whisper. "I just want my wife to recover, and I'll cooperate fully with the investigation."

The officers nodded in acknowledgement, their demeanour remaining professional yet compassionate. They assured Robert that they would handle the investigation diligently and expressed their hopes for Victoria's recovery.

The police conducted interviews, examined the scene, and consulted medical professionals to gather a comprehensive understanding of the incident.

"She had a terrible fall, the process for her recovery would take long, but we hope for the best." The Doctor said in a calm voice.

"Thanks so much, Dr., we will still come back to gather information from the victim of the domestic accident when she's fully stable."

"No problem, you can always come over to know how she's fairing."

Exiting the doctor's office, the police officers encountered a visibly distraught Robert, pacing restlessly in the hospital's reception.

Beads of sweat formed a sheen on his forehead, some trickling down the back of his neck. "How can I protect Alex from the fallout?" he agonized internally. "If he's taken in, they might charge him with attempted murder. It was a terrible mistake, a burst of uncontrolled anger, something that could befall anyone. I can't let this compound the disaster Victoria's incident has already brought!"

As Robert ruminated, lost in his tumultuous thoughts, trying to figure out how best to approach the matter, the officers approached him. "Mr. Robert", one began, "we'll need to accompany you home to interview any witnesses present during the incident. Are you ready to proceed?"

Caught off guard, Robert stuttered, "Y-e-s…" He managed to hold himself together, despite feeling as though he was on the brink of a breakdown. The journey home felt surreal, his mind a whirlwind of dread and anticipation. When they arrived near his residence, he was jolted back to reality.

Upon entering the house, the first face he saw was that of his mother-in-law. Etched with concern, she held the younger children close, their tearful eyes wide with fear. Taking a step into the room, Robert's weary gaze met hers.

"What happened? How's Vicky?" she implored; her voice filled with anxiety. Before Robert could muster a reply, the officers made their entrance.

"Good evening, madam", Officer Stevens began, his tone formal yet empathetic. "We're here to investigate Mrs. Victoria's accident. Can you point us to the eyewitnesses?"

Both children hesitantly moved forward. The tension was high, and Diana's anxiety grew. She feared the children might inadvertently say something that could land their family in deeper trouble.

Officer Thompson knelt to the children's level. "What are your names?" he asked kindly.

Each child responded in turn.

"Now, can you tell us what happened?" he continued gently.

Robert's heart raced; he felt a sick sensation in his stomach, dreading what might be revealed next.

Alex took a deep breath before explaining, "Anna and I were arguing. It was getting loud, and Mom came in to see what the fuss was about. In my haste to get away from the heated argument, I didn't realize Mom was right behind me by the stairs. I accidentally bumped into her, and... she fell."

"Oh...that was serious but did you have any altercation with your mother before that incident happened and you felt that might have triggered your reaction to what happened?"

At that point, Robert's heart was pounding hard, 'bum bum bum', its frantic beats echoing loudly in his ears, like the relentless pounding of a heavy hammer against metal. Even in the room's cool ambience, beads of sweat formed on his brow. He desperately tried to catch his son's eye, seeking a silent plea of reassurance, but Alex was not looking towards his side.

"No", Alex responded firmly, "The only issue we had was the disagreements about her euthanasia choice, but that was settled long ago. We haven't broached the topic since she was moved to the psychiatric ward, and even when she was released, it remained a closed chapter. The accident was an unfortunate coincidence, not driven by any prior dispute."

As the officers continued their questioning, Robert felt a growing relief with each word Alex spoke. When it was all said and done, his rapid heartbeat had settled, replaced with a quiet hope. The case was brought before the court, and it became evident that the incident was a tragic accident, rather than a malicious act.

Thankfully, the judge was discerning and compassionate, seeing the situation for what it truly was. Instead of punitive action, Alex was directed towards therapy, a move to help him manage his emotions. Robert couldn't have been more grateful, as a harsher verdict could have derailed Alex's education and future, tarnishing his reputation.

During the court proceedings, Victoria's well-being was never far from the family's thoughts. They visited her frequently, providing the comfort of familiar faces. Adam, too, extended his support, praising Robert for standing steadfast despite the tumultuous events. He lauded him for his unwavering dedication, even when faced with Victoria's sometimes obstinate decisions.

With the ordeal nearing its end, the family was quick to arrange for Alex's therapy sessions. Thanks to their lawyer's assistance, he was soon enrolled in a nearby program, marking the first step in their collective healing journey.

Chapter 16

It All Went Blank

Anna's eyes welled with tears as she spoke, "Dad, seeing Mom like this terrifies me! It feels like she's not really responding to the treatments. She didn't even open her eyes!"

Alex's voice trembled, "I share your fears, Anna. Every time I close my eyes, I see that moment replaying. I wish I could turn back time!" Alex said, hanging his head thoughtfully.

"Dad, I am scared of the condition of Mum. The way things are going, I hope she survives it. She's not responding to treatment!" Anna said tearfully.

Robert sighed, pulling his children into a gentle embrace. "It wasn't your fault, Alex. Ever since your mother mentioned euthanasia, it's been a weight on my mind too. But both of you have been my rock through this. We'll face this together."

Anna responded, "She just wanted to exercise her freedom of choice, Dad."

"I know, sweetheart", Robert said, looking sombre. "I need to head to the hospital now. The last time I saw her, she seemed so... distant, almost like she was unresponsive to treatment. Just taking shallow breaths at intervals..."

Before leaving for the hospital, Robert turned to Anna and Alex with an urgent plea, "Listen, both of you! It's vital that you don't discuss what happened with anyone, understood? For your own sake, I want to keep you away from any further complications!"

He quickly dialled Victoria's mother. "Diana, please come over to stay with the kids. I'm headed to the hospital and they shouldn't be alone right now."

Afterwards, he hurried out to where he parked his car, whistling as he tried to open the door. But midway to his car, he realized he'd forgotten something. Doubling back, he pushed the door open and called out, "Anna, Alex! Remember, speak only with your grandma when she arrives. No one else. Am I clear?"

Together, they responded, "Yes, Dad!"

He hurried towards his car and drove off. While driving, many thoughts flooded his mind, and soon, it was obvious that he was unhappy. "Victoria, how did you get here? I did not know at the very point that you started making such a grave mistake. Was it something you read or some external influence?" He struggled with the memories of their recent past. "I thought her time in the psychiatric ward might have changed her mind, but she stood firm even in court. I could not believe it was my wife who was arguing over the impossible in the court of law. We even tried to distance ourselves, hoping she'd see the consequences of her choices, but nothing swayed her." The weight of his thoughts pressed down as he continued his drive.

Upon Robert's arrival at the hospital, he hurried to the ward where his wife was, but he was requested to wait outside as medical professionals were still administering treatments to improve her health. Robert was disturbed as he paced up and down the corridor. He saw some people sitting on the long metal chair, many of them wearing grave looks while some looked calm, based on the medical conditions of the people they had brought for treatment.

He seemed not to care about the people who sat nearby watching him. He stood there with his arms folded and his lip ground at intervals, wanting to know his wife's condition. At last, he became calm and sat down with a middle-aged woman who just walked into the ward a few minutes ago. "Is everything fine, sir?" She asked Robert because she saw some of his anxiety display a few minutes after sitting down. "I am fine, ma'am." Robert replied without looking at the woman's face. He was not ready for any conversation; he only cared about his wife's health.

After sitting for a few minutes, a ring interrupted his thoughts. Robert pulled out his phone, recognizing the caller ID as his mother-in-law's, he walked down the corridor seeking a quieter place. "Hello, Diana", his voice tinged with worry. He filled her in, "Doctors are still with her. I haven't been able to see her yet... No, you don't need to come over, I'll stay with the kids and take care of necessary things. We'll come together tomorrow." After a few more reassurances, he hung up. As he pocketed his phone, he spotted a doctor emerging from Victoria's room. Heart pounding, he dashed over. "How is she?", he asked.

The doctor, with a deep sigh, motioned for Robert to follow. Robert's concern deepened as he trailed behind, observing the solemn expressions of the medical team leaving Victoria's room. "Doctors always maintain a professional mannerism. Maybe it's just routine", he tried to reassure himself.

Realizing he had fallen behind, Robert hastened to catch up. Upon reaching the doctor's office, he was motioned to take a seat. The doctor, after a brief wash, began drying his hands. The heavy silence was disturbing. Unable to contain his anxiety, Robert finally blurted, "Please, tell me, how is she? What exactly is happening?"

"Mr. Robert," the doctor began, "Victoria hasn't responded to our treatments as we'd hoped. We're doing everything in our power, but her journey to recovery may be long. While her present condition is worrying, with her immobility and closed eyes, she still breathes, offering a glimmer of hope. It's not uncommon for patients to awaken after extended periods of unconsciousness. Patience is paramount." He gently placed a reassuring hand on Robert's shoulder.

Swallowing hard, Robert asked, "Can I see her now?"

"Of course", the doctor replied softly. "I'll arrange for a nurse to accompany you."

The sight of Victoria, fragile and unresponsive, weighed heavily on Robert. He stood beside her, struggling to contain his emotions, before quietly leaving the room. The attending nurse gave a sympathetic nod, sensing his deep anguish.

Driving home, a whirlwind of thoughts consumed Robert. Upon arriving, he was surprised to find Adam, his brother-in-law, waiting. "Adam! I wasn't expecting you. When did you arrive?"

"I've been meaning to come, but work has been relentless. Now that I have a break, I came straight here. You've been incredibly strong for Victoria."

Robert sighed, "I just got back from the hospital, and, to be honest, she's not doing well. Let's head inside so I can fill Diana in."

Inside, Diana looked up, "How's everything?"

Robert hesitated, then said, "It's challenging. She's not showing signs of improvement. I wish I had better news, but I need to be upfront about where things stand."

As Diana's tears flowed freely, both Adam and Robert instinctively drew closer to offer comfort. Collecting herself after a moment, she asked, "What's our next step?"

"Honestly, I don't know," Robert replied, a hint of helplessness in his voice. "I'm relying on the doctors, and they seem to be giving their best."

As the adults discussed Victoria's situation, the children approached, eager to learn the latest and their eyes searching for reassurance.

Recognizing their need for hope, Robert gently said, "We're waiting and hoping for the best."

"But is mom improving?", Alex's voice wavered.

"We're hopeful she will", Adam answered swiftly, aiming to protect the young minds from undue stress. "Tomorrow, your dad and I will visit her, and hopefully, we'll see positive changes."

That night, sleep eluded Robert. He roamed the living room, consumed by worry and what-ifs. The haunting thought of potentially raising the children without Victoria tormented him. "We were meant to grow old together", he mused bitterly. "Now, because of her choices, our family faces this unimaginable trial. I truly wished this never happened. I had thought that we would both grow old together but now, her stubbornness had cost us a huge price and at this point, it seems that nothing is redeemable unless..."

As he was in deep thought, Adam walked up to him because he had been unable to sleep too. He was first afraid because he never thought that anyone would come to interrupt him at that moment. He had been engulfed in his thoughts and did not know until Adam touched him. He jumped back into reality! "Oh...Adam, why aren't you sleeping?". He tried to smile and act calm so that Adam would not suspect that he had been in deep thought.

Adam sighed, "I have tried sleeping, but it's quite impossible with all these thoughts about Vic. Based on what you shared, her recovery seems slim. What if she remains like this for months? It's terrifying."

"Adam..." Robert continues while putting his hands on his shoulders. "I understand your fears. The harsh reality of it all saddens me deeply. Let's hold on to hope that things will improve because the harder I try to evade my fears, the more I feel them encroaching upon me."

Adam nodded, "Stay strong. We must endure this situation together. I'll be by your side for an extended period, so you won't have to confront this on your own. It's crucial that we offer each other support, particularly given how much this is affecting Mom."

Drawing strength from each other's presence, they shared a glass of wine, discussing potential steps to support Victoria's recovery. The following morning, united in purpose and hope, Robert, Adam, and Diana left early to be by Victoria's side.

At the hospital, Victoria's condition remained critical. The doctors worked tirelessly to stabilize her; their expressions were grave with concern. News spread quickly among family and friends, and they gathered at the hospital, united in their shared anguish. Victoria remained in a deep coma. Her loved ones stood vigil by her side, praying for her recovery. The guilt weighed heavily on Robert because he didn't prevent the argument and did not foresee what might happen if he didn't interfere. Because of his negligence, Alex had his heart burdened by the consequences of their argument.

Some colleagues from her company had visited to check up on her, praising what a wonderful and brilliant woman she is. "It's truly heartbreaking that she had to go through this. We were all hoping for her to recover strongly after the hospital experience, only to be faced with another difficult situation", Yasin expressed.

As days turned into weeks and weeks turned into months, her condition showed no signs of improvement. It became clear that the hope of her recovery was slipping away, and her family faced an agonizing decision.

The weight of sorrow and despair settled heavily upon them as they gathered in a solemn meeting with the doctors. The room was filled with tears and broken hearts as they listened to the medical professionals explain the gravity of Victoria's condition.

The lead physician, Dr. Johnson, asked Robert to follow him into a private consultation room, the weight of the news heavy in the air. They both took a seat; the room permeated with tension and anxiety.

Dr. Johnson's voice was filled with compassion as he began, "Robert, I want to be completely transparent with you. Victoria's condition has shown no improvement despite our best efforts. She remains in a deep coma, and her chances of waking up are exceedingly slim."

Robert's heart sank as he absorbed the gravity of the situation. His eyes welled up with tears, his heart pounding like the military boot while they march to war, his ribs clenched together as his blood seemed to rush up, and his hands were already shaking on the table on which he placed them as he waited for the doctor's response. Still, he maintained his composure, ready to face whatever lay ahead for the sake of his beloved wife.

The doctor continued; his voice gentle, yet firm. "Given the severity of Victoria's condition and the prolonged duration of her coma, we need to discuss the next steps. Continuing life support and medical intervention may only prolong her suffering without a reasonable chance of recovery or any meaningful quality of life."

Robert's hands trembled as he tried to grasp the enormity of the decision that now rested in his hands. He took a deep breath, his voice quivering as he asked, "What are our options, Doctor?"

Dr. Johnson's gaze was one of genuine understanding. "There comes a time when we need to consider withdrawing life support. It's an intensely personal choice, and we'll stand by whatever decision you make. Choosing this path would mean allowing Victoria to depart peacefully, without further medical interventions. However, it's important to consider all possible options. We're discussing the possibility of organ donation."

A mix of anguish and determination washed over Robert's face as he struggled with the weight of this life-altering decision. He was torn between the agonizing reality of the present and the knowledge of what Victoria had wanted. She had always been an advocate for choice, battling societal norms and expectations. She hadn't envisioned her departure like this, but she'd hoped for understanding and a loving farewell. She had pictured a graceful farewell, encircled by those who cherished her.

Tears streamed down his face as he mustered the strength to speak. "Doctor, if her chances of meaningful recovery are slim and if she's destined to endure endless pain... I can't stand by and watch. She deserves peace. I believe we should respect and honour her wishes. Given everything she's endured - from her time at the psychiatric facility to the devastating fall - I think it's time we consider sparing her further suffering. My wife has always been so kind and giving. If donating her organs is something she would have wanted, I... I have to consider it."

Dr. Johnson nodded understandingly, placing a supportive hand on Robert's shoulder. "By donating her organs, she can leave a legacy of kindness and hope. Her choice to help others can make a significant difference in their lives. I know it's a heartbreaking choice. We will ensure that her passing is as peaceful and dignified as possible. Take all the time you need to discuss this with your family and loved ones. We are here to support you every step of the way. I hope that you and your family can find the strength to surpass this pain and reach a place of acceptance."

Emotion overwhelmed Robert as he contemplated the immense responsibility resting on his shoulders. He knew he had to consult with their children and Diana and seek their input, but deep down, he understood that this decision ultimately lay with him.

He thanked the doctor for his care and guidance with a heavy heart, knowing that the road ahead would be filled with heartache and grief. But he also held onto the belief that by releasing Victoria, he would be granting her the greatest act of love and compassion he could offer.

As Robert left the room, he carried with him the weight of the world, knowing that his decision would forever shape their lives.

Swirling thoughts consumed him. "She faced an untimely demise in that accident. But do any of us genuinely understand our last moments? If life is snuffed out suddenly, or if we drift into an eternal sleep, there's no sensation of pain, no fear... Perhaps she was onto something, suggesting that we should accept death rather than dread it."

On that particular day, he felt deeply troubled as he pondered how to approach the matter with her family members, especially her broken mother. Initially, he opted to call Adam, requesting him to come over so they could discuss the crucial matters at hand. Robert began by discussing the issues with him, and together, they wholeheartedly agreed to follow the doctor's recommendations.

"Robert", Adam began, his voice choked with emotion, "we're at a pivotal juncture regarding my sister's fate. Isn't it more merciful to let her find peace rather than languishing in this limbo? But now, feeling the weight of her pain, I believe we shouldn't prolong her agony. She's endured enough. She could bring hope and life to others who are in desperate need. It's a way to honour her values and the love you both shared. It's time we grant her the peace she deserves."

"Hmmm...", Robert sighed deeply. "Thank you, Adam, but I'm really anxious and scared. If she's allowed to rest, there are still so many challenges left for me to handle—the children, your mother, and even myself. I'm not sure how I'll manage all these emotional demands."

Adam continues, "I completely understand your concerns, but have you considered that her current state of lying there is also causing emotional trauma? How much longer can she endure this without a solution?..." He paused and walked over to stand by the window. "You know that the doctors must have exhausted all options, and unfortunately, what they've presented is the only choice we have left. The legacy of kindness from both you and her would keep inspiring goodness in the world."

Eventually, a meeting was convened, and all the family members gathered together. At first, Robert was too overwhelmed with sorrow to find his voice. As he carefully conveyed what the doctor had told him, a heavy atmosphere settled over the room, and for a few moments, a profound silence hung in the air.

"We are all in agreement with the doctor's decision. They have exhausted all options, and it appears that they have reached the end of the road. Though she might be unconscious of the situation, I believe it would bring her peace, and her spirit would find solace in the afterlife", aunt Kathy shared.

With a heavy heart, Robert signed the necessary forms, giving his consent for Victoria's organs to be donated. It was an agonizing decision, but he knew it was the right one. Victoria, even in her absence, would continue to bring hope and life to others.

At that point, Anna started crying as she rested her head on her father, who was seriously disturbed. He did not utter a statement as everyone was bringing different suggestions. Alex did not cry; he only went limp and stirred into the space like someone still trying to figure out what was happening. Diana was also crying as Adam's wife kept consoling her.

It was a choice no family should ever have to make, but they believed it was the most compassionate course of action for

Victoria. A sombre silence filled the hospital room as they gathered around Victoria's bedside for one last time. Their hands knotted, a symbol of the unbreakable bond they shared, and their tear-streaked faces revealed a mixture of anguish, love, and acceptance. While standing, they sang a heartfelt song.

"God be with you till we meet again; By His counsel's guide, uphold you; With His sheep securely fold you.

God be with you till we meet again."

The rest responded with the chorus, "Till we meet, till we meet; God be with you till we meet again."

After singing it, the doctors finally emerged. It was the most agonizing moment for everyone present, a dark and dreaded moment they all wished to overcome. Anna's heart pounded in her chest, and she struggled to suppress a scream. Aunt Kathy and another distant cousin, whom she had never met, held her tightly. Alex clutched his father's hand, seeking comfort. Diana remained surprisingly calm, though tears streamed down her cheeks. Robert remained silent after the song ended. The beeping of machines ceased. A profound sense of loss enveloped the room, and grief washed over them like a tidal wave. The pain they felt was immeasurable.

Victoria was now at peace, free from the pain and struggle that had consumed her. Most of those around her blamed her for not dealing with her mental confusion, a problem that modern society often confronts, but it's not taken very seriously. At the same time, she requested her death in a decent way, but not accepted. I wonder why soldiers are sent to certain deaths in wars that are not necessary.

Nobody forbids wars! Those who resent war are judged and accused of not being patriots. They don't wish to die. They don't want to kill people that never harmed them. When strangers send troops to certain deaths is legal, accepted and moral, but choosing your death upon wish is illegal, unacceptable and immoral. That hilarious. This world is crazy, and I had the misfortune of living at the wrong time.

"Ultimately, she has won her battles", uncle Tom said, lowering his head. Tears trickled down his cheeks, but he quickly wiped them away, attempting to hold back his emotions. He didn't want to break down, especially knowing that Robert was entering another mourning phase. Uncle Tom approached Robert offering support. "Be strong...I know how deeply pained you are, but we must accept the will of God over human life, and in this case, death has prevailed."

"On behalf of the medical team and the individuals whose lives will be profoundly impacted by your generosity, I want to extend our heartfelt gratitude for your decision to donate Victoria's organs.

While this is an incredibly difficult time for your family, your choice to give the gift of life in the face of loss is a testament to your love, kindness, and the legacy of Victoria's compassion. Your decision will have a lasting, positive impact, and we are deeply thankful for your remarkable act of generosity. I want you to know that she did not lose the battle, even though her beliefs contrasted ours but I think she fought for what she understood to be the best for her. God rest her soul". Dr. Johnson told them as he stepped out.

Following that, one by one, they all left the room with tears in their eyes. Passersby, who had patients in the hospital, unaware of the incident, glanced at them with pity, sensing that they had experienced a significant loss. This sight instilled fear in those whose loved ones were in critical condition, and they could only hope for their swift recovery. In the weeks that followed, Victoria's organs were transplanted into individuals who desperately needed them.

The solemn atmosphere was unmistakable to all they crossed paths with. They talk about how Victoria was an exceptional woman with top-notch brilliance that radiated even in darkness. While they were talking, Alex left them and went to sit in the car, his heart still pricking him about the death of his mother. Even though he had sought therapy, the passing of his mother appeared to initiate a new stage of mourning. Immediately his father noticed that he had disappeared from the scene; he went to the car and found him crying.

"Alex, I've already explained that we made every effort to try and save your mother. Your focus now should be on moving forward with life and supporting your younger sister. I know it's not easy, and I'm facing the same uncertainty about the future. But I believe that whatever lies ahead cannot be worse than what has already happened. Please, stop blaming yourself for everything. After the burial, I suggest that you consider counselling as a way to work towards emotional stability." With these words, he rose from his squatting position and embraced his son.

Ultimately, Victoria's lifeless body was transferred to the morgue while the family left the hospital to initiate the preparations for her interment.

Chapter 17

Black Memories

The world seemed to dim in the days after Victoria's passing. The sun lost its usual brilliance, and the nights were devoid of the moon and stars' usual glow. Rain poured, as if the heavens were mourning too, and the Rock family prayed its cascades might cleanse their anguish. Each day felt like a weary drag, and Robert found himself caught in the grasp of his relentless sorrow. Sleep evaded him, and the more he tried to fend off his tormenting thoughts, the heavier they weighed on his spirit.

His house had grown as silent as a cemetery, with the children responding to the grief even more profoundly than he had anticipated. Anna had withdrawn to herself completely. No more the laughter that filled the atmosphere, no more those running around the house whenever she played with Alex, no more watching her favourite TV shows and documentaries. She no longer found interest in her novels; the preferred dishes that salivated her became like gall to her memory.

Alex remained rather silent, spending each day in the little garden his father had lovingly created in memory of his mom. As he walked checking some of the flowers, he often said, "I remember how Mom cherished these flowers while she was with us… I recall the shoes and clothes Mom brought on many occasions while she was on a trip for her company. I wish she was here!"

After his melancholic monologue, he would only sigh and would go inside the house whenever anyone called his name. Robert was deep in thought, too; he had lost himself completely. His sleep was scanty, and he ate sparingly while grandma Diana was mostly with her Bible, reciting many comforting verses. Adam was often calling to check on Robert and the kids. Family members would return in a few weeks to prepare for Victoria's burial.

"We aren't ready for another funeral right now. If grandma is not well taken care of, then...". Adam sternly mentioned not neglecting his mom.

In the immediate aftermath of the family's departure, the emptiness of the house felt more pronounced. The once lively atmosphere grew stiflingly silent, amplifying the family's pain. Alex's cherished basketball seemed to mock him, and Anna found no solace in her beloved books or her usual online research.

Robert's gaze drifted aimlessly as he pondered, engrossed in his thoughts while tending to his household chores. Throughout the week, memories of his time with Victoria continually flooded back.

Lying in bed one evening, staring at the ceiling, he remembered the passion and excitement they shared while designing their home. Victoria might be gone, but her spirit lingered in every nook and corner. Their dream home, with its exterior marked by crisp lines, expansive windows, and a minimalist colour palette, was an embodiment of their shared vision.

They had chosen natural elements like wood and stone to harmonize with nature, grounding the house in its surroundings. Inside, they opted for an open floor layout, flooded with natural light, and decorated with a blend of contemporary and rustic design elements. Sleek furniture met rustic wooden beams, merging their individual tastes perfectly. Even in her absence, the home stood as a testament to their shared dreams and love.

I, on the other hand, paid attention to sustainable practices. The house needed to incorporate energy-efficient features, such as solar panels, smart thermostats, and insulation techniques, reducing its environmental impact while providing comfort and cost savings. We were such a good team in building our forever home.

Outdoor living spaces were an essential part of the design. We wanted a safe space for our children, so we chose expansive decks or patios that seamlessly connect the interior with nature. These areas feature natural stone fireplaces, cosy seating arrangements, and landscaping that blends modern and rustic elements. I loved the architecture of our unique home: a balance between modern sophistication and rustic charm. It offers a timeless appeal and a welcoming atmosphere, showcasing the best of both worlds and providing a distinctive living experience.

Everyone who visited us felt welcomed and at home. "I used to feel comfortable here, but without her, it now seems like just an elegant but ordinary house. Ahhh!!! Stop running your thoughts around- you need to focus"- Robert told himself.

As Robert paced back and forth, preparing for the speech, he whispered to himself, "I want to honour her the way Demosthenes did with his orations... She deserves a tribute that echoes her essence."

"How do I approach her beliefs? Should I touch on them? Or do I address the broader idea of personal freedom versus societal order?" He pondered aloud. "The judge had made a compelling point. He said that while personal freedom is an intrinsic human right, allowing us to make choices and express ourselves, it's not without its boundaries. Such freedom shouldn't come at the cost of others. For even in nature, boundaries exist. Consider the seas, they don't flood the earth, nor the sun which doesn't shine relentlessly. Similarly, there are natural rhythms to how we live, eat, and sleep. If even nature, observes limitations, shouldn't we as humans too?"

Robert inhaled deeply, collecting his thoughts. "Victoria was undeniably intelligent and passionate about her beliefs. Yet, was she entirely right when judged against the societal framework? After all, the law exists to instill order, ensuring a balanced society."

He continued, "While cherishing our freedoms, we must also recognize the need for responsible actions and reasonable constraints. The consequences of overlooking these can be vast - from strained relationships to mental distress. Drawing boundaries, even in freedom, is crucial for the well-being of both individuals and society."

Satisfied, Robert nodded to himself, feeling more prepared and grounded in his message for the gathering.

"While we all cherish personal freedom, it's imperative to pair such liberty with accountability and respect for societal norms.

Overlooking the delicate balance between individual autonomy and communal responsibility can lead to a spectrum of repercussions, from fractured relationships and tarnished reputations to emotional distress for those involved.

Finding the right balance between individual autonomy and societal needs is far from easy. It's like walking a tightrope, balancing our desires on one side and the greater good on the other. True freedom doesn't mean living without rules but living responsibly within them. This ensures that while we enjoy our individual rights, we also preserve the harmony and well-being of the community.

Every individual plays a part in this intricate dance. Our duty to society is to be mindful of our actions, ensuring they don't disrupt the delicate equilibrium. While laws and regulations might seem constraining at times, they're designed to ensure that our freedoms don't impinge on others. Even as these rules evolve to reflect the changing needs of society, their core purpose remains unchanged: to foster a community where personal freedom and collective welfare thrive side by side.

Personal freedom holds immense value, as it allows individuals to exercise their autonomy and freely express themselves. However, it's imperative to recognize that personal freedom cannot be absolute, as unrestricted behaviour can lead to severe consequences. By embracing responsible conduct and setting reasonable limits, we can protect individual rights, maintain privacy, preserve trust, and promote society's overall well-being. Balancing personal freedom with societal responsibilities is essential for creating a harmonious and functioning community where individuals can thrive without causing harm to others. If everyone is to exercise what they feel their rights are, then we are heading for a chaotic environment. Thieves would boldly tell you that they have the right to steal, and gangsters would say to you without feeling any guilt that they can misbehave since it is their right or freedom. That is why the law sometimes sanitizes and tries to force itself on people. If there were no enforcement of the law, the world would be in a state worse than a jungle, where animals can prey on each other or act in any way they please without any oversight.

What makes the law inherently significant is its persistence, even in times of war when there is a complete breakdown of order. There are situations where the law expressly forbids harm to women and children, demonstrating its adaptability while maintaining a resolute stance. This underscores its supremacy over all individuals. In instances where one seeks to be resolute, the law will either compel conformity through coercion or gently guide individuals into compliance with its dictates. In the end, the law possesses more power than any individual, and this is what fosters a rational society.

I agreed with it—nothing to argue about. We cannot choose what reality is. The day is the day; the night is the night. The sun is warm; the moon is shady. Winter is cold; summer is hot. Depression is what it is, and these people need help, but we cannot do anything without their screams for support. I don't know Vic… were you sick? Were you depressed, or did you feel that life was irrelevant? So many thoughts that make me feel overwhelmed. Was there any difference between you and those who showed their mental disorder? Maybe, it doesn't matter when exploring the connection between quantum physics and life after death like David Bohm did. Perhaps his speculations about linking quantum physics and metaphysical concepts are something to explore more deeply. His ideas were not popular within the scientific community when he proposed that consciousness and matter are deeply linked, suggesting that thoughts and consciousness are integral components of a fundamental cosmic intelligence. Maybe you were a Chubbuck, but it didn't manifest yet. Who knows? If Vic was distorted, she should have asked for help, but to choose so easily to perish away, I'll never understand. My uncle said that her illusion might have stemmed from the numerous books she had read, but could that be true? We have many more knowledgeable people who have done much research on tough topics, even on death.

Checking about the history and ethics of euthanasia, one would know that it was originally from Greece and Rome, and it started gaining ground. Physicians started advocating for the use of aesthetics and morphine to deliberately end a patient's life to relieve the pain of death. It was Samuel Williams who first proposed the act in 1870. After that, there were debates about it in the United States and Britain, and this birthed the 1906 Ohio bill to legalize it. However, it was ultimately defeated for many reasons. Could it be that the people who made a strong argument against it knew initially were afraid of something? In any case, that's a minor point, and I believe I might be overanalyzing this. For the sake of Alex, Anna, and Grandma, I must find inner strength. Ever since Vicky's passing, their moods have been unpredictable. I empathize with their pain and recognize the need to keep my emotions in check, especially when they're with me, as breaking down would only intensify their distress. I'm grateful that Adam has taken Grandma under his wing, as coping with the emotional burden of all three would be exceptionally challenging, especially when I'm grappling with my own psychological upheaval."

Robert stood up and walked down to the big mirror by the side of the big bed frame; he assessed himself and sighed deeply. "You have lost so much weight within a few days!" I have never felt this hollow and emptiness in this heart. Victoria's passing has undeniably taken a piece of me, and I'm certain she carried those pieces with her to her resting place. Victoria, my Victoria, heaven knows how much I love you even in death!"

He moved abruptly from the mirror as if someone had caught him in an unlawful thing. He checked the time on the golden wall clock and exclaimed, "Ohhh! So, I have been awake for that long! My God! I need to start rushing things in preparation for Vicky's funeral."

He grabbed his phone and left his uncle some messages regarding certain aspects of the funeral preparations. Shortly thereafter, he received a phone call and promptly offered some suggestions to his uncle. The conversation extended for nearly an hour before he hung up. Afterwards, he retreated to the living room, taking a seat as he attempted to jot down notes about the entombment.

Adam later called to know about how far Robert had gone with his part of the arrangements. "I am fixing things. Don't worry…", Robert tried to console his brother-in-law.

"Yeah… I never thought though that I would be the one attending my sister's funeral." Adam attempted to steer the conversation in a lighthearted direction to alleviate his overwhelming sorrow.

"How is grandma coping?", Robert asked.

"Hmmm... we are having a distressed experience trying to calm her… Uncle Ned was here and he also took some time to talk to her. My wife is making an effort to support her by keeping her company whenever she returns from work. I consistently avoid her when I'm experiencing grief because I know that if she witnesses me in that condition, she would become emotionally distraught."

After they spoke for a few minutes, they ended the call.

"Have you not been sleeping, Robert?" He looked back as Aunt Kathy emerged from the room. "Aunt, I am trying to put some things together. I just finished speaking with Uncle Tom and Adam, and we have some mapped-out plans for the burial..." He tried racking his head to think of other ideas to add. "Aunt Kathy, I don't even know what next to think about; I am serious. It is like I never saw her death coming, but I now know that no one is fully prepared for the grief, emptiness, and shocks that come with the death of a loved one. With each day that goes by, it feels as if I lost her only moments ago. I had never thought that I would be so deeply shaken!"

Gazing at the horizon, Aunt Kathy began, "Death, Robert, holds its enigmatic reverence. Words often falter in expressing the profound pain of losing a loved one, be it a newborn or an adult. Everyone recognized the deep bond you shared with Victoria."

She glanced at the clock, adding, "But look at the time, Robert. Dawn has broken, and I can't recall the last time you had a peaceful night's sleep. Grieving is natural, but you must pace yourself. I recall the despair that gripped me when I lost my son, merely three years after my husband passed. I doubted if I'd ever find solace. Yet, here I am, drawing strength from those trials. We can't question fate. Grieve, yes, but also remember the strength within you. You've barely been eating, and neither have the kids. I had to coax Anna to eat a sandwich yesterday. Of the two, Alex seems to be slowly finding his footing. I've been talking to them, trying to provide solace. Remember when you were my pillar of support during my time of loss? Your kind words and genuine care still resonate with me."

Robert nodded appreciatively. "Thank you. They say time heals, and I'll cling to that hope, especially for my children." They embraced, their shared grief strengthening their bond.

The scene then shifted to 9 a.m. on that sombre Friday morning. A procession of vehicles moved solemnly, the hearse carrying Victoria's remains leading the way. Dressed in an elegant dark rose gown with pristine white gloves and socks, Victoria looked serene. As a tribute, Alex had placed one of her favourite books beside her in the coffin. Robert and the children, all clad in black, followed closely. Anna held a wreath close to her heart, preparing to lay it at her mother's final resting place.

Amidst the procession, cars filled with family and close friends followed closely behind. A separate bus carried some of Victoria's colleagues who had come to pay their last respects. For health considerations, Grandma had been allowed to be present, her attendance sanctioned by her doctor's recommendation.

As they arrived at the cemetery, a solemn silence enveloped the area. One by one, they disembarked and formed a quiet line, moving in unity towards Victoria's final resting place. The headstone was already in place, engraved with the words: "In Loving Memory Of Victoria Rock, a Cherished Wife, Mother, and Daughter. Rest in Eternal Peace."

Standing patiently by the grave, the priest awaited in his black cassock, his white collar distinct against the backdrop. The ceremony began without delay. Robert stepped forward, taking a deep breath, and began his tribute.

"Today, as we gather to bid farewell to Victoria, my heart is heavy with grief. I stand before you to share a belief that transcends the boundaries of this earthly existence and embraces the profound nature of our universe. In the depths of my sorrow, I find solace in the notion that parallel dimensions may hold the key to our eternal connection. Quantum physics, with its enigmatic principles and exploration of the fabric of reality, hints at the existence of realms where time, space, and our very beings intersect in extraordinary ways. Within the cosmos' vastness, I envision a tapestry woven with infinite threads, where aeons of time and parallel dimensions combine to bring souls together once more. I hold onto the belief that the love Victoria and I shared transcends the limitations of this earthly plane and finds expression in the boundless expanse of the multiverse.

While our human understanding of alternate realms may be limited, I embrace the hope that time and space are not immutable barriers.

Instead, they may be interwoven, bending and flexing to unite kindred spirits across the ages.

In this moment of farewell, I urge each of you to hold onto the memories, the laughter, and the love that Victoria brought into our lives. Let us mourn her passing and celebrate the indelible mark she left upon our souls. And as we navigate the complexities of grief, may we find solace in the Universe's infinite possibilities. I find comfort in the thought that her spirit, energy, and very being will patiently wait for me in the otherworldly expanses of the cosmos. The ether once believed to carry the essence of all existence, may hold the fragments of her beautiful soul, yearning for our paths to cross once again.

The profound bond that Victoria and I shared was not confined to the fleeting moments of this lifetime. It transcends the boundaries of space and time, delving into the core of our being. In the grand cosmic symphony, where quantum physics dances with the infinite, I choose to believe that our souls will one day reunite, embraced by parallel dimensions that intertwine our destinies.

Today, we say goodbye to Victoria's physical presence, but we carry her spirit within us. As we embark on our journeys, let us cherish the moments we shared, drawing strength from the love and memories that transcend the limits of this earthly realm.

In the face of loss and the mysteries of the universe, I embrace hope and the belief that love goes beyond the limitations of our physical existence. May the ethereal realm cradle the fragments of Victoria's essence, safeguarding them until we reunite through the cosmic dance of eternal connection.

She wrote an epitaph for herself while waiting for the judges' deliberation.

She asked me to engrave it on her gravestone when the time comes:

And I will walk through soul and tears…
And I will dance on smiles and flowers…
And I will fall asleep in your thoughts,
But when they all disappear forever,
I will hike through crucified hearts
Following me eternally to infinity.

I will forever miss my Victoria; I'm sure you all will! Thank you."

Robert's voice held a tremor as he concluded, "My Victoria will always have a special place in my heart, and I believe she touched all of you deeply as well." As he spoke, a sombre hush enveloped the gathering, and many wiped away tears, deeply moved by his words.

The priest then gently asked if anyone else wished to share memories or sentiments about Victoria. Alex, brimming with emotion, made his way forward. But as he began to speak, his grief overwhelmed him, and he sobbed openly. With encouragement from those around him, he found the strength to continue, "My heart feels an emptiness like never before, losing my beloved mother. I cringe! Every day feels hollower without her infectious smile, her loving admonishments, rebukes and her unwavering love. While I believe she is now at peace, the void she has left is profound…" He managed to continue his speech but he was overcome once more with emotion; he had to be gently led away from the scene.

When it was Anna's turn, she only managed to say, "I love you, Mom!" before crying again. Adam also gave a short speech about the wonderful sister he had and how he would greatly miss her.

The priest then began the burial rites. As Victoria's casket was lowered into the ground, a huge silence fell upon the gathering, as if time itself had paused and the world stood still. The soft strains of the hymn, "God be with you till we meet again", gradually filled the air, serving as a poignant reminder of the love and memories that would forever bind them all to Victoria.

That was followed by the "earth to earth, and dust to dust" as the children and her husband paid their last respects to her. Anna placed the wreath she carried on the grave, and the people started dispersing slowly; with a funeral look, everyone went to their cars.

Leaving the cemetery felt like stepping out of one realm of grief and into another. For Robert, it was a whirlwind of emotions. Victoria's absence was a gaping void, and the weight of the days ahead pressed heavily upon him. "She's at peace now, away from life's troubles. And I'm left here, grappling with this crushing reality. My heart is filled up, overburdened; my body trembles." He thought, the gravity of his loss sinking in. "How do I move forward? I think it is now that I am seeing the reality of losing a wife. How do I cope?" He settled into the car with a sigh, clearly feeling the weight of these thoughts.

As they slowly drove away, Anna and her siblings cast one last look at the cemetery, the final resting place of their beloved mother. Though they left behind her physical presence, they carried with them the hope that her essence, through cherished memories, would guide them in the days to come.

www.ingramcontent.com/pod-product-compliance
Lightning Source LLC
LaVergne TN
LVHW021559060726
842527LV00015B/3869